# Dial W For Witch
## A Wicked Witches of the Midwest Mystery Book 22

### Amanda M. Lee

WinchesterShaw Publications

Copyright © 2023 by Amanda M. Lee

All rights reserved.

No part of this book may be reproduced in any form or by any electronic or mechanical means, including information storage and retrieval systems, without written permission from the author, except for the use of brief quotations in a book review.

❧ Created with Vellum

# Prologue

## 14 years ago

"That's not going to work."

At first, I thought my great-aunt Tillie was talking to me, and I jerked my eyes away from the full-length mirror and shot her a dirty look. I was a big fan of my Winter Festival dress, and there was no way I was giving it up. I, Bay Winchester, was taking a stand. Yes, she might wipe the floor with me—she was surprisingly spry for her age—but I was not backing down this time. Thankfully, her eyes were on my cousin Clove, not me.

"What's not going to work?" Clove, her long dark hair pulled back in a bun and offset with a glittery silver hair pick, jutted out her lower lip in defiance as she regarded Aunt Tillie.

"Your dress," Aunt Tillie replied. "There's no place to hide a potion. That top is so tight I'm convinced something is going to burst."

"What potion?" I demanded. At sixteen, I had big plans for the Winter Festival dance. I was raised by witches, and I was certainly familiar with potions, but they weren't part of my plans for this evening.

"You know what potion," Aunt Tillie said. She was dressed in black pants and a shiny top. In fact, it was so shiny, it was almost distracting. I kept finding my eyes drifting with the reflections.

"I don't know what potion you're referring to," I countered.

"Yes, you do."

"No, I don't."

"Yes, you do."

"No, I don't."

"What did I say?" Aunt Tillie's voice was shrill.

"What an illuminating conversation," my cousin Thistle drawled as she entered the room. She'd opted for a simple blue dress that offset her dirty-blond hair. Unlike Clove, who had a lot going on upstairs, Thistle was less well endowed, and the thin spaghetti straps of her dress didn't look as if they were fighting a losing war to keep her top in place. Clove had enough cleavage in her pink dress to make the *Baywatch* babes drool.

"Nobody asked you, mouth," Aunt Tillie shot back. She eyed Thistle's dress with unreadable intent. "Can you fit a potion in that bra? There's not much else in it, but that makes camouflaging it all the more difficult."

Thistle glared at her. "There is no bra. I don't need one."

"Figures." Aunt Tillie shook her head. Much like Clove, she was blessed in the breast department. "You inherited your mother's lack of charms. Maybe we can find a way to tape a potion in there."

Thistle's mouth dropped open. "You want to tape a potion to my boobs?"

"Only for a little while." Aunt Tillie's smile was quick. "I heard Margaret was going to have security at the door to make sure no contraband makes it inside. I don't care who's running the door, feeling up a fourteen-year-old is a no-no."

"I'm not doing it." Thistle folded her arms across her chest. "I don't know what you have planned, but I'm totally not doing it."

"I was thinking I would throw the potions at all those silver snowflakes Margaret spent the last two weeks making," Aunt Tillie replied. "The potion would slowly shred them into glitter."

Margaret Little was Aunt Tillie's nemesis—her word—and they'd been going at each other for years. Since we were little, Christmas was our busiest time torturing the town kvetch. That was another word Aunt Tillie liked to throw around when dealing with Mrs. Little. After learning what the word meant, I had to agree it was a good choice.

In addition to being the town kvetch, Mrs. Little fancied herself the mayor. She designed all of Walkerville's pageants and festivals and took great pride in doing so—almost as much pride as Aunt Tillie took in dismantling her efforts.

Hey, nobody ever said their rivalry was mature. My cousins and I ranged in age from fourteen to sixteen, and even we marveled at how immature Aunt Tillie and Mrs. Little could get. Of course, that didn't stop us from joining in on Aunt Tillie's antics when we were bored, which happened often during a Northern Lower Michigan winter.

"I kind of like the sound of raining glitter," Clove admitted.

I didn't hate the sound of it. The problem was, I knew Aunt Tillie. There was no way her only plan was to ruin the stars. There was more.

"What else?" I demanded.

"Whatever do you mean?" Aunt Tillie was the very picture of innocence. That wasn't going to work on me.

"You might be doing the glitter thing, but there's something else." I crossed my arms over my chest, which was caught somewhere between Thistle's and Clove's when it came to size. I was happy with where I fell on the spectrum, but Aunt Tillie hadn't asked me to shove anything in my bra.

"It's horrible that you're so suspicious of your favorite aunt," Aunt Tillie sniffed.

"Tell me what's going on, or we won't help you."

Clove's mouth dropped open at my fortitude. Thistle looked smug.

"I could make you help me," Aunt Tillie warned.

"Not if we tell our mothers what you're up to," I shot back.

"Oh, geez, I was wrong," Aunt Tillie whined. "You're going to be the kvetch tonight. I thought for sure it would be Clove.

On a normal night, that might be true, but I didn't trust Aunt Tillie. She had mayhem lighting her eyes.

"Hey," Clove shot back. "I'm not a kvetch. I'm sitting here minding my own business."

Aunt Tillie eyed her and then handed over a potion. "Hide that in your cleavage."

Clove, obviously wishing she hadn't opened her mouth, eyed the potion. "What is this? Is this the glitter potion?"

"No, the glitter potion is smaller." Aunt Tillie rummaged in her own cleavage and came back with another vial. This one she handed to Thistle. "You have to take the small one because you don't have a lot to serve as camouflage up there."

"Thanks for the reminder," Thistle said dryly.

"Just do as I say."

Rather than concede to Aunt Tillie's demands, Thistle mimicked my stance and crossed her arms. "Let's hear the rest of it first."

"Goddess, you're such a pain." Aunt Tillie clucked her tongue. "Why are you such a pain?"

"Because I'm good at it," Thistle replied. "Now talk."

"Margaret has decreed that no alcohol can be served at the dance," Aunt Tillie replied. "Now, I hate a bad drunk as much as the next person."

"Unless you're the bad drunk," Thistle muttered.

Aunt Tillie ignored her. "Margaret doesn't have the right to tell people what they can or can't do. She sucks the fun out of everything. She's been that way since we were in grade school. I just want to have a little fun with her." She pulled out another potion. This one matched the one Clove held.

"There's alcohol in that?" I asked. I wasn't an expert on alcohol—my mother and aunts took that title on wine nights—but it didn't seem like the vials were big enough to do any damage. A couple of shots wouldn't make the night fun for anybody.

"There is ... *fun* in those bottles," Aunt Tillie replied.

"You bottled fun?" Thistle didn't look convinced.

"Yes, and I'm going to give you a double dose because you haven't been fun since you were two and removed your own diaper in Margaret's store and threw it at her."

Thistle scowled. "I hate that story."

"You shouldn't. That was your one crowning achievement in this life."

I eyed the bottle Aunt Tillie held. "What will the potion do?"

"It will allow everybody to have a good time."

The answer was evasive. "Even the kids?" I tried to picture my mother's face if she found out we'd helped Aunt Tillie intoxicate the under-twenty-one crowd.

"Actually, it's uniquely directed at the adults," Aunt Tillie replied. "I'm not an idiot."

"Will people actually get drunk?" I was a worrier by nature and couldn't stop myself from doing just that now. "What about the people who are sober?"

"Nobody is getting drunk," Aunt Tillie promised. "I don't trust people who are sober for obvious reasons, but I wouldn't risk pregnant mothers or people who have other health concerns. This is simply a way to ensure everybody has a good time."

I remained suspicious. "Everybody is going to act drunk but not really be drunk?"

"That's it in a nutshell."

I glanced at Thistle to gauge her response.

"It sounds kind of fun," Thistle noted. "If all the adults are drunk, they won't have time to worry about us. We'll be able to have a good night, and Aunt Tillie will get one over on Mrs. Little. I don't see a downside."

"That's the spirit." Aunt Tillie pumped her fist.

"Of course, I also don't want to encourage Aunt Tillie because I prefer her miserable and pouting," Thistle added.

Aunt Tillie's eyes narrowed. "Do you want to be on my list? I'll make sure you don't have fun if you ruin my fun."

I debated for only one more moment and then held out my hand. "We'll make a trade," I warned her. "We'll smuggle in the potions for you, but once inside we're handing them over, and it's your show. You're going to leave us alone and do your thing. You'll also make sure that we're not blamed when our mothers find out."

"And they *will* find out," Thistle added. "They always do."

"You're a lot smarter than you were when you were eight," Aunt Tillie lamented. "You just did whatever I wanted back then and never figured out I would make you the scapegoats. Ah, good times."

I had to bite back a smirk. "Agreed?"

"Agreed." Aunt Tillie preened as I tucked the potion in my cleavage.

"Not only will I make sure that your mothers don't blame you, I'll make sure they don't interrupt your smooching time with your dates."

My cheeks burned. "Nobody is planning on smooching time."

"Speak for yourself," Clove shot back. "I brought ChapStick. I'm going to need it."

"You'll be the first one pregnant," Aunt Tillie muttered as she shook her head at Clove. "You'd better wait until you're at least twenty."

Clove feigned hurt. "You don't get pregnant from kissing. I've taken health class." Even as she said it, she looked uncertain and flicked her eyes to me. "Right?"

"Yeah, you shouldn't do anything other than kissing before you've had a refresher course," I said. "As for smooching, don't worry about it," I commanded Aunt Tillie. "We've got everything under control on our end. You just handle your end, and we shouldn't have any problems. Can you do that?"

Aunt Tillie had the audacity to be offended. "Don't I always?"

"No," I replied.

"Hell no," Thistle said at the same time.

Aunt Tillie managed an impressive glower. "As soon as this night is over, you're both on my list. Prepare yourselves because it's coming."

That was the night of the Great Intoxication, which still lives in infamy in the former Walkerville.

We might've profusely apologized to our mothers after the fact, but we regretted nothing.

That was the true gift Aunt Tillie blessed us with that night. Raining glitter was great. Drunken adults were hilariously disturbing. But no regrets? That was the best reward ever.

That's what the Winter Festival was all about.

# One
## Present Day

Christmas is not my favorite holiday—Halloween will always bear that title—but there was something homey about drinking peppermint mochas while watching Thistle hang silver stars in Hypnotic, the magic shop she owned with my cousin Clove, as Christmas music played and snow flurries fluttered past the shop window.

Christmas is stressful, and yet there is something magical about the time of year.

"What do you think?" Thistle climbed down from the stepladder and planted her hands on her hips to study her handiwork. The calendar had just flipped to December, and that meant Christmas decorating.

"Nice," I said from my spot on the couch, my mug gripped in my right hand as I flipped through a catalog with my left. "What do you think I should get Landon? This is our first Christmas as a married couple, so it should be something good."

"I got Sam a baby," Clove replied as she checked the portable playpen on the other side of the couch. Hypnotic's central real estate was taken up by a couch and chairs, the retail shelves spread around it, and her son Calvin was now used to taking naps amid shopping chaos.

The kid was only a few months old but already a pro at dealing with Winchester mayhem. "That's the greatest gift of all."

"Should we all expect the baby to be our Christmas gift?" I asked.

"You should," Clove fired back.

Thistle made a face. "Good grief. Are you really not getting Sam anything? You popped out that kid forever ago. How long are you going to pretend that he's a pooping, crying gift? If I were Sam, I would already be looking to trade up."

We weren't always certain that Sam Cornell, Clove's husband, was a friend, but in the time we'd known him, he not only turned out to be an important ally—he had a bit of witch in his blood—he'd also taken Clove off our hands. Now he had to put up with her daily kvetching. That pretty much elevated him to sainthood in Thistle's book. I would never agree audibly, but I was right there with Thistle for a change.

"Hey!" Clove's dark eyes flashed. "I created human life out of nothing. How is that not a gift?" She looked to me for confirmation. "Right?"

I chose my words carefully. "Sam will probably shower you with gifts because that's who he is. You're going to feel like an idiot if he doesn't have a single thing to open."

Clove's lower lip jutted out. "I don't have time to shop."

"That's why you do it online, numbnuts," Thistle said. "Not only have I already ordered all of Marcus's stuff, most of it will be here by the end of the week. I'm storing it at the inn until I can wrap it."

That was so unlike Thistle. "You already have all your shopping done?"

"I have all of Marcus's shopping done," Thistle clarified. "I still have a few other people to shop for."

"Who?"

"Everybody else."

I snorted. That sounded more like the Thistle I knew and loved. "I'm struggling with Landon too," I admitted. "I'm thinking of getting him a dog."

Clove made a horrified face. "Do you know how messy dogs are? They're twice as messy as kids."

I'd seen her kid eat. That wasn't even remotely true. "He's in love with Peg, so he needs something to dote on."

"Doesn't he have you for that?" Thistle asked.

"Yes, but I'm serious about the dog. He might need someone to watch sports with, and it's not like the dog would be stuck at the guesthouse when he's at work. I can take it to the newspaper office with me."

"I like dogs," Thistle said. "But Marcus runs a petting zoo, so we're good."

"What did you get him for Christmas?" I asked.

"Oh, I'm not telling you." Thistle solemnly shook her head. "Nobody in this family can keep their mouth shut."

I wanted to be offended, but she was right. "I'm thinking about planning a trip for Landon and me," I said. "In February to break up the winter doldrums."

"Where to?" Clove asked.

"I'm not sure. We've made a list of places we want to visit. I was thinking New Orleans, but that's when Mardi Gras takes place, and I think we're too old to get the appeal of Mardi Gras."

"You could go to the Florida Keys," Thistle suggested. "It's warm there. It's Bohemian. It would be a nice break. It's not hurricane season, so you would be good."

"That's an idea," I agreed. "I need to think about it. If I get him a dog, a vacation feels out of the question."

"There's that," Thistle agreed. She was quiet for a moment. "Or you can leave the dog with us. It's only a week. Marcus would happily include a dog with all the other animals he's taking care of."

It was a surprising offer, and I shot her a grateful look. "Thanks. Mom volunteered to take the dog at the inn for a week. With Peg running around, there's no reason a dog can't be part of the fun."

Peg the pig had become a fixture at The Overlook, the inn my mother and aunts ran. My mother had sworn to the Goddess the pig wasn't staying. That was so long ago I'd lost count of the months that had passed. Peg was going nowhere.

"Have you bought your other gifts?" Clove asked.

"I got a nice watch for Dad. I have something ordered for Mom. She desperately wants a new KitchenAid blender. While I don't happen to think that's a good Christmas gift, she does."

"A blender isn't my idea of a good Christmas gift either, but your mother will love it," Thistle assured me. "What do you think about the changes to the Winter Festival? Did you see the pamphlet Mrs. Little sent out last week? She's changing a bunch of things."

I scowled at mention of Mrs. Little. She was no longer just Aunt Tillie's nemesis. She was also my nemesis. "I saw. Some of the ideas aren't terrible—Landon loves the hot chocolate kissing booth—but the rest is weird. What's the thing with the gingerbread men again?"

"She took the old Gingerbread man and woman decorating booth for the kids and turned it into a gingerbread house decorating booth," Thistle replied. "Apparently, last year, the Davis boys had just learned about sex thanks to a visit from their grandfather and his HBO Max account. They piled all the gingerbread men and women on top of each other or something."

"I heard they put them in sexually suggestive poses," Clove added. "Some of the parents complained, and Mrs. Little melted down. Now it's gingerbread houses."

"Which are going to be hell for the kids to transport home," I mused. "I foresee a lot of tears."

"You and me both," Thistle agreed. "I was a big fan of the gingerbread couple doing it doggy style. I took a photo. Makes me laugh just thinking about it."

I grabbed the pamphlet from the coffee table. "This is the part I don't get. It says they're bringing the Happy Holidays Players to town—although Mrs. Little wants everybody to know that it wasn't her decision to change the name of the group from the Merry Christmas Troubadours, and she's not waging a war on Christmas, so don't blame her. They're planning a big pageant or something. We usually don't have anything nearly that structured at our festivals."

"I'm curious about that too," Thistle said. "I meant to look them up online. It sounds as if they're going to do multiple rounds of caroling downtown and perform skits in the town square. They said they're going to be looking for locals to perform walk-on parts. Guess whose mother wants to be one of the locals." She made a face. A walk-on performance in a Christmas pageant was right up her mother Twila's alley.

"Aw, poor you," I said with a laugh. "At least I don't have to worry about that."

"No, but they're having a Christmas pie baking contest," Clove noted. "Your mother and my mother will be all over that. And given the fact that they're convinced Mrs. Little cheated when she won the Thanksgiving contest, I expect the fur to fly."

My mother was still complaining about losing that contest. "At least it will keep them distracted."

"Are you going to cover the pageant?" Thistle asked.

I owned and operated *The Whistler*, Hemlock Cove's only newspaper. It was more of an advertorial really, with a handful of pages dedicated to news and community announcements. The locals cherished it, which is how I stayed in business. "Probably." I was rueful. "There's not much else going on. I'll arrange for photos to be taken of the locals in their walk-on parts. That will keep people happy."

"And give Mrs. Little something to use as a marketing ploy for Christmas later this month," Thistle added. "She'll be happy with that."

I narrowed my eyes. The last thing I wanted to do was give that woman a reason to be happy. She'd been nothing but terrible all year, even when we saved her from killing herself when she'd been afflicted with a bad luck curse. That didn't even take into account the djinn she'd called upon to ruin our lives. "I wish she would just hibernate for the winter," I muttered.

"But then what would we laugh at in January when Aunt Tillie plows in her driveway and fills it with yellow snow?"

She had a point, but still.

"I liked when Aunt Tillie dropped all the red in the snow," Clove volunteered. "Mrs. Little thought there'd been a murder in her yard and assumed someone had left with the body. That was funny."

That *was* funny. She spent a week trying to track down whoever in town could be missing.

"What about Calvin?" I asked, opting to change the subject. It was the baby's first Christmas. The family would spoil him rotten. I wanted to get Clove necessary items before the kid was buried in toys the following Christmas. "Do you want anything specific for him?"

"Yes." Clove bobbed her head. "I sent emails this morning with a shopping list."

I blinked. "You sent a shopping list?" I hadn't checked my email yet. Now I had something to look forward to.

"I created a registry," Clove confirmed. "Make sure to tell your friends. You know ... Stormy and Scout."

Well, that was presumptuous. Stormy Morgan and Scout Randall lived in different towns, but they'd become good friends. They both had their own issues to deal with, however. "Why do you assume they're buying Calvin gifts?" I asked as I darted a look to Thistle.

"You've seen him." Clove gestured to the sleeping baby. "Nobody is cuter. I get that you guys are bitter, because whatever kids you add to the mix don't have a shot of being that beautiful—especially you, Thistle. He's too cute not to shower with gifts."

Thistle narrowed her eyes to murderous slits. "Why especially me?"

"You know," Clove replied breezily.

"No, I don't know."

"You know," Clove repeated forcefully.

"I think you'd better tell me."

The sigh Clove let loose was one for the record books. "Everybody knows that Marcus is the pretty one in your relationship, but we have the dominant genes. So, the baby will look like you." The way she wrinkled her nose told me exactly how she felt about that. "I'm sorry. I'm sure the baby will have a great personality."

I had to bite the inside of my cheek to keep from laughing at Thistle's murderous expression.

"So you're saying that if Marcus had the dominant genes, we'd be fine," Thistle gritted out.

"He's very attractive," Clove said. "I don't know what he sees in you, but he's a beautiful specimen of a man."

"I'm going to make you eat so much yellow snow," Thistle growled.

Rather than acknowledge the threat, Clove turned to me. "Your kids will be adorable. They'll all be blond like you, and they'll definitely have blue eyes because both of you do. But they're going to have that weird thing once they hit puberty, so it won't be all smooth sailing."

Now I was offended. "What weird thing?"

"You know."

"I don't think I do."

"*You know.*"

I was going to throttle her. "Clove!" I barked.

Another sigh greeted my response. "I don't know why you're getting so upset. You clearly grew out of that phase. Landon is a good-looking guy too, but your kids won't get any of his coloring. That's too bad because he's going to age better than you. It's probably good that he won't care about any of that. Well, as long as someone keeps him in bacon and cake."

"Get the shovel," I ordered Thistle.

She was already on her feet. "You'd better start running, Clove."

Rather than flee in terror, she clapped her hands and giggled like an idiot. "You guys are so easy. I'm allowed to say whatever I want. You can't get mad. I gave birth. That gives me a free pass."

"Since when is that the rule?" I challenged.

"Since now. When you have kids, you can say whatever you want too."

"Whatever." Thistle meandered to the cash register counter when her phone lit up. Her forehead creased as she read an incoming message. "Turn on the television," she ordered.

I didn't bother arguing. If Thistle thought there was something we should see, she meant it. I grabbed the remote from the coffee table and aimed it at the television. It was already set to a local channel—they didn't bother paying for cable at the store—and the screen filled with a familiar newswoman's face.

"It's unclear at this time how many prisoners have escaped," she said in a grave voice. "All we know is that there has been a breach, and that at least one prisoner is unaccounted for. A name has not been released, but law enforcement officials are warning all motorists in the areas of Hemlock Cove, Hawthorne Hollow, Shadow Hills, Bellaire, Mancelona, and Alden against picking up hitchhikers or leaving their doors unlocked. Again, if you're just tuning in, there has been a prison break at the Antrim Correctional Facility. At least one prisoner, maybe more, is unaccounted for. Residents in the area are urged to take precautions. All schools are locked down for the next few hours. We will keep you apprised of any updates."

I worked my jaw as *General Hospital* returned to the screen.

"What should we do?" Clove asked. All of her previous bravado had vacated. Now she was her normal whiny self. "What if he's already outside? What if he wants to steal my baby and use him as a shield? Oh, Goddess, protect my son." She clasped her hands together and looked to the ceiling.

"I'll threaten you if you don't cut the theatrics," Thistle barked. "Seriously, what do we do?"

It took me a moment to realize she was talking to me. "Why are you asking me? I'm not an expert on prison breaks."

My husband Landon Michaels, an FBI agent, picked that moment to push open the door and stick his head inside. Instead of the flirty greeting he'd normally bestow upon me, he was grim. "I assume you've heard," he said.

I nodded.

"I need you to come with me, Bay. If there's a chance you can use one of those locator spells, we can end this soon."

I grabbed my coat.

"You two should lock up the shop and go home," Landon ordered, his gaze falling on Thistle and Clove. "We're urging everybody to stay inside until we know more about the situation. You'll be safer at home."

"I can't go to a lighthouse in the middle of the woods," Clove said. "You just know that a prisoner would find that's a fine location to perform his ritual serial killings. There's no way I'm subjecting my baby to that."

Landon blinked twice. "Take her to The Overlook," he ordered Thistle. "Winnie can deal with her."

Thistle offered up a saucy salute. "I'm on it, Bossy McBossypants."

Landon didn't smile. "I don't know how late we'll be. Don't hold dinner for us." He held out his hand for me. "Come on, Bay. We need to get moving."

# Two

Landon dropped an absent kiss on my forehead before opening the rear door of Chief Terry's official vehicle and helping me inside. Chief Terry was behind the wheel, and he looked agitated.

"What took you so long?" he barked at Landon.

"I had to explain to Clove that a prisoner wasn't coming for the baby," Landon replied.

Apparently, that was a good enough explanation for Chief Terry because he let it drop. "It'll take about twenty minutes to get to the prison. Buckle up because I'm going to try to cut that down to fifteen minutes."

I did as instructed, trying not to cringe when Chief Terry spun out of the police station parking lot and headed toward M-88. "What do we know?" I asked when I was certain my stomach wasn't about to stage a revolt. All those doughnuts and the ultra-sweet peppermint mocha were starting to feel like a mistake.

"More than one prisoner escaped," Landon replied. He didn't look over his shoulder to make eye contact. "They're not releasing numbers yet because they have to do a head count."

"Even after the head count, all the nooks and crannies of the prison have to be checked," Chief Terry added. "Antrim isn't a big facility—two hundred inmates. Some work in the laundry. Others are on cleaning crews. There's an outbuilding where they repair machinery. All of that has to be checked and double-checked."

"How did they escape?"

"We don't know," Landon said. "It's maximum security, but maximum security doesn't mean the same up here as it does down south. Most of the inmates aren't violent offenders."

"There were some," Chief Terry countered. "Don't kid yourself, there are murderers in Antrim."

"Why wouldn't they keep the violent offenders down south?" I asked.

"Overcrowding," Landon explained. "Any prisoners transported up here would've had a long stretch of good behavior. This place is considered a reward compared to prisons like Jackson."

"I still don't understand."

"I'm not sure I do either," Landon said. "I've never given the proximity of the prison much thought. Most of the men here are near the end of their runs."

"Or they're drug offenders," Chief Terry added. "Drug offenders aren't considered violent offenders. The problem you have with that is, a lot of the time, plea bargains are made. But that doesn't mean they don't have violent incidents in their past."

"Okay." I blew out a sigh. "What happens if a bunch of prisoners escaped?"

"Nothing good," Chief Terry replied. "They'll scatter. That will put all the surrounding communities in peril. We'll have to lock down Hemlock Cove to be safe."

That wouldn't go over well. "And you expect Mrs. Little to just cancel the Winter Festival?"

"Margaret Little is not the boss of this town!" Chief Terry exploded, thumping his fist against the steering wheel. He'd been surly for a few weeks since a local FBI agent had gone undercover with a meth gang under his watch ... and not come back.

I had sympathy for him—he'd been more of a father figure to me than my own father when I was growing up—but he was taking Kevin

Gallagher's death hard. Kevin was gone before we'd even realized we had an evil djinn on our hands. There was nothing we could've done.

"I'm sorry," Chief Terry offered in a low voice when the silence had stretched almost two minutes. "I didn't mean to snap at you, sweetheart. It's just ... Margaret Little is on my list."

The statement would've been funny under different circumstances. Aunt Tillie was normally the one putting people on her list. It was rare for Chief Terry to lose his cool. He'd always been the calm adult presence in my life. Because of that, I figured he deserved a pass.

"It's okay," I assured him. He wasn't the only one grappling with Kevin's fate. So was Landon. They were both used to winning. Losing, and in such a profound way, wasn't something they could easily overcome. "My feelings aren't hurt."

"It's still not okay." Chief Terry was firm. "You didn't deserve that."

I searched for something that would cheer them up. "Did you hear Mrs. Little is upset because she believes the war on Christmas is hitting Hemlock Cove? Apparently, the Merry Christmas Troubadours changed their name to the Happy Holidays Players, and she's complaining to anyone who will listen."

Chief Terry didn't respond for a moment. When he did, he sounded a bit lighter. "Will she blame that on Tillie?"

"Probably not. There will be plenty of other things to blame on Aunt Tillie by the end of the month. The first significant snow could hit any day. As soon as that happens and Aunt Tillie has her plow out, it's going to be war."

Chief Terry managed a chuckle. "I do so love when Tillie turns Margaret's snow yellow. When she started that, when you were kids, I was horrified. It's something of a Christmas tradition now."

"It's awesome," I agreed. "She already told us we have to go on a sabotage mission with her for old time's sake on Christmas Eve. We've been trying to beg off—she doesn't need us to torture Mrs. Little—but she won't have it."

"I don't like that idea at all," Landon complained. "I have big plans for you Christmas Eve. They involve alcoholic cocoa—I already ordered a bag of those freeze-dried marshmallows—and nudity. I got some special mistletoe too."

"Don't make me hurt you," Chief Terry warned. "That's my little sweetheart. I don't need you being gross."

A year ago, Landon might've balked in the face of Chief Terry's animosity. Now he brushed it off. "Any other gossip?"

"Um..." I scrambled and then remembered Clove's list. "Apparently, Clove is sending links to a registry for Calvin's first Christmas. She's even sending links to Stormy and Scout."

Landon chuckled. "Sounds like her."

"She said that because she's given birth, she can do whatever she wants. She makes it sound as if she's single-handedly fought a war, and we should all be grateful for her deigning to spend time with us."

"Are you going to shop from the registry?"

My shoulders slouched in shame. "Yes."

"Then I don't think you have much ground to stand on."

Of course he would say that. "If you're not careful, you'll get a lump of coal in your stocking," I warned.

"As long as I have you, I don't need anything else."

"Aw," I crooned, going warm all over as I tried to ignore Chief Terry's mimed vomiting from the driver's seat. I sat up straighter when the razor wire-topped prison walls came into view.

"Look there." Landon pointed to a section of fence surrounded by prison personnel. "They must think they escaped from that spot. It looks as if there's a bit of a gap between the razor wire sections."

I narrowed my eyes as I studied the section that had caught his attention. "That's not much of an opening," I noted. "Can someone fit between those two sections?"

"You'd be surprised what somebody can do when motivated."

Landon turned to me. "Listen, I need you to act meek and not open your mouth." He was firm. "We don't have control of this situation. If asked, we'll say that you were already with us when we got the call. The warden and his men won't be excited to see you."

"Do you want me to stay in the truck?"

"No." Chief Terry shook his head as he pulled up to the main entryway. The man in the guard shack waved us through. We wouldn't be the only representation from local police departments joining the hunt. "We want you to get a feel for the people and the situation. Just don't draw attention to yourself."

I chewed my bottom lip. "This place is pretty stark." Everything was gray, no hint of color other than the multitude of police vehicles parked in front of the main building.

"It's a prison," Landon said as he unbuckled his seatbelt. "It's not meant to be cheery." He was already at my door when I pushed it open. "Stick close to me."

He was genuinely worried my presence would be questioned. "I won't say anything unless asked a direct question," I promised. "I won't make you look bad."

"You never make me look bad. I wanted you with us in case you could help. But these people won't understand the sort of help you can offer."

"I've got it."

Chief Terry led the way, Landon following closely behind. He flashed his badge as we approached the group at the gate.

"I'm Warden Brad Childs." A bull of a man—he was at least six and a half feet tall with broad shoulders and a bald bowling ball of a head—extended his hand to Chief Terry.

"Terry Davenport. I'm chief in Hemlock Cove. This is Landon Michaels. He's with the FBI office out of Traverse City. We were out for lunch when we heard the news." Chief Terry dipped his chin toward me. "This is Bay, Landon's wife. She won't get in the way. We didn't have time to take her home."

"Ma'am." Brad nodded in greeting to me, but he didn't linger. "We're still counting inmates. We believe as many as fifteen made it over the fence, but that number could change. We have teams sweeping the prison and grounds. We have dog teams in the woods. We're hopeful we can round them up before they even get a mile from here."

"But not all of them," Landon said.

"No." Brad scowled. "I think that at least some of our escapees had plans in place for a while. They would've thought ahead about transportation. It's likely several inmates were swept up in this at the last second. We'll have an easier time tracking them down. The others, well..."

"How long between the time they escaped, and you realized they were gone?" Landon asked.

Shame flooded Brad's features. "We don't count the inmates several times a day. We count for lockdown at night. We've never had a problem."

"I'm not casting blame," Landon assured him. "If you're right and the majority of the escapees are on foot in the woods, our net should be relatively tight."

"They were gone four hours before we realized it." Brad looked as if he would've preferred a hole open beneath him rather than provide the answer he did. "We checked the security camera feeds, but there are gaps."

"Gaps?" I blurted before realizing I was going to open my mouth. I shrank back when Landon shot me a quelling look. "Sorry ... it's a horrible thing."

"It is, ma'am," Brad agreed. "Almost half our cameras went down at the same time. We thought it was a system error, and we were working on it. The camera angle on the lone monitor that was still working jumped every ten seconds. That's why we can't be certain how many escaped. We only had two monitors with feeds, and the one at the back of the property didn't catch anything because they all fled on the east side of the grounds."

"How did they get over the fence?" Landon asked.

"They fashioned footholds somehow. They were prepared. They hammered pegs into the wall as they went up. Then they used sheets pilfered from the laundry room to protect them from the razor wire.

"There's some blood up there," he continued. "At least one of them snagged on the wire. This is a fluid situation."

Landon cast me a wary look. "What do you want us to do?" he asked.

"We have teams amassing in every town in the area. You know Hemlock Cove best. We're asking you to check any houses that might've been vacated for winter. Snowbirds and such take off in December and don't return until March. Some of the escapees might hole up in those empty houses and hunting shacks. Deer season is over. The odds of a hunter stumbling across an inmate in one of the shacks seem long. We'd obviously rather armed professionals conduct searches than residents."

Landon rubbed his chin. "Do you have any reason to believe any inmates managed to get their hands on weapons?"

"I would like to say no," Brad was grim. "They'll sharpen toothbrushes into daggers to stab someone if they have to. And they must have at least one hammer because of the pegs in the wall."

"We'll head back to Hemlock Cove," Chief Terry said. "I know a few places—most right off the highway—that might appeal to someone trying to lay low. Should we mark the cabins to show that we've already searched them?"

Brad nodded. "I hadn't thought that far, but it's a good idea.

"I have decals in my truck from last year's Winter Festival," Chief Terry offered. "Snowflakes. I haven't had a chance to dump them."

"That's a good idea." Brad managed a smile, but it didn't touch his eyes. "I appreciate your help. I have no idea how this is going to play out, but it won't be a happy ending for everyone."

Chief Terry agreed. "The sooner we start wrangling up these inmates, the better. We'll be in touch."

# Three

I used my magic as soon as we were clear of the prison, unleashing the tracking spell Aunt Tillie had taught us and I'd grown adept at. We were barely two miles down the road when I got my first hit.

"There." I pointed to a narrow dirt road.

Chief Terry pulled down it without asking a single question. He drove slowly, allowing me to direct him, and when we reached a small clearing, I had him pull over.

"What are you doing?" Landon demanded when I shoved open the rear door. He looked panicked.

"Catching an escapee." I smiled at him as I hit the ground, ignoring the noise as he and Chief Terry scrambled behind me.

"There's nobody here," Chief Terry argued.

He was wrong. The locator beacon wouldn't have led me here for no reason. I tracked the woods around the clearing, reaching out with my senses. Weirdly enough, my magic told me our source was directly on top of us. When I looked up, into the tree branches spreading above our heads, it took me several seconds to realize what I saw.

"Is that a deer blind?" I asked.

Landon moved next to me and nodded, his eyes narrow and shrewd. "It is. Good find."

"How do we know someone is up there?" Chief Terry demanded.

"We could ask," I suggested. I cleared my throat. The air was cold enough my breath was visible. "Excuse me," I called out. "If you could be so kind as to climb down, that will make things easier on all of us."

I thought I heard a faint shuffling.

"It would be best if you didn't make us implement step two of the search," I said. This time I was certain I heard shuffling.

"There's definitely someone up there," Landon noted. "I don't see a ladder."

"Probably a rope ladder," Chief Terry said. "He would've pulled it up with him after making the climb."

I pressed my lips together, debating, and then let loose a sigh. "Well, I can only think of one way to get him down."

Landon shot me a curious gaze. "You are not going up there."

"I wasn't suggesting that."

"I'm all for the girl power," he insisted. "I know you're the strongest one here, but you can't go up there. He might have a shiv or something."

"I just said I wasn't going up there." I formed a fist with my right hand and engaged my magic. "*Come*," I intoned.

The wind picked up at the same moment my spell grew in power, and when Viola, the ghost of my newspaper office, appeared she looked annoyed.

"I was watching *General Hospital*," she complained. "I just know Lulu is going to wake up at any moment and get her husband back. How can you ruin this for me?"

I feigned patience. "There's an escaped prisoner in that deer blind." I pointed up. "I need you to scare him out. That's way better than any *General Hospital* episode."

"Says you." Viola sniffed and cocked her head as she regarded the blind. "There really is someone up there. I hear him."

Did ghosts have superior hearing? In life, Viola had only heard what she wanted to hear. I tucked the question away to consider later. "Can you scare him down?"

"Do you want him down in one piece?"

"That would be preferable."

"Okay. Give me a second."

Landon cast me a sidelong look. "Is she going to help?"

"Yeah. She's mad about me interrupting *General Hospital*, though."

"Priorities." He moved his hand to my back to give it a reassuring pat and then drew his service weapon.

When the tree branches started swaying, I was impressed. Viola had been practicing her ghostly abilities to affect the physical world. She was getting good at it.

"Woo!" she yelled as she pounded her fists on the side of the blind. "Woo! Woo!"

"What is she doing?" Chief Terry asked. "Is she ... wooing?"

I was amused. "She *is* wooing. I'm impressed you can hear that."

"It's hard to miss."

It took another thirty seconds before the prisoner was at his limit. The sound of a trap door opening beneath the structure became apparent, and a rope ladder fell through the opening.

"I'm coming down," a frightened voice announced. "Don't shoot me. I'm unarmed."

Landon grinned when a figure appeared on the ladder. "This is why we should take a witch with us wherever we go."

"She's going to give me an ulcer," Chief Terry complained. He moved forward and grabbed the prisoner as soon as the man was on the ground. "Hands up," he ordered.

The prisoner, still in his orange jumpsuit, didn't struggle. He was pale, his eyes wide, and he looked as if he was eager to return to prison rather than deal with the ghost. "There's something up there," he whispered.

Landon trained his gun on the prisoner as Chief Terry searched and cuffed him. "The world is a frightening place," he acknowledged when the man was subdued. "What's your name?"

"Ted Arnold."

"What are you in for, Ted?"

"Armed robbery. I have five years left."

"Something tells me you're going to have a bit more time added to your sentence." Landon slid his eyes to me. "That was pretty impressive, sweetie. Have I mentioned you're my favorite partner ever?"

"I'm pretty sure I should be offended by that remark," Chief Terry groused.

I smirked despite the serious situation. "That was pretty good."

"It was," Landon agreed. "Let's get him back to the prison. Bay, you're in front with Chief Terry for the drive. I'll be in the back." His tone told me arguing wouldn't be allowed. That was fine. I didn't want to be in the back anyway.

"Maybe we'll have them all captured by the end of the day," I suggested.

Landon nodded, but his expression told me he didn't believe that would be the case.

**BRAD'S FACE WAS ALMOST COMICAL WHEN** we returned with a prisoner thirty minutes after we'd left.

"We got lucky," Chief Terry explained. "We saw the two-track and went down it on a hunch. We stumbled across him."

"Wow."

When we left again, I tapped the locator spell a second time. It led us to an abandoned machine shop. From the parking lot, it was impossible to tell how many prisoners were inside, but I was convinced there was more than one.

"Maybe we should call for backup," Chief Terry suggested as we stared at the building. I could imagine that prisoners were scrambling inside to fortify their location. Of course, that could've been the fact that I liked to watch a lot of television fueling my imagination.

"If we do that, I won't be able to use my magic," I reminded him.

"Yeah, but if there are five prisoners in there, your magic might not do us any good."

I wasn't prepared to acknowledge that. "I think there are two of them." I cocked my head as I tried to reach out with my senses. "Hold on."

I called Viola again. This time she wasn't quite as annoyed.

"Is this going to be an all-day thing?" she demanded.

"Maybe." I shot her a rueful smile.

"Well, *General Hospital* is over, and Lulu still hasn't woken up, so I have an opening in my schedule."

"Great." I nodded to the building. "Can you pop in there and tell us how many prisoners are present?"

"Sure. Do you want me to scare them out?"

"Not yet. I want to see what we're dealing with first."

"Okay." Viola was gone in an instant.

"Is she doing it?" Chief Terry asked after a beat.

"She's inside checking things out." I kept my gaze on the building. "I bet you never thought you'd be tracking down escaped prisoners with a ghost in tow."

"I never thought I'd be doing it with you in tow," Chief Terry grumbled. "I love you, Bay, but when I pictured your future, this isn't what I had in mind."

I was curious. "What did you want for me?"

"I don't know. I thought maybe you would end up in a castle."

That was unbelievably sweet and ridiculous. "A castle, huh? Have you ever considered that maybe the castle is yet to come? I mean, it won't look like a castle. It will look like a log cabin house on the lake—and there's a very real chance the furniture will be fashioned out of bacon—but castles come in different shapes and sizes."

"I never wanted you in danger." He looked momentarily morose. "I wanted you safe ... and happy ... and warm. Right now, we're sitting outside an old machine shop waiting for a ghost to report back on escaped prisoners."

"Did it ever occur to you that being in the thick of action makes me happy?"

His eyes were soft when they locked with mine. "I want you happy, but you need to develop some boring hobbies. You're going to give me an ulcer."

"I'll do my best." I flicked my eyes to the open spot in the backseat when Viola reappeared. "Well?"

"Two," she replied. "They've armed themselves. One has a huge pipe. The other has made some sort of spear fashioned from a rusty pole. I think if you were to get stabbed by it, you'd need about ten tetanus shots."

I repeated what she'd told me to Landon and Chief Terry.

"We should call for backup," Chief Terry announced.

"What do you think, Bay?" Landon asked.

"We can take them," I replied. "Viola can tell us where they are. We can get in, knock them out with magic, and cuff them. No muss, no fuss."

Landon flicked his gaze to Chief Terry. "I agree with Bay."

"Of course you do," Chief Terry groused. "You want her to cuddle with you on the couch later. She won't do that if she's annoyed."

"Yes, my whole life is about cuddling on the couch," Landon drawled.

I didn't meet his gaze. I was afraid he would see the truth. He was a big cuddler. "We can take them out relatively easily. They won't be at the same door. They'll split up, so it will be easy to take them one on one."

Chief Terry grumbled. "Fine," he said, flashing a tight smile. "You're going to do what I say for a change. Landon and I will be the first through the door. You follow us."

I was expecting the edict. "Okay." I didn't tell him that if I thought he and Landon were in danger that I would do whatever was necessary to save them. "You can go first."

Chief Terry blew out a breath and met Landon's gaze. "Let's do this."

Landon looked more relaxed than Chief Terry when we met in front of the truck. "Remember to do what we say," he reminded me.

"I've got it."

Instead of heading toward the front door, we circled to the back. Chief Terry looked to me for permission to enter the premises.

"Where are they?" I asked Viola as she emerged from the building.

"One is behind some sort of machine directly on the other side of the door," she replied. "The other is over that way." She gestured to the far end of the building. "The one with the spear is at the other door."

I smiled in thanks and repeated the information to Landon and Chief Terry.

"Remember that we're first," Chief Terry ordered. "Don't even think of pulling a Tillie."

That would've made me laugh two years ago. Unfortunately, it had become glaringly obvious that I was starting to emulate Aunt Tillie in some respects. Nobody was more surprised—or upset.

Landon moved to the door and slammed his foot into the jam to break the lock. It was old and gave almost immediately. The door groaned when he tugged it open. He gripped his gun, cast me one more look, and then started barking orders.

"I'm Landon Michaels with the FBI. Put your weapons down. Put your hands in the air. Don't make this more difficult than it has to be."

A grunt not far from the door caught my attention. There was a big piece of machinery in the way. It could easily hide a man. Two men I loved were about to put themselves on the line, so I decided to insert myself into the battle without permission.

"*Purgo*," I hissed, magic coursing through me.

The piece of machinery slid across the floor with more than a little reluctance, revealing a wide-eyed inmate in an orange jumpsuit behind it. He gripped a piece of pipe as Viola said, but he appeared so surprised by the shifting machinery that he froze.

"Hands up!" Landon ordered, leveling his gun on the escapee. "Don't make this worse."

The inmate took a moment to consider, and then he threw the pipe on the floor and raised his hands. I was just about to comment on how easy it had been when I sensed something behind me.

I swiveled, prepared to take on the second prisoner and his rusty spear, but it wasn't a physical threat.

The inmate had crossed to us rather than flee when given the chance—I would have to think about that later—but he wasn't worried about Landon and Chief Terry, who hadn't yet noticed him. He was interested in me.

Magic rolled off of him in waves, a dark shadow power rippling beneath his surface, and I had a full moment to consider how out of place that was before the prisoner tossed aside the spear and grabbed me by the throat. He lifted me off the ground as my oxygen supply was cut off, but I barely registered that. It was the magic licking at my skin that caught my attention.

"You shouldn't be here," he rasped.

I sensed rather than saw Landon realize that the second inmate hadn't hidden himself in the dark recesses of the building as we assumed. "Bay!"

I couldn't focus on him. I reacted the only way I knew. "*Venio*," I intoned, watching with grim satisfaction as Viola, and the two other ghosts I'd summoned, grabbed the prisoner's arms and wrestled him back.

He had no choice but to release his grip on me. He fought the ghosts, but they overpowered him. I took two steps forward, stared into his glowing yellow eyes for several seconds, and then slapped my hand to his forehead.

"*Sopor*," I ordered.

The prisoner's legs went out from under him. Landon rushed to my side.

"Are you okay?" he asked, breathless.

"I'm fine," I assured him.

He took a moment to run his fingers over my neck, which would be sore later, and then turned to the fallen prisoner. "What the hell was that?"

"I'm not sure." I cast a look over my shoulder, to where Chief Terry had the first prisoner cuffed, and then reached out a hand to touch the prisoner who had attacked me. "*Manifesto*," I whispered.

Immediately, I was plunged into his head. "His name is James Barker," I whispered as the images assailed me. Most of them were easy enough to make out, but some were confusing. "Someone helped them escape. Someone somehow shrouded."

"Someone magical?" Landon asked as I emerged from Barker's head.

I nodded and gripped the man's wrist. "Yes. He's under a spell."

"Can you remove it?"

"I can try." I looked again at the first inmate, who seemed to have given up the fight. There was no magical aura surrounding him. "Does this strike anybody else as odd?"

"Is that a trick question?" Chief Terry demanded.

I shook my head. "No. It's just weird."

"Do what you have to do," he ordered. "We'll figure out what's weird and what isn't when we're safely removed from this situation."

"*Exsolvo*," I whispered as I attacked the spell holding Barker in thrall. Holes appeared in the glowing net almost instantly. Within seconds, the magic that had been fueling the man was gone.

"Are we good?" Landon asked.

"Yeah." I studied the unconscious prisoner. "I have no idea what that was."

# Four

When we arrived with two more escapees, the scene in front of the prison was bedlam. Both escapees were cuffed. One was unconscious. I drove so Chief Terry could keep his eye on the situation in the back with Landon and the prisoners. The warden was dumbfounded.

"You caught two more?" he asked as I hopped out of the truck.

"It was luck," I lied. "Chief Terry remembered the machine shop. We checked it on a lark."

Brad's gaze was heavy when it landed on my face. Was he searching for a lie? When he broke into a wide grin, I let loose the breath I'd been holding. "Maybe you're their good luck charm."

"She's always my good luck charm," Landon said as he handed over the conscious inmate, who hadn't spoken since his arrest. He'd seen how things had played out. While he might not have been able to ascertain the magical aspects, he had to know that his takedown had been far from normal.

"We have one unconscious," Chief Terry volunteered. "Can you get a gurney out here to collect him?"

"Sure." Brad studied Barker's unconscious form. "Did you have to knock him out? I mean ... did he attack you?"

"He moved in behind us," Landon replied. "There was a scuffle when he grabbed Bay, but he kind of fell over, and not just because we hit him. I think he might've had a medical emergency."

"You took Bay into the machine shop?" Brad's expression was difficult to read.

Landon realized his mistake.

"We didn't want to leave her in the truck in case there were more escapees watching from the woods," Landon explained.

"Uh-huh." I felt Brad's eyes on me but didn't look up to meet them. "Well, come with me." He wrapped his hand around my elbow and gave me a light tug. "That's a nasty bruise forming around your throat. We should have it checked out."

I didn't bother arguing. Brad led me to the lobby and directed me to sit on one of the couches.

"Let's see what we've got here." Brad's fingers were gentle as he touched the skin around my throat. "Does that hurt?"

I nodded. "I'll be fine, though," I promised. "My aunt is a holistic medicine proponent. She has this great magical balm." I glanced around for Chief Terry and Landon and found they were near the door, several representatives from the Michigan State Police grilling them. The looks Landon kept darting toward me reflected worry.

"You know, I've been to Hemlock Cove a few times," Brad volunteered. He smiled at a man in medical scrubs as he approached with what looked to be a bottle of ointment. "I used to live in the Ann Arbor area but moved up here when there was an opening. I've always loved this area."

I did my best to remain calm. "Do you like Hemlock Cove?"

"I do. I knew it as Walkerville when I was a kid. When I first heard about the rebrand, I thought it was the dumbest thing ever."

I swallowed hard. This conversation felt pointed.

"Obviously, I was wrong," he continued. "The town is thriving, especially compared to some of the others in the area. Mancelona is a shadow of the town I remember from my childhood. It used to be bustling with activity. Hemlock Cove is the place everybody wants to visit now."

"It's a good town," I agreed. "We love it a great deal. I remember when it was Walkerville. When I was a kid, it was harder to see the way people were struggling. My mother and aunts were struggling, but they kept it from us. Things are definitely better now."

"My understanding is that your family owns The Overlook," Brad said. "That's supposed to be the premiere inn this side of Charlevoix."

"My mother and aunts work very hard," I said. I had to be careful.

"I was so surprised when you brought back that first inmate that I decided to do a little research," Brad volunteered. "I was waiting for a head count anyway, and there was very little I could do. I wanted to be out there searching, but as the warden, that's not my job. Bureaucracy is a pain."

"I bet."

"When I was reading up on Landon and Chief Terry, I noticed something interesting," he continued. "Your name was on most of the articles regaling their exploits." He had a pretty impressive vocabulary. Some might call it hoity-toity. He was obviously well read, and he was setting a trap.

"Well, it's easy to write articles celebrating them when they do such a good job." I smiled. "They make it easy. Chief Terry has always been close to my family. Now he's even closer."

"Oh?" Brad's smile was easy, but there was an edge to his eyes. "How so?"

"He's dating my mother."

Brad barked out a laugh. "How ... fun. That sort of makes him Agent Michaels's father-in-law, doesn't it?"

"My father and uncles are in town. They run another inn. The Dragonfly." All of that was public record, so there was no point in withholding the information.

"I didn't know that. What I did read—and found fascinating—is that your family has a very specific reputation."

"We're famous," I agreed, uncomfortable.

"There are a lot of rumors about you. Some people say you're magical."

"The whole town is magical," I reminded him. "It's witches as far as the eye can see."

"Fake witches," he clarified. "The town is full of fake witches ... except a lot of the online chatter says your family is the real deal."

I darted a worried look to Landon, but he was still talking with the Michigan State Police contingent. "Are you asking if I'm a real witch?"

"I'm just curious. I've always been a believer of certain things. That's one of the reasons I like visiting Hemlock Cove. The stories that fly around that place, well, they're downright delightful. Most of those stories revolve around your family."

"I'm sure."

"Your great-aunt, for example, is considered terrifying."

"Try living with her."

"Do you live with her? I noticed Landon's home address is the same as that of the inn."

I frowned. If he'd dug that deep, he was *really* interested. "We live in the guesthouse on the property. I used to share it with my cousins, but they've both moved out. They're still in town, but they've moved in with their significant others. Landon and I took over the guesthouse. We plan to build our own house in a few years."

"The cousins you lived with," he prodded. "They own the magic store, right?"

I was over this game. "If you have a specific question, now would be the time to ask it," I said in a sharp voice that had Landon jerking his chin in my direction.

Brad handed me the tube of ointment. Clearly, he wasn't comfortable applying it himself. "Are you psychic, Bay?"

Of all the questions he could've asked, that wasn't the one I expected. "I ... you..." I trailed off, debating.

"I already told you I'm a believer."

"That doesn't necessarily mean anything," I hedged. "I don't really consider myself psychic."

"But you get feelings? Your instincts point you in a certain direction." Panic set in, but Chief Terry and Landon were still talking with the other officers. I was on my own.

"Everybody has feelings." I chose my words carefully. "I was taught at a young age to listen to my inner voice."

Brad worked his jaw, seemingly debating, and then nodded. "You're afraid. I don't blame you. It's okay. I really am a believer. I'm asking because I thought maybe if you saw the cells of the inmates still missing you might pick up on something."

Yup. This was definitely taking an unexpected turn. "I can look." I made the offer without thinking about it. "I can't promise anything."

"Your results this afternoon speak for themselves." Brad stood. "Tell me when you're ready, and I'll take you back."

I uncapped the ointment and put some on my fingers before rubbing it into my neck. "Chief Terry and Landon are responsible for catching those inmates." I was desperate for the men in my life to get their due recognition.

"I think you did it as a team, but I'm impressed with what they pulled off," Brad said. He cast a look toward a wary Landon, who had finally torn himself away from the Michigan State Police. "Your wife seems like an amazing individual."

"She is," Landon confirmed. "Is everything okay?" He took the ointment from me without asking and dabbed some on his finger before transferring it to my neck. His gaze was dark when it landed on the bruising. "That guy is lucky he's already unconscious. I would kill him and enjoy it right now."

"Everything is fine," Brad assured him. "Two other inmates were found in the woods thanks to the dogs. We believe ten inmates are still out there. We're putting deputies and local officers on every road within a fifty-mile radius."

Landon nodded. "The remaining ten won't be easy to catch. The longer this goes on, the more time they'll have to entrench themselves in remote locations."

"We're holding a news conference in an hour. Your wife has agreed to check the cells of those still missing. I hope that's okay with you."

Landon's eyes didn't leave my face. "If you think she can be helpful. It's her decision."

"She's already agreed, so I assume she's fine with it."

"I am," I said, smiling for Landon's benefit. "It's a great idea."

"Then we'll head down." Brad bobbed his head. "Just the three of us." He was offering me cover, but it felt like something else. He wanted me to perform. This could go sideways fast. I had to be very careful.

"I need to hit the bathroom first," I said. "Five minutes, and I'll be ready."

"Of course. Take your time. I'll be waiting."

**LANDON FOLLOWED ME INTO THE PUBLIC RESTROOM.** He checked all the stalls before speaking.

"What in the hell, Bay?"

I held out my hands. "He checked up on us after we brought the first inmate back. Ted Arnold. He thinks I'm psychic. He got to that piece of information in a roundabout way, but that's obviously his belief."

"Did you confirm that?" There was no censure in Landon's tone.

"I just said that I was always taught to embrace my feelings."

"Okay." He leaned in and pressed a kiss to my forehead. He brushed his fingers over my neck, which looked horrible when I caught sight of my reflection. "We need to get that fixed as soon as we get back to the inn or I'm going to melt down."

That nudged a smile out of me. "What do you want me to do when checking the cells?"

"Go with your gut."

"I prefer more direction."

"I don't want you opening yourself up to undue attention, Bay." Landon spoke from the heart. "I fear that if word spreads about what you can do, every law enforcement agency north of Bay City—and some south—will try to tap you as a consultant. That will screw up our lives."

"Because they'll be bothering us all the time?"

"That and the first time you screw up, you'll be attacked and called a fraud."

I hadn't considered that. "I'll keep it to myself for now."

He pulled me in for a hug, his lips moving over my cheek. "I love you. Ultimately, this is your decision. I'll stand by you no matter what."

"I love you too."

"I know. I'm a catch." He grinned as he pulled back. "Are you ready?"

"As ready as I'll ever be."

. . .

**I DON'T KNOW WHAT I** expected, but the prison was dark and depressing. It was clean—Landon explained the inmates were responsible for keeping it clean, and since that meant more time out of their cells, they were keen to do it—but that was about all I could say.

Brad took us from cell to cell. There was a lot of catcalling from the inmates. Landon didn't hold my hand, but he stuck close, shielding me.

The cells were mundane. Some of the inmates had taped lewd drawings to the cinder block walls. It wasn't until we got to the last cell that I alerted on magic again.

"This cell belongs to Steven Mitchell," Brad said. "He murdered his girlfriend twenty years ago, was a model citizen in Jackson, and was transferred here about six months ago. We've never had a problem with him behavior wise."

Magic bounced off the walls and the bed. It was enough that my stomach constricted.

"Anything?" Brad asked hopefully.

"I don't know what you want me to say," I replied, keeping my eyes on the drawings affixed to the wall. They were the same illustrations I'd seen in other cells. "He draws nooses around all the women's necks," I noted.

Brad followed my gaze. "We don't actually frown upon art as a therapeutic tool, but some of it is distressing."

"It's interesting that he killed his girlfriend and was still considered nonviolent enough to end up here," I mused.

"He was twenty when he killed her. He's just over forty now. He hasn't had a single violent incident while incarcerated. He killed the girlfriend in a fit of rage because he thought she was going to break up with him. It was a crime of passion."

"That doesn't make her any less dead," I pointed out.

"No, but there's a big difference between premeditated crimes and crimes of passion. You understand," he prodded Landon.

"I do, but I'm not comfortable with this guy being here." He put his hand to my back. "You don't have to stay in here, sweetie."

I looked around again and then nodded. The traces of magic

remained, but there was nothing I could do about them given where we were and who was watching. "Sorry I couldn't be more help," I offered softly.

"It's fine." Brad held his hands palms out and shrugged. "I was hoping you might be able to figure something out. I guess that was just wishful thinking because my job is on the line."

My shoulders jolted. "I didn't realize that."

"It's a prison break. Someone will be blamed. If we can get all the prisoners back without anybody on the outside getting hurt, I have a shot at keeping my job. But the second someone is hurt, I'll lose all hope of staying here."

I remembered what he said about being excited to move here. "I hope you get to stay."

"Me too."

"I can't help you."

"It was worth a shot."

"I really am sorry."

"You did your best. That's all I can ask."

# Five

I told Landon and Chief Terry what I had really felt in Mitchell's cell during the drive back to Hemlock Cove. Chief Terry dropped us at the police station. He had things to organize but promised not to be too late to dinner.

Landon let me think in silence for the drive to the inn. We'd left my car downtown—I could catch a ride with him the following morning. He was alert navigating the roads to The Overlook, but there was nobody out. I couldn't imagine the remaining escapees hiding out in this area, but he was going to fret, so there was no point trying to stop him.

When we got to the inn, I was excited to realize it was empty. My mother and aunts had guests coming in, but apparently not today. It was a relief, because that meant we could discuss the prison break without worrying about freaking out guests.

"What are you doing?" I asked Aunt Tillie when we walked into the dining room. Landon immediately headed to the wine table, which was to be expected, and I sank into my usual chair.

"I'm debating the meaning of life," Aunt Tillie snapped. "What does it look like I'm doing? I'm waiting for dinner."

*Snort. Snort.*

Peg the pig was under the table at Aunt Tillie's feet. She perked up when she saw Landon.

"There's the happiest face on earth," Landon gushed when he caught sight of her. He stopped by me long enough to deliver a glass of wine and then dropped to his knees to kiss the pig. "Who loves me best?"

*Snort. Snort.*

I rolled my eyes. Getting jealous of the affection he slathered on Peg was a losing proposition, but it still irritated me at times. That was one reason I was seriously considering getting him a dog for Christmas.

"What happened to your neck?" my mother asked as she emerged from the kitchen with a platter of fried chicken.

"I had an interesting day," I replied. "It's fine, although I wouldn't mind a bottle of that healing ointment you've been making," I said to Aunt Tillie.

"I made a double batch this year. If you keep finding trouble, it might not be enough, so maybe try to pace yourself." Despite her bold words, she looked concerned when she peered at my neck. "Those are finger marks." She leaned back in her chair to glare at Landon. "You didn't do anything freaky, did you?"

Landon scowled at her. "Yes, I grabbed my wife by the neck and gave her a squeeze for fun. Do you really think I would do that?"

"It depends on if she slathered herself in bacon grease."

"Then I would lick her to death, not strangle her." Landon was surly when he got up from the floor and claimed his chair between Aunt Tillie and me. "Don't be weird."

"There was a prison break at Antrim Correctional," I volunteered as my aunts Marnie and Twila emerged from the kitchen with the rest of the food. Apparently, it was going to be just us tonight—no Thistle or Clove, who had returned home before our arrival—and I was secretly relieved. Clove would melt down at the thought of prisoners on the loose. "We managed to track down a few. There was an incident with one of them."

"I heard something about that on the radio," Mom said as she sat. Her gaze was dark. "I didn't realize you were going to be in on the search. Is that where Terry is? He said he'd be late for dinner and not to wait for him."

"He's making sure that the patrols are aware of what they should be looking for," Landon explained. "He won't be long."

"I thought they would catch the prisoners right away," Marnie admitted.

"Five were caught," Landon confirmed. "We're responsible for three. Er, well, Bay is." He shot me a soft smile. "There are still ten on the loose."

"Ten?" Mom was flabbergasted. "How could fifteen prisoners escape?"

"They still don't know." Landon reached for the tongs on the chicken platter. He stacked my plate first, which showed the boundless depths of his love because he was a food-oriented individual. "It looks to have been an inside job."

I jolted at the words. "Who said that?"

"That's what the state police troopers were telling me while you were with the warden. They said that the cameras going down and nobody sounding an alarm for almost four hours suggests that somebody—maybe multiple somebodies—inside the prison helped."

I watched as he added carrots, potatoes, and bread to my plate. I was capable of getting my own food, but this was his way of doting on me following my injury. Two years of being together had taught me a thing or two about balance. I needed independence in some things, and he gave as much as he could considering the trouble I found.

"Are they thinking the warden did this?" I asked when he was done heaping my plate full of food. It was enough for two people, but I was hungry enough to eat all of it.

Landon tilted his head, considering, and then shook it. "I don't think so," he said after several seconds. "The warden has only been on the job two years. He doesn't have nearly enough time accrued for retirement. Even if he got payment from several of the inmates, it wouldn't be enough to live out the rest of his years."

"Then it had to be someone working for him," I surmised.

"Pretty much," Landon confirmed.

"What are our options?"

"Obviously, we don't know." Landon slathered a slice of bread with enough butter that I shot him a dirty look. "It's been a rough day," he protested. "I need comfort food. It's not as if it's bacon."

"You need to monitor your cholesterol."

"Yeah, yeah, yeah." He waved off my concern. "It's almost Christmas. We'll worry about my cholesterol after the cookies have been packed away." He bit into his bread, groaning because it was still warm, and waited to swallow to speak. "I have to think it's one of the guards."

"Wouldn't it make more sense to be one of the service providers?" I countered. "What about food delivery? Or the laundry service? What about the medical professionals who come in for more serious cases?"

"All of those people will be looked at," Landon confirmed, "but logistics suggest it can't be any of them. It must be someone who has regular contact with the inmates. This isn't just something that happened on the spur of the moment. It was planned."

"Do you think some of the inmates were swept up in the escape and not part of the plan?"

"Absolutely." Landon tapped the side of my plate. "Eat. I want you to eat every bit of that. Then we'll take dessert home, put that ointment on, and I'll cuddle the crap out of you in the safety of our own home, so I don't look like a wuss."

He was impossible not to adore. He had the best heart of anyone I knew, and he was willing to own his schmaltzy feelings. "I'll eat, but I don't know if I can put all of this away."

He beamed at me. "Good girl." He sobered when grabbing his wine. "All of the service providers will be questioned. The inmates we captured today will be questioned. Deals will be offered to get dirt on the others, and whoever helped them."

"How would you have worked it?" I asked. "You're not a criminal mastermind, but you understand the logistics."

"I would've gone for one of the guards. They don't make much money. This prison is quiet—at least as far as prisons go—and they're not as diligent when it comes to checking visitor logs or watching which guards interact with which prisoners.

"If I had to guess, I would say that the original plan was between one guard and one inmate," he continued. "The others were added in later as cover."

"How will they narrow it down?"

"It won't happen overnight. Even if the captured inmates barter information for lighter sentences, not all that information can be taken at face value."

"So we have to wait it out," I mused. "We won't know anything for days."

He ran his hand over my back. "It's okay. We'll figure it out."

He was right. Dwelling on it now wouldn't do any good. "When do the guests arrive?" I asked my mother. "I was surprised to find the parking lot empty. I thought they were coming in today."

"Tomorrow," she said. "Hearing all this, I'm relieved about it. This prison break is going to have to be spun, I guess. Thankfully, we don't have tourists, just the acting troupe."

My eyebrows hiked. "The Happy Holidays Players are staying with you?"

"Yes." Mom's smile was enigmatic.

"I'm going to get a part in the pageant," Twila volunteered, her eyes sparkling. "A big part."

I was confused. "Do you know which parts are going to be offered?"

"No, but she's convinced she's getting a big one," Marnie replied. "She doesn't realize I'm going to get the big part."

"Oh, please," Mom scoffed. "We all know I'm the best actress under this roof. That's why the guests gravitate toward me. I will be getting the big part."

I skirted my eyes to Landon and found him grinning. "You still haven't told me how you know there's going to be a big part," I pressed.

"They always have a few bigger parts at all their stops," Mom replied. "Twila looked it up on the internet."

"Oh, well, you know it's true if it was on the internet," I groused. "Before we get off the prison break, there's something you need to know." I'd debated leaving out the magical bits while bringing them up to date, but that would put them at a disadvantage if they crossed paths with one of the escapees. "There's one more problem."

Mom's eyes were expectant when they landed on me. "I'm not going to like this, am I?" Her mood switched from teasing to dark in an instant.

"The reason the guy in the machine shop managed to get his hands on me is because I was distracted by the fact that he was swimming with magic."

Aunt Tillie showed genuine interest in the conversation for the first time since we'd sat down. "What sort of magic?"

I lifted one shoulder in a shrug. "I've never seen anything like it. I can say it was dark. I don't know how much power he truly had. He grabbed me by the throat, and I used my magic to knock him back and out.

"I looked in his head while he was out," I continued. "I was looking for signs of what he was. All I saw was human. There was a shrouded figure helping him escape. There wasn't a face to go along with the body."

"That's probably a byproduct of the magic used," Aunt Tillie noted. "Whoever did it messed with his memory. It's possible the face is in there, but we would have to dig hard to find it."

"Well, he's outside of our reach now. He's back in the prison. I removed whatever spell was placed on him. At least I think I did."

"He was fodder," Aunt Tillie surmised. "He was meant to slow the search parties down as the real culprit gets away."

She was prone to hyperbole, but I didn't disagree. "The warden seemed to sense there was something different about me. He ... um ... believes I'm psychic."

Mom's face filled with alarm. "I hope you shut that down right away."

"I was kind of vague." I glanced at Landon. "I didn't want to completely shut him down because he gave me access to the cells."

"It's fine," Landon interjected when Mom opened her mouth to argue. "He doesn't know the truth. He can't. If he wants to believe she's psychic, that might benefit us."

"And what happens when the dust settles and he's bored one day?" Mom challenged.

"Everybody in the area has a Winchester story. This will just add to the mystique." He squeezed my knee under the table. "Don't get crazy.

We don't have a reason to worry yet. Besides, as far as he's concerned, Bay didn't find anything in the cells."

"As far as he's concerned?" Mom's eyebrows shifted toward one another. Of course she would pick up on that caveat.

"Steve Mitchell." I'd come this far. It was best to finish it. "His was the last cell we were in. He killed his girlfriend twenty years ago. He's been a model prisoner ever since. That's why they moved him north."

"I take it he's one of the escapees."

"He is, and I felt magic in his cell," I replied. "There were some disturbing drawings of women with nooses around their necks taped to the walls. The warden didn't seem all that upset about them, but I was less than thrilled. The magic was not fresh. It was fragments of a bigger magic clearly used over a stretch of time."

"What do we know about this Mitchell?" Mom asked Landon.

"Not much," Landon replied. "I have a request in for his full file from the Department of Corrections. I'm hoping to have more tomorrow."

"So there's at least one more supernaturally enhanced prisoner on the loose and just in time for the big pageant," Mom said. "That's just great."

"It had better not ruin my starring moment," Twila groused. "I'll be mad forever if it does."

"Yes, that's what we should be worried about," Mom shot back, rolling her eyes. "Good grief." She turned to Aunt Tillie. "Should we strengthen the wards on the property?"

Aunt Tillie looked intrigued. "I don't see the point. The current wards will keep a murderous human off the grounds. Without knowing what sort of magic we're up against, I don't see the point in trying to keep out magical beings. That's like firing an arrow into an ocean and expecting to hit a shark."

Mom nodded. "Well, we'll leave that decision for later. Hopefully, this won't be an issue after tomorrow."

She was an optimist when she wanted to be. I was more of a pessimist at heart. I knew we wouldn't have all the escapees in custody anytime soon. "Just keep your eyes open for anybody you don't recognize. A prisoner won't look like a tourist, no matter how hard he tries. If somebody stands out, call Landon and Chief Terry and let them handle it."

"Like you let them handle it without you today?" Mom challenged.

"Let's talk about something else." I forced myself to look at Aunt Tillie. "Are you going to try for a part in the pageant?" I already knew the answer. I was just desperate for a different conversation. An Aunt Tillie rant would be welcome.

"Screw the pageant." Aunt Tillie made a face. "I'm more interested in the prisoners. Are there rewards for catching them?"

"No," I answered.

"Yes," Landon replied at the same time. He didn't shrink down in his seat when I glared at him. "What?" he demanded after a beat. "If she wants to catch a few escaped prisoners, I won't stop her. She can take that vampire she's so fond of, and they can catch them all. It will save me a bunch of headaches."

The vampire in question, Evan, had become Aunt Tillie's sidekick in recent months. When he wasn't in Hawthorne Hollow helping the monster hunters there, he was with Aunt Tillie, helping her wreak havoc on the community. As far as sidekicks went for tracking down killers, he was as solid as they came.

"That's the deal," I said. "If you go hunting prisoners, you take Evan."

"You're not the boss of me." Aunt Tillie was haughty. "I want to take him, so I'll let it slide." She rubbed her hands together. "Now, about those rewards."

"Catch a prisoner first, and then we'll talk," Landon replied. "Until then, keep your nose out of trouble and don't do anything weird."

"Oh, right," Aunt Tillie scoffed. "Like that's going to happen."

# Six

Landon's diligence in checking security at the guesthouse amused me. The property was warded. Sure, we didn't know what sort of magic was flitting about, but I wasn't too worried. He was another story.

"If you're here in the afternoon tomorrow, keep the door locked," he ordered. "That way no one can burst in on you."

"If that doesn't work on my family, what makes you think it will work on an escaped prisoner?"

"That's a fair point, but I still want you to be careful."

"I'm always careful."

"Oh, you're full of it." He kicked off his shoes and dropped his pants, leaving them in the middle of the living room before grabbing me around the waist and dragging me to the couch.

"Well, that's romantic," I offered sarcastically.

He chuckled. "That comes later. I need to digest. Right now, it's snuggle time."

I laughed as I rolled onto the couch with him. He grabbed the blanket we always kept draped over the back and tucked me in. His eyes were thoughtful as he took in my face. "Where's that ointment from Aunt Tillie?" he asked.

"In my coat pocket."

I'd dropped my coat on the arm of the couch. He secured the ointment without having to get up. He dabbed the medicine on my neck, the fierceness in his eyes telling me he had something important on his mind.

"It was a fluke," I assured him. "Don't get worked up."

"Who says I'm worked up?"

"Your face."

"I happen to think my face is perfect." He screwed the cap back on the ointment and dropped it on the coffee table. "I've been told that I look like one of those Greek statues."

"Who told you that? If it was your mother, it doesn't count."

"Women the world over have fallen for this face, Bay." He sounded deadly serious, but it was impossible to miss the twinkle in his eyes. "Thankfully for you, I'm a one-witch sort of guy. I only care what you think now."

I didn't respond.

"This is where you're supposed to say that I'm the handsomest man you've ever met," he prodded.

I laughed again because it was expected. "You're unbelievable," I said when I'd recovered. "Does that mean I'm the most beautiful woman you've ever met?"

"Yes." He answered without hesitation. "That's what I thought when I met you in that cornfield. *Look at her. Could anybody be more beautiful?*"

"Then you wondered why I wouldn't shut my mouth."

"Yes, well, I've grown to love that mouth." As if to prove it, he kissed my upturned mouth. "I love you, Bay, but we need to be careful now."

"You're worried the warden will spill our secret."

"I'm worried that he's going to try to use you and your abilities to his advantage as the walls close in on him. The odds of him keeping his job are slim. He'll get desperate."

I could see that. "He seemed earnest, as if he meant what he said."

"That's probably true, but when people feel they're losing something, beliefs change. He doesn't want to lose his job. As the investigation turns internal, he'll be on the hot seat."

"How do you think they managed it?"

"I honestly don't know." His hands moved over my back so he could rub. "Is it possible some sort of witch was involved? I mean ... you sensed magic."

"I did, but I've never come across the type of magic I felt when I was fighting off Barker. And he didn't use the magic to attack me. He used his hands."

Landon growled.

"I'm fine," I reminded him.

"You could've been seriously hurt. He's bigger than you. If he'd grabbed harder, started shaking..." He trailed off. "I don't want to think about it."

"I know you don't, but I'm in this now." I was firm. "You can't cut me out because you had a scare."

"I *could* cut you out." There wasn't much conviction in his tone.

"You need me."

His sigh was soft. "Oh, Bay, I always need you. Before you, I managed to solve cases all the time. Now that rarely happens."

"That's because you didn't see the magic before. I'm sure there were cases that flummoxed you, and looking back, you have to wonder if magic was involved."

"Maybe a few." He didn't look happy at the realization. "Everything is magical now. Even meth heads bent on murder."

My heart went out to him. "If you want to talk about Kevin, we can."

"There's nothing left to say. He got caught up in a situation beyond his control, and now he's gone. It's not as if we can bring him back." He shifted his eyes to my face. "You're a necromancer, but you can't do it?"

"No. Dead is dead. But there are stories about necromancers who could raise the dead."

"Seriously?" Landon looked intrigued.

"There was a guy in South America who supposedly raised the dead to work his farm. You should keep in mind that he raised them as zombies and not as full humans. In general, though, dead is dead."

"And Kevin is at peace. You made sure of that."

"He's not suffering, Landon," I promised. "You're suffering because you can't let him go."

Landon looked momentarily pained. "I'll get over it. I'm just feeling surly." He blew out a sigh. "Let's go back to talking about the prison break. You asked how it might be done. I'm guessing one of the prisoners—perhaps it was Mitchell—crossed paths with a witch. She used her magic to help him escape, and they pulled other inmates into it to serve as fodder. If the focus of the search parties split, it would be easier to escape the net."

"Could they already be gone?"

Landon hesitated and then shrugged. "If it were me, I would get out of the immediate circle and hole up in a cabin somewhere for at least a month. Traveling right now anywhere in the state will be difficult. Cops will be looking everywhere."

"He needs to change his appearance," I said. "That means growing a beard, maybe shaving his head. He needs new clothes. All of that would have to be in place right from the start."

"If it were me, I would've had the getaway vehicle parked down the road away from the cameras and potential traffic. I would've broken away from the rest of the inmates, gone to the pre-arranged rendezvous point, gotten in the back seat, changed clothes while the other person was driving, and immediately gone to a cabin or house already picked out.

"The driver would've arranged for food," he continued. "I keep picturing a woman because now I've gotten it in my head that it's a witch, but Sam has witch in him, so I know it's stupid to ignore the possibility that it's a man. I just ... don't know."

He looked frustrated enough that I reached up to press my palm to his cheek. He kissed my palm and then settled into the touch.

"It could've been a family member," I said. "Maybe Mitchell's mother is a witch. Or maybe witch runs in his blood, and he has a sister."

"I'm pulling all of those files tomorrow," Landon assured me. "Right now, they're tied up in bureaucratic nonsense."

"We might luck out. Maybe more prisoners will be caught overnight."

"That's a distinct possibility. It's getting cold tonight. Some of them won't be prepared. One or two might actually turn themselves in."

"Do you want me with you tomorrow?"

He took a long moment to consider it. "I'm tired, Bay. Seeing your neck like that makes me irrationally angry. Can we wait to have that conversation in the morning?"

It was a reasonable request. "Does that mean you're ready to move on to the romance portion of our evening?"

A devilish gleam came into his eyes. "You read my mind."

**THE NEXT MORNING, OTHER THAN FAINT** bruising I could easily cover with makeup, my neck was back to normal. Landon still glared at the now-covered marks as he drank his coffee.

We drove to the inn because we would be leaving from there. I had no idea what was on the agenda, but I knew that there would be nothing quiet about our day. The dining room bustled with activity, and one look at Aunt Tillie told me things were about to get rough.

"You're not wearing that," Mom barked. She had her hands on her hips as she stood next to Aunt Tillie's chair and glared at her.

Aunt Tillie didn't look worried. She was dressed in camouflage pants, a black top that showed more cleavage than usual—she'd been doing that a lot lately since hooking up with Whistler in Hawthorne Hollow—and she had a strange utility belt holding up her pants.

"What's with the belt?" I asked as I tried to get a better look. She had numerous potion vials attached to it. There was also what suspiciously looked like a grenade tacked on the belt near her right hip. "Are you going to blow something up?"

Landon, who had apparently not seen the grenade at first glance, did a double take. "Is that real?"

"You bet, Sparky." Aunt Tillie winked at him. "I'm loaded for bear."

Landon darted his eyes to Chief Terry. "You're going to do something."

Chief Terry looked bleary eyed and beyond it all. "I've opted to pretend I don't see it."

"Well, that seems healthy." Landon rolled his eyes and planted his hands on his hips. "You cannot walk around with a grenade. Where did you even get that thing?"

"Don't worry about it." Aunt Tillie's eyes flashed with annoyance. "Who designated you the weapons police?"

"Um ... the federal government."

I held up my finger to silence Landon and tried a fresh approach. "What's wrong with your stick? Why can't you use that instead of the grenade?" Something occurred to me. "Wait. That's not for Mrs. Little, is it?"

"Like I need a grenade for her," Aunt Tillie scoffed. "It's not a grenade—not that I owe 'The Man' an explanation—so don't get your panties in a twist."

Landon didn't calm down. "If it's not real, what is it?"

"A magical grenade."

Landon turned to me. "Did she just explain something?"

I was as confused as him. "What's a magical grenade?"

"It's a bunch of magic that will go boom when I need it to." Aunt Tillie looked far too happy with herself, so I knew she was leaving pertinent information out of the explanation.

"What is it for?" I pressed.

"It's for the prisoners." She lifted her chin when Marnie emerged from the kitchen with a platter of scrambled eggs and bacon. Twila followed with the hash browns and toast. "Yay. Here comes my fuel."

"You're going on a prisoner hunt?" Landon demanded.

"Last night you said it was a good idea," Aunt Tillie reminded him.

The look of betrayal Chief Terry shot Landon would've made me laugh under different circumstances. "You told her it was a good idea?" he hissed.

"I said that it was an interesting notion," Landon lied. He looked to me for help.

"You're on your own." I plopped down in my usual chair and reached for the juice carafe. "Only three slices of bacon today," I reminded him.

"I have to hunt for prisoners all day. That requires more than three slices of bacon."

"You had cake and two servings of potatoes last night," I argued.

"When did you turn so cruel?" Landon was morose when he sat.

"About the time you decided to cut me out of the prisoner hunt," I replied as I ladled eggs onto my plate.

Next to me, Landon froze. "How...?" He trailed off.

"How did I figure it out? You've been evasive this morning," I replied. "If you were going to include me in the hunt, you would've already been making plans. You've been careful not to mention anything about your day. I'm not an idiot."

If I thought Landon looked morose before, it was nothing compared to his expression now. "I just think it's not smart to have you with me two days in a row, Bay. I'm afraid of the message it will send to Warden Childs. He's already suspicious. If you're not with us when we check in today, it might disrupt his radar."

"Sure." I refused to meet his gaze as I purposely added four slices of bacon to my plate.

Landon's mournful glare almost made me laugh. "Why do you get four slices?"

"Because I don't overindulge in bacon five times a week," I replied. "Plus, I'm the one getting cut out of the action."

"Is that wise?" Mom asked. She'd seemingly forgotten about Aunt Tillie's grenade because she was focused on Chief Terry as she sat. "If one of the prisoners really is magical, shouldn't Bay be with you?"

"I want her safe," Chief Terry replied. He didn't look up, and I was suddenly suspicious. Was he the reason Landon had decided to cut me out of the action? "After what happened yesterday, I've reassessed how I want to handle this. Bay has her own job to do. She doesn't need to be part of ours." He gestured between Landon and himself.

My eyes were narrow slits of suspicion as I stared at Landon. He refused to meet my gaze and instead focused on his three bacon slices.

"You know, one of the reasons I was so ready to marry into this family was the food," he lamented. "I feel as if I've been bamboozled."

"You'll live." I patted his knee. "That's the reason I'm trying to teach you moderation."

"Whatever." Landon poured his own glass of juice. "Even though you're irritated with me, I need you to promise me something, Bay."

He sounded serious.

"If you go out looking for prisoners—and by if, I mean when—I don't want you going alone. Take Aunt Tillie. Evan would be even better."

I was floored. "Since when do you purposely want me hanging out with other guys?" I asked.

"He's not another guy. He's a vampire, and he can fight magical and nonmagical prisoners. He's fast enough that you can't even see him unless he wants you to."

"Hey!" Aunt Tillie was incensed. "Evan is my sidekick. If Bay wants a sidekick, she needs to find someone else. I suggest Thistle. Maybe put her on a leash and make her bark like a dog."

The joke would've landed better if Thistle had actually been in attendance for breakfast.

"I have a few things I need to get done today," I replied. "The Happy Holiday Players arrive, and I need to interview them. On top of that, I have some listings for Christmas because it's right around the corner."

Now Landon was suspicious. "Are you seriously going to sit there and pretend you're not going to search for the escapees?"

"I'll send Viola out looking," I replied. "After that, who knows."

Landon made a face and then very pointedly reached over to the bacon heap and grabbed three more slices. "You're lying."

"I'm not lying, and you put that bacon back," I warned.

"He already touched it," Mom interjected. "He either has to eat it or toss it."

Throwing away bacon was akin to a war crime to Landon. He stuffed all three slices in his mouth at once. "When you're willing to tell the truth, I'll moderate my bacon intake," he garbled around his full mouth.

I glared at him. "You're ticking me off."

"Welcome to the club." He swallowed. "If you go out chasing prisoners, I don't want you alone. Take backup."

Was that the end of the argument? "Are you mad?" I asked after a few seconds. "Are we good?"

"We're always good. But I know you're lying. You have every intention of going after those escaped cons. You can't help yourself."

Deep down, I knew he was right. That didn't stop me from feigning innocence. "You don't know. The Happy Holidays Players could be so fascinating that I won't want to chase prisoners."

"Now you're lying to yourself." Landon grabbed another slice of bacon.

# Seven

Landon was sulky when he dropped me at the police station.

"You will be careful?" He rubbed his stomach as he regarded me.

I dug in my purse for the acid reducer and handed it to him. "I think you learned a lesson about eating too much bacon," It was hard not to be smug. "As you get older, these things will happen more frequently."

"Thanks, Mom," he drawled, grudgingly accepting the acid reducer. "You still haven't promised you'll be careful. That's part of why my stomach is upset."

"I'll be careful, Landon." I meant it. "You do the same. I won't be there to protect you if you find one of the magical prisoners. More than one might be magical. Keep that in mind."

"Bay, I'll be fine." He managed a smile. "Without you, we probably won't even find any prisoners."

The way he said it made me suspicious. "This is all Chief Terry, isn't it?"

Landon shifted his gaze to the town square. "They're all ready for the Happy Holidays Players. It looks nice. I love when the Christmas stuff is out."

I folded my arms across my chest. "Landon Michaels."

He sighed. "He texted when you were in the shower this morning. He's worked up about what happened. I can't force him to bring you with us."

"But you would if you could?"

"I prefer you were with us," he acknowledged. "You're powerful. I like having you as a partner, but I can't ignore his feelings. He thinks of you as a daughter, and you don't want your daughter finding trouble."

That made me feel a little better. Well, at least with him. I was angry with Chief Terry. I would have to wait until later to confront him. "You do realize that when we have a daughter, she's going to find constant trouble?"

"That's why I have to enjoy my bacon now." He managed a rueful smile. "Don't go anywhere alone if you can help it. Promise me. I'm going to be antsy all day."

My stance had softened without me even realizing it. "I promise." I leaned in and pressed a kiss to the corner of his pouty mouth. "I'll even text if I get a lead."

"Thank you." He stroked the back of my head. "Do you know what I was thinking last night?" His eyes were intense, but his lips were curving.

"That you're lucky to have me?"

"Bay, I've always thought that. I was thinking about Christmas. This is our first Christmas as a married couple."

"And our third Christmas overall."

"Yes, but the first one was kind of tense because I was still dealing with some of the witch stuff. I was silently freaking out, but I didn't want you to know it."

"Well, you hid it well." He hadn't hidden it well at all, but there was no reason to bring that up now. We were in a good place. We had been since he'd not only decided he could handle the witch stuff but also wanted to learn about it as much as possible. That made him a hero in my book ... even if he was a glutton with impulse control problems.

"I want it to be a perfect Christmas, Bay. I know we have weeks yet, but it's important to me. Make sure nothing happens to you that will ruin my Christmas."

He'd purposely said it that way to get a rise out of me. All I could do was laugh though. "You do the same."

He planted a hard kiss on my mouth. "I'll be in touch. Maybe we can swing lunch?"

"The Happy Holidays Players arrive around ten o'clock. They'll be downtown surveying the pageant area. Mrs. Little made sure to send me a note. I'm not sure how long the interviews will take."

"Will Mrs. Little be present for the interviews?"

"Probably." I scowled at the possibility. "Isn't she always there when I don't want her to be?"

"I'm thinking that might be even more dangerous than hunting escapees." After yet another kiss, he pulled away. "Be good. I'll let you know if we find anything."

"Tell Chief Terry we're going to talk later," I said as I moved toward my car. "There's no escaping it."

"I'm sure he'll be thrilled."

**THE WHISTLER OFFICE WAS QUIET**. Down the hallway, I heard the faint whispering of a television and knew Viola was present. Before tracking her down, I set the security system because Landon would want that—and it was the smart thing to do—and then took a photo of the panel to text him before heading to the kitchenette.

Viola was in her usual chair watching television. It was early, so she had the news on, and she didn't look happy with the reports.

"The world is going to Hell in a handbasket," she noted. "Prisoners escaping. Lou Metcalf apparently got drunk at the bar in Hawthorne Hollow last night and got himself arrested for flashing all the women in town. It's a sin factory over there."

"Poor Lou," I noted. "Has he been released yet?"

"I have no idea." Viola used her ghostly powers to turn off the television. "What's my mission today?"

Surprise washed over me. "What makes you think I have a mission for you?"

"There are still prisoners on the loose, and I saw what happened with that one at the machine shop yesterday. He wasn't normal. You won't rest until all of them are back behind bars. The news said there are ten still out there. That means a prisoner hunt."

"Wait ... none of the prisoners were captured overnight?" That went against what Landon and I had surmised the previous evening.

"Is that important?"

"I thought for sure they would find one or two more. I guess they all managed to find places to hole up for the night."

"Do you want me to go looking for them?"

"Actually, I do, but I'm not sure where to have you start." I went to the map on the wall. "Here's the prison." I pointed. "How far do you think they could've gotten on foot in a few hours?"

Viola shrugged. "How should I know? I'm not a math wizard."

"We have no way of knowing if these men are together or if they're on foot. Some probably managed to get into vehicles. So where are they?"

"I would head home. I know that's not the smart thing to do, but I wouldn't be able to help myself."

"Right. We need information on the individual prisoners. None of that was provided last night. I'll have to get Landon on that."

"Where do you want me to start looking?"

I could think of only one place. "The lake," I replied without hesitation. "There are houses out there closed up for the winter."

"Okay. I'll check downtown too when I get back. What do you want me to do if I find them?"

"Nothing. Just come back and tell me."

"That's kind of boring."

"That's what I need." I flashed a smile I didn't feel. "One more thing," I prodded before she could disappear. "If you see Aunt Tillie, tell me. She managed to escape when everybody was distracted this morning. She took her plow truck."

"There's no snow yet. We're supposed to get an inch tonight, but that's not much."

"That's what worries me. I can see her using that plow to mow down prisoners."

Viola nodded sagely. "I'll be on the lookout for her." After a saucy salute, Viola was gone. That left me to deal with advertisers and emails.

Thanks to the size of the town, it took me less than an hour to get through both. By that time, I was looking to stretch my legs.

A huge bus chuffed on Main Street when I exited the building. It reminded me of a tour bus. Like ... rock stars would've been jealous. Well, other than the cheerful holiday scenes painted on the outside. That wasn't very hardcore.

"There you are, Bay," a prickly voice said in front of the police station. When I turned, I found Mrs. Little standing next to one of the tinseled benches. She was dressed in her warm winter coat, and she didn't look any happier to see me than I was to see her.

"Mrs. Little," I replied stiffly.

"Bay."

I frowned. She'd already said my name. "Mrs. Little."

"Bay." Now she looked amused. "Is that all you're going to say? I thought for certain you would have something nasty to throw at me."

"I'm all out of knives," I replied darkly. "What are you doing here?"

"The same as you, I imagine. The pageant people are a big deal. This is the second biggest festival. The Christmas Festival later this month is our biggest, but this needs to be a success if we want to keep drawing people in during the cold months. January is a bit of a dead zone for us when it comes to tourism."

"Perhaps you could call a djinn to fix that for you."

Her eyes narrowed. We hadn't talked much since she'd admitted to unleashing a djinn on the area to wreak havoc on our family. People had died as a result. While she hadn't wanted innocent people to die, I held no illusions about her wishes for my family. "You just won't let that go, will you?"

"I won't." I saw no reason to lie. "People are dead, Mrs. Little."

"There's nothing I can do to change that."

"Your need for vengeance caused unnecessary death," I insisted. "Maybe take just a little responsibility for that."

If looks could kill, I would be dead. "Responsibility? All I do is take responsibility for this town. Was a mistake made? Yes. If you would keep Tillie on a leash, I wouldn't feel the need to protect myself. And, yes, Bay, that's exactly what I was doing. Protecting myself."

She was full of it. "You keep telling yourself that. You're the only one who believes it."

"I believe this conversation is a waste of time," she said primly. "You'll never see my side of things."

"I could say the same about you."

"As far as I'm concerned, you don't have a side. You do what you want, when you want, and expect no repercussions. What happened is on you."

"That's rich." The sound of the bus door opening drew my attention to our incoming guests. Allowing them to see us going at each other wouldn't benefit anybody. "Do what you want to do, *Margaret*. Just know, we're watching you."

"Right back at you." Mrs. Little was all smiles as she slid forward to greet the festive-looking woman who stepped off the bus. She was regal —her hair was long and silvery gray, pulled back in a complicated twist —and her smile was bright enough to illuminate the darkest night. "You must be Mary Stratton," Mrs. Little said. "It's so nice to meet you face-to-face finally. So sorry about the war on Christmas and having to change your name."

Mary blinked several times—Mrs. Little was a lot to take, even on her best day—and then smiled. "Oh, it was my idea to change the name. Christmas is for everybody, but if we narrow our offerings down to just Christmas, we have a problem. By encompassing more holiday time, we can do more performances. That means more money."

Mrs. Little looked flummoxed. "I didn't think about that."

"Yes, well, now you can think about it." Mary turned to me. "And you are?"

I introduced myself, explained about the newspaper, and asked if I could do a few quick interviews. She was all for it. Any free publicity was good publicity in her book. There were more players than I expected, and the interviews took longer than I anticipated.

As I finished up—more than an hour after I'd started—I was exhausted and ready for some coffee. Thistle, apparently expecting this, arrived on the sidewalk with a warm peppermint mocha.

"What do you think?" she asked as she handed it over.

I was grateful for the chocolaty goodness and sipped before

responding. "They're more business oriented than I thought," I said. We were across the street from the group, which was garnering attention from multiple residents. "The leader, Mary Stratton, basically put Mrs. Little in her place the second she got off the bus."

"Oh, so she's our sort of people," Thistle said with a laugh.

"She seems to be. I think she can read people well. She would probably have to do that in her line of work."

"Who do we have?" Thistle asked as she nodded her chin toward the actors.

I whipped out my reporter's notebook. There was no way I could keep them straight without help this early in the game.

"That's Thomas Avery." I pointed to a strikingly handsome man with a bit of scruff and a warm smile. "He's thirty-four, and he's been with the group two years." I pointed to a flirty blonde who couldn't seem to get enough of Thomas. "That's Ava King. She's twenty-seven and clearly wants a slice of Thomas's pie for dessert."

Thistle burst out laughing. "Even I could pick up on that, and I'm not always the best at reading people. As far as I'm concerned, all people are evil. Even the good ones."

"You're nowhere near as snarky as you pretend." I pointed to an older gentleman who bore a striking resemblance to Sam Elliot. "That's Lenny Stewart. He's got a gravelly voice to match the face, and I kind of love him. He's blunt."

"That means he's our people too," Thistle noted.

"The final two actresses are Robin Blanchard and Renee Palmer. They answered questions but didn't seem all that excited about it. I get the feeling this is a lifestyle for Mary, an opportunity for Ava and Thomas, and just a job for the others."

"You can't hold that against them. Too much forced holiday cheer would annoy almost anybody."

"True." I let loose a sigh. "You haven't seen Aunt Tillie, have you?"

"No, and it's been a good day. Why? Is she up to something?" Thistle made a face. "Oh, why am I even asking? It's been two weeks since she's found trouble—that we know of—so of course she's up to something."

"She had a grenade strapped to her belt this morning."

Thistle choked on her mocha.

I laughed at her response. "She said it's a magical grenade. She's on the hunt for missing prisoners."

"Should we be worried about that?"

"Just keep the door to the alley locked," I suggested. "I can't imagine wandering around downtown will be on any of their lists of things to do, but stranger things have happened. Also, at least two of the prisoners are magical."

I caught her up, including how bitter I was at Chief Terry for cutting me out of the action. When I finished, she looked caught between amusement and worry.

"You get more like Aunt Tillie every day," she said. "That was totally an Aunt Tillie rant when you went off on the Chief Terry maneuver."

I glared at her. "That's the meanest thing you've ever said to me."

She continued, unbothered. "What do you think the magic stuff means? Are we in danger?"

"I don't know that we are," I replied. "Just be careful. I think the odds of any of them ending up in this area are slim but keep your eyes open."

"I think I can manage that." Thistle let loose a breath. "What do you think Aunt Tillie is going to do with that grenade?"

"I don't want to find out."

"You and me both. It's going to be ugly."

"Then here's hoping she throws it at Mrs. Little."

# Eight

Viola hadn't returned when I got back to *The Whistler*, so I wrote the article about the Happy Holidays Players and sent it to our part-time page designer. The actual pageant wouldn't be covered until the next issue. I was about to call it a day and head to Hypnotic to gossip with my cousins—and maybe eat some of the good chocolate Clove always had on hand—when an excited Viola popped into existence in the middle of my office.

"There's a freaky dude in the alley behind your cousins' store," she announced.

I remained calm. "Oh, please tell me it's not Lou. Is he still drunk?"

Viola emphatically shook her head. "It's not Lou. It's a guy I've never seen before, and he looks to be hunting trouble."

I straightened. "Is it a prisoner?"

"He's not wearing a jumpsuit, but he looks the type."

"Are you sure it's not a deliveryman? The stores on Main Street get a lot of deliveries this time of year."

"Do deliverymen often have homemade tattoos on their necks?"

Viola was prone to melting down over nothing in particular so it was possible she was overreacting. Still, I couldn't ignore the possibility.

"Thanks." I shut down my computer and grabbed my keys. "I'll check it out."

"I'm going with you." Viola's tone was no nonsense. "You know, just in case you need some muscle." She flexed, which came across more Bugs Bunny than Arnold Schwarzenegger. Landon had insisted I go nowhere alone, so I took her up on the offer.

The Happy Holidays Players were still in the town square. I pasted a bright smile on my face as I passed them, intent on making sure I didn't cause a panic. Mary's gaze was curious.

"You're in a hurry," she called out.

"I need some caffeine," I replied easily. "I usually hang out with my cousins in the afternoon and overdose on coffee and chocolate."

"Ah, a family bonding exercise I can get behind." She winked and waved goodbye, seemingly happy with the town's fawning over her.

I waited until I got to the end of the block, glanced over my shoulder again to see if anybody was watching, and then rounded the corner of Hypnotic instead of going inside. I could've grabbed Thistle for backup—Landon would've much preferred her as my sidekick rather than Viola—but if there really was danger in the alley, I didn't want to leave Clove and Calvin alone in the store. It was better Thistle stay with them.

Everything looked quiet. I shot Viola a questioning look. "He's down by the ell."

The ell was directly behind Hypnotic's back door, and it made me nervous. "Keep your eyes open," I hissed.

"I always do. I sleep with my eyes open. I'm just that good."

"Now I know why you and Aunt Tillie were always at each other's throats," I groused as I edged forward. "You both say the same ridiculous stuff."

"I'm way better at sleeping with my eyes closed than Tillie."

"Yeah, yeah, yeah." I rolled my neck and took another two steps. I was barely in the alley when a wave of magic washed over me. It wasn't an attack. It was my detection senses kicking into overdrive ... and it wasn't a good feeling. "Well, hell."

I blew out a breath and gripped my hands into fists at my side. I took another step, but it wasn't enough to let me see around the corner.

Then I took another step, and my heart rate picked up a notch as a warning whisper assailed my senses. I reacted on instinct, dropping to my knees as a barrage of red hit the wall directly next to the spot I'd been standing in. If I hadn't ducked, the magic would've hit me full on.

"Well, that's interesting," I muttered as the brick where the magic had hit turned black and grimy. "That's not fire magic."

"I told you I found something freaky."

"And you were right." I rubbed my sweaty palms over my knees, cursed my luck, and then crawled to the left. I didn't allow the prisoner to see me. Once I was near the opposite wall, I pushed myself to my feet and pressed my body flat against the fence that separated the alley from another row of businesses.

"I was thinking we should talk," I called out. I wasn't comfortable sticking my head around the corner in case he tried to blow it off. If I could get a sense of where his head was at, I could decide how to handle the situation.

"You want to talk?" a gravelly voice demanded from somewhere just out of sight. He was much closer than I realized. He couldn't be behind the dumpster. He was right at the corner, which wasn't good. If he moved fast enough, he could get his hands on me, and then I would be in a world of hurt. I took a step away from him. If he wanted to play games, I would make him work for his prize.

"I want to talk," I confirmed. "Do you have a name?"

"Blow me. That's my name."

"Is that hyphenated?"

"Do you think you're funny?" The growling he let loose was more animal than human.

"I have it on good authority that I'm quite often funny," I replied. "Obviously, you don't think so. Either way, we need to come to a meeting of the minds here. You really don't belong in the alley."

"That's convenient because I don't want to stay in the alley. I don't suppose you have a car? I'll make a trade. You can leave with your life, and I'll leave with your vehicle."

"Yeah, that doesn't work for me." I narrowed my eyes when I caught a hint of movement. He was right at the corner, preparing to make his move. He had magic at his disposal, which made him dangerous. "You should turn yourself in." I backed up a bit more, trying not to think too hard about the stuff I had likely gotten on my hands and knees when on the ground.

"That's not going to happen, little girl," he rasped. "There's no way I'm going back. I'm free, and I'm going to stay that way. Now, either give me your car, or you're going to give me a little something else."

My blood ran cold. "I think we have to part ways there." My voice wasn't as shaky as I felt. "That's not going to happen." I said the words and then scrambled to the other side of the alley. I wouldn't be where he was expecting when he rounded the corner.

"We'll just see about that." His voice boomed as he appeared. Sure enough, his gaze was where he thought I would be, not where I'd ended up.

"*Glacio*," I intoned, freezing him in place.

His eyes went wide, and to my surprise, he fought the spell. He wasn't strong enough to break free of it, but he struggled mightily.

My breath came in ragged bursts as I shifted closer to him. The tension in his muscles told me he was still fighting the spell. How long would it take for him to break free? "Who did this to you?" I demanded.

He didn't respond.

"Are you Steve Mitchell?"

There was a flash of recognition in his eyes. "Well, I guess I'll find out the answer to that soon enough." I stepped in front of him and slapped my hand to his forehead. "*Ostendo*."

He dropped like a stone. I looked around to make sure nobody had wandered over to take a gander down the alley. I dropped to my knees and placed my hand on the inmate's forehead. A series of images assailed me almost immediately.

His name was Jordan Fox. He was an arsonist. He'd learned to love fire at a young age. As a young man, he'd let the fire get away from him and started burning buildings instead of trees. He killed three people— all tangentially—by the time he was caught. He'd been receiving therapy in prison. And had been a decent prisoner. He wasn't looking to run.

Then the shadow had found him the day of the prison break. It had whispered to him, enticed him, and before he even realized what was happening, he was climbing the fence. The magic had infused him but not fueled him. He wasn't completely aware of what he was doing. In the time since he'd escaped, he'd been holed up in a recreational vehicle sales lot. He'd managed to get inside a vehicle, but he wasn't comfortable staying there with no access to electricity ... or news. That's why he'd ventured into Hemlock Cove. He was looking for a vehicle to escape in, but he also wanted an update.

I plopped down on my bottom and removed my phone from my coat pocket. Landon was not going to be happy. Chief Terry was going to lose it, but I had no choice but to call it in.

"Do you miss me?" Landon asked when he answered. I heard the smile in his voice. "I'm sorry I couldn't make it to lunch."

"Every moment without you is hell," I said. "Where are you?"

He must've picked up on the edge to my voice because he sobered quickly. "Where are you?"

"I asked you first."

"I'm in the car with Chief Terry. We're on our way to check some vacation rentals by the river."

"I need you to come to town instead."

"Okay." Landon addressed Chief Terry now. "Go back to town. Bay needs us."

I heard Chief Terry viciously swearing.

"Tell me what's going on, Bay." Landon sounded as if he was forcing himself to remain calm. What I had to tell him wasn't going to make things better.

"I have one of the prisoners. His name is Jordan Fox."

"You have the arsonist?" Landon's voice ratcheted up a notch. "What did he burn?"

"Technically, he tried to burn me, but with magic. We're in the alley behind Hypnotic."

"Do I even want to know what you were doing in the alley behind Hypnotic?"

"Probably not."

Landon muttered a series of unintelligible words. "We're ten minutes out. Are you okay until then?"

"I'm just peachy."

"You'd better be."

. . .

**JORDAN WAS STILL OUT** when Landon and Chief Terry came racing into the alley. They pulled up short when they saw me. Landon looked torn between going to the prisoner or me. Ultimately, duty won out.

"Handcuffs," he said as he pulled them off his belt. "What happened, Bay?" he asked as he fastened the handcuffs on the downed man.

"Viola told me there was a strange man back here," I replied. My butt had gone numb in the cold, and I wasn't certain I could get back up. "I came to check it out. He threw magic at me right away." I gestured to the mark on the brick wall. "I did what I had to do."

Landon turned from the now-cuffed Jordan Fox and hunkered down in front of me. "Are you okay?"

"I think my butt is numb from the cold."

He arched a brow.

"I'm fine," I said. "I might have gross stuff on my hands and knees from crawling, but otherwise I'm unharmed."

He took my hands and studied the palms. "What did you hear when I asked you to take backup?" he asked quietly.

"I did bring backup. It was just of the ghostly variety."

"Ghosts don't count, and you know it."

"And yet I could've ordered her to rip him limb from limb."

Landon stilled. "I hate that you have a point." He pressed a kiss to my forehead. "We're going to have a talk about what is and isn't acceptable backup later. A ghost doesn't work, even if you can order her to dismember people. Do you want to know why? I'll tell you why. Because a ghost can't call us to help if you get into trouble."

I knew he wasn't referring to a ghost when he'd made me promise I wouldn't go anywhere alone. "I hadn't thought about it that deeply," I admitted. "I just knew I was safe. The other part, well, I didn't consider it." I was appropriately contrite. "I'm sorry."

Landon studied me a moment, his lips twitching. "Well, that was a good way to defuse an argument." He gave me another kiss. "Don't scare me again."

"I honestly didn't think about it. I knew I would be fine with Viola. But had he been able to knock me out with that first magical burst, he could've taken me ... and he made some noise about what he would do if he got his hands on me, so I wouldn't have liked that."

Landon gripped my hands and squeezed. "Please don't torture me."

"I'll do my best. Honestly, I knew I was in trouble right away. I had to protect myself at that point. That meant taking him out, not running away."

"I know." He rested his forehead against mine. "It's okay. I should've put my foot down and kept you with me."

Chief Terry, who had watched the scene from five feet away, threw his hands into the air. "You have got to be kidding me!"

I jolted. I'd almost forgotten he was there. "What's wrong now?"

"You're just so ridiculous. I made the decision that you weren't going with us this morning. It was me, not him."

Even though I'd been angry about that decision earlier, now I was amused. "I'm well aware. Landon told me."

"Tattletale," Chief Terry muttered.

"Hey, who was right?" Landon demanded. "She should've been with us. This would've never happened if we'd included her."

"Maybe not," I said. "But what would've stopped him from going into Hypnotic? He wanted a vehicle and was determined to get it. I'm actually kind of glad I was here."

Landon shook his head. "We'll talk about that part later." He kept his gaze on Chief Terry. "I know you want to protect her because you still see her as your little angel, but she found trouble without us. That's what she does."

Chief Terry made a testy sound. "You're giving her a pass when she did a reckless thing. She should be punished."

"Oh, yeah?" Landon's eyes lit with a wicked gleam. "Do you want me to punish you, sweetie? Do you want a spanking or the rack?"

"You're so gross," Chief Terry muttered. "Just ... so freaking gross."

I didn't disagree with him. "He's not the prisoner I alerted on when we were at the prison," I interjected. "That means more of them could be magical."

"Any suggestions on what we do about that?" Chief Terry asked.

I held out my hands. "I need to think about it. Have you caught any of the others?"

"No." Landon shook his head. "They're off the radar screen."

"That shouldn't be possible. At least one of them should've screwed up and gotten caught."

"You would think, but that's not the case," Chief Terry said. "They appear far more organized than any other escapees I've dealt with."

"That's because they're being used to distract us," I said. "They're going to dole out people to catch to give themselves more room to breathe. I looked inside his head. He only vaguely knew what was happening. Before he was dosed with the magic, he had no interest in escaping. He actually liked prison."

"So how do we find them?" Landon asked. "What do we need to do?"

"I don't know, but we'd better figure it out fast. They could get bolder. If that happens, all bets are off."

# Nine

Landon and Chief Terry had to transport Jordan Fox to the prison. They didn't think taking me along would go over well, and I was not interested in watching the melee downtown. Residents I hadn't seen in months had come out of the woodwork to hang out with the Happy Holidays Players ... my mother, Marnie, and Twila among them.

I made a disgusted sound in the base of my throat before taking off for home. Because everybody was downtown—except maybe Aunt Tillie, and I had no idea where she was ... or what she was doing, thank the Goddess—the inn was quiet. I made myself a cocktail and settled in the library to go through some magic books.

"I didn't realize you were here," a female voice said, jolting me out of my reverie. When I looked at the library door, I found Mary watching me with curious eyes. "Are you staying here too?"

It was natural she would have questions. "No. Well, kind of." I shut the book. I wasn't getting anywhere anyway. "I live on the grounds with my husband, in the guesthouse. My family owns The Overlook, and we eat dinner here most nights."

Mary broke into a wide smile. "That sounds nice." She ventured into the room, her gaze appraising. "This is a nice corner. I bet you spent a lot of time reading in here growing up."

I wanted to ask how she knew I was a reader, but given where I was when she found me, that was a stupid question. "This part of the inn didn't exist when I was growing up. The old homestead at the back, where my mother and aunts still live, was our house. Everything was renovated when they decided to open the inn. This is all relatively new."

"Ah." Mary bobbed her head. "That's lovely. There's nothing better than keeping family close. Are you the only child?"

"I'm an only child, but I was raised with my cousins. Clove and Thistle own the magic store in town."

"Hypnotic. I saw the window. That's where you were heading this afternoon when I saw you. I definitely want to visit when things die down. We were kind of mobbed downtown today. I wasn't expecting it."

"The competition is fierce for spots in the pageant."

"So I noticed." She let loose a low chuckle as she sat. "I saw you this afternoon. The police came screaming in, lights flashing. I couldn't figure out what was going on. Then I saw you exiting the alley behind your cousins' store with the chief of police and another man."

"That would be my husband." Talking about it made me uneasy, but I had to do some damage control. "He's an FBI agent."

"In this area?" Mary's forehead creased.

"He works out of the Traverse City office, but they let him keep his base of operations here."

"That's nice." She leaned back in her chair and crossed her knees. "Tell me about these escaped prisoners. My people are worried."

"There are nine still on the loose last time I checked. More might've been captured. They're a concern, of course, but I can't see where you guys would be in danger. If you were trying to avoid being caught and sent back to prison, would you go to a winter festival?"

"Probably not."

"I think the one being here was a fluke. He was looking for a vehicle."

"You talked to him?" Mary's eyebrows hiked.

"He took me by surprise in the alley. I was heading into Hypnotic through the back door, and there he was."

"How terrifying."

"It was okay. Landon and Chief Terry swooped in."

As if knowing I was talking about him, Landon appeared in the doorway and glanced between us. He looked concerned.

"Landon, this is Mary Stratton. She's with the Happy Holidays Players. They're staying here."

"Ah, the FBI husband." Mary got to her feet and extended her hand. "It's fascinating that you live in a town this size. You must have worked out a great arrangement with your boss."

Landon was calm. "I'm good at my job, and my boss knows it's important for me to be here with my wife every night. Bay can't be away from the newspaper—or her family—so this is the compromise we struck. It works well."

"It seems to." Mary shuffled to move around him. "I'll leave you to your husband-and-wife stuff. I was just looking around. The inn is lovely. We have backstage staff staying at the Dragonfly, and they say that inn is lovely too. Apparently, Hemlock Cove is full of lovely vacation destinations."

"We built the town on tourism," I confirmed.

"Well, I'm going to take a break in my room. Today was hectic. I'm looking forward to dinner, though. I hear you present your own type of theater at meals."

The Winchester dinner theater was famous in certain circles. "I think you'll be happy with the performances," I assured her. "We've been honing them for years."

Her laugh was bright enough to take over the entire room.

Landon waited until she was gone to shut the door and move to the couch with me. "Come here." He pulled me in for a hug, his hands roaming my back. "You didn't get hurt, did you? It occurred to me, that in all the talk of ghost backup and father figures melting down, that I didn't ask. I was annoyed the whole ride to the prison."

"I'm fine. I didn't even get all that dirty." I kissed his cheek. "How did the transfer go?"

"Brad was impressed we found another one. That was the only prisoner brought in today. He thought we did it on our own, but we couldn't omit your part in it because if someone were to stop in town and ask, enough people saw you with us to blow the story out of the water."

"What did he say about that?"

"He asked if you were okay." He pulled back and brushed my hair out of my face. "He made a few jokes about you being the true power in our little search group. I could tell he was intrigued, though. I don't know what he's going to do with the information, but he's definitely interested."

My stomach was uneasy. "The exposure will reflect badly on you."

"I don't like when you say things like that." Landon was stern. "You don't ever reflect badly on me. I need you to understand that. It's just ... people think all the witch stuff in Hemlock Cove is for show. They're willing to embrace it as long as it's all fake. It's when it gets real that things take a turn."

"What do you want me to do?"

"I don't know." He tugged me against him and reclined on the couch. "I don't know the answer, Bay. I think missteps can be made in both directions. Can I have a bit of time to think about it?"

"Sure."

He rested his cheek against my forehead, and we stayed like that for several minutes. I was almost ready to settle in for a nap when Chief Terry appeared at the door and fixed us with his darkest glare.

"So let me get this straight," he drawled, his disdain obvious. "There are nine prisoners on the run. Bay took down a magically enhanced arsonist and almost got herself killed three hours ago. Tillie is running around with a grenade strapped to her belt. Twila, Marnie, and Winnie are all threatening to drown one another in syrup over that stupid pageant. The warden thinks Bay is some sort of magical homing device. And you two have decided to deal with all of this mayhem by playing a game of grab ass in the library. Do I pretty much have all of that covered?"

It was hard to hide my smile. "There's also a pig living in the inn, and the Happy Holidays Players are staying here," I added. "I think that about covers it, though."

Chief Terry's expression was murderous. "You're on my list."

I feigned innocence. "What did I do?"

"Not you." His nose wrinkled. "You're my angel. You always have been. Even when you screw up, it's not your fault. I blame him." He gestured to Landon. "He allows you to do stupid things. That's on him."

He might've thought he was placating me, but it didn't work. "So he controls everything I do? I don't have a mind of my own? I can't make my own decisions because I'm too stupid? Or is it because I'm too female?"

Chief Terry froze. "I walked right into that one, didn't I?"

"You did, and I want to hear your answer."

"Oh, Bay, it's none of those things." He threw his hands into the air and made a hilarious face. "I don't want you getting hurt. I don't want you being exposed. The fact that you stumbled across a magically enhanced prisoner behind Hypnotic scares the bejeezus out of me."

Even though I was irritated, I couldn't help taking pity on him. "It's going to be okay. I can take care of myself. I think I proved that today."

"And what if there had been two prisoners instead of one?"

It was a fair question. "I won't go after a prisoner without physical backup again," I promised. "I didn't think about the part where a ghost can't communicate with you guys. I'm sorry."

Chief Terry stared hard and then sighed. "You're forgiven."

I knew he meant it. "Thank you."

"Am I forgiven too?" Landon asked. He didn't look bothered by any answer he would receive.

"No. You're gross and paw my sweetheart with alarming regularity," Chief Terry replied. "I'll never forgive you for that."

"And all is right with the world," Landon teased as he kissed my forehead before standing. "Come on." He held his hand out to me. "Let's see what your mother and aunts are cooking up for dinner. I worked up an appetite today, and if they're in competition for pageant roles, that means they're probably competing in the kitchen. That can only mean good things for me."

I shook my head. "You're unbelievable."

"I am."

The dining room buzzed with activity. Most of the Happy Holidays Players were already at the table. Aunt Tillie had apparently ordered them to steer clear of our chairs because they were at the far end of the table, and she was in her usual spot glaring. The performers seemed excited about how the day had gone.

"This town is amazing," Robin enthused as she poured herself a glass of wine. "Growing up here must've been great."

I considered the statement longer than was probably necessary. "It had its moments," I said after a bit. "We had a few wild years when we were teenagers. That's one thing that small towns struggle with. There's not a lot for the kids to do, so partying in fields and by lakes becomes the norm."

"Still, look at this place." Robin was effusive, her eyes sparkling with unmitigated glee as she gestured around the dining room. "It's right out of a Hallmark movie."

Aunt Tillie stirred. "Why is she insulting me by saying things like that?" she demanded. "A Hallmark movie? Good grief."

I shot her a quelling look. It wasn't Robin's fault that she was excited. Most people could only see the good in an idyllic setting like Hemlock Cove. The bad parts only became apparent after extended time.

"Oh, this must be the dinner theater you're famous for," Thomas said as he stood at the far end of the room. He had a glass of wine in his hand and looked far too happy, making me wonder exactly how much wine they'd imbibed before our arrival. "Do you work from a script? Do you decide the day of what you're going to do during each meal? It's fascinating when you think about the sustained performances you maintain."

"Yes, that does sound fascinating," I agreed as I plopped down in my chair and turned to Aunt Tillie. "Where did you spend your day?"

"Why do you care?" Aunt Tillie challenged. "You're not my keeper."

Maybe not, but her surly attitude told me something had happened. "Were you with Evan?"

"No, Evan was with me."

"Well, at least that's something." I darted a look to the end of the table, frowning when I realized all the Happy Holidays players already at the table were focused on us. "Where's the thing you had on your belt this morning?" The grenade had conveniently disappeared. "You better not have used it!"

"Again, why do you care?"

"Don't make me lose my cool," I threatened under my breath. "I want to know where that grenade is."

"Well, don't worry about it." Tillie flicked her gaze to the swinging door that separated the dining room from the kitchen as Mom made her entrance with a huge platter of ribs.

"Oh, wow!" Landon brightened considerably. "It's barbecue night? Why didn't anyone tell me?"

I ignored him and went back to staring at Aunt Tillie. "Did you get anywhere today?"

"No, but I heard you did." Aunt Tillie gave a morose sniff. "I can't believe you beat me."

"It wasn't a competition."

"Says you. We were on the hunt for that guy all day. He kept evading my locator spells. He'd pop up one place, and we would go there, but he was always gone by the time we arrived. It was maddening. Then you just happen to stumble across him when you weren't even looking. I'm pretty sure you cheated."

"First, it's not a competition," I growled.

"Says you." Aunt Tillie raised her chin. "You're up four to none. If that's not a competition, I don't know what is."

I forced myself to remain calm. "Second, what do you mean the locator spell didn't work? That's what I was using yesterday, and it worked fine." I kept my voice low in the hope the others at the far end of the table couldn't hear. Landon was already elbow deep in spareribs—they hadn't even brought out the sides yet—and I hoped the sound of his chewing helped drown us out.

"It didn't work," Tillie replied. "It would give us a clear location but then falter."

I frowned. "Meaning someone managed to screw up the spell."

"I don't know. I'm going to have to come up with a different plan tomorrow. I can't let your good luck ruin my hard work."

"Uh-huh. And where is the grenade?"

"Yes, where *is* the grenade?" Mom growled as she leaned in close. "She came home without it. Maybe she hid it on the grounds before coming in. Either way, she knew I was waiting to ambush her this afternoon. She didn't have it on her."

"I'm not a rookie," Aunt Tillie said pointedly. "Clove might've fallen for that trap you laid this afternoon, but nobody else in the family would have. Well, maybe Twila."

As if on cue, Twila emerged from the kitchen with a platter of potatoes. "Are you talking me up to the pageant people?" she asked. "That's so sweet, Aunt Tillie. I always knew you were on my side."

"Yes, that's what I was talking about." Aunt Tillie's eye roll was pronounced. "She definitely would've fallen for Winnie's lame trap. Nobody else, though."

I glanced at my mother, who looked ready to throw down. "She may be old, but she can still take you," I warned.

Mom didn't look convinced. "We're going to talk about this later," she warned Aunt Tillie before sliding into her chair. "Is everybody here?"

"Everybody except Mary," Renee volunteered. "She'll be down in a few minutes. She took a shower and is changing her clothes. She said to start without her."

"There's plenty of food," Mom assured her. "We always make more than we need." Her dark glare fell on Landon, barbecue sauce smeared on his cheeks. "For obvious reasons."

Landon barely blinked. "Hey, it's been a long day. Your daughter almost gave me a heart attack. I've earned a big meal."

Mom could never stay irritated with Landon for long. She broke into a wide smile. "Yes, well, eat up. We have more sides on the way. Marnie made the creamed spinach you love so much, Bay."

I did love creamed spinach. Barbecue, on the other hand, wasn't my favorite. I would've preferred pot roast, or maybe even a taco bar, but I would live. "I want to talk to you before bed," I said to Aunt Tillie as I accepted the tongs from Landon. "Don't run off after dinner."

"I never run off," Aunt Tillie shot back. "Don't start spreading that rumor." She was in a foul mood. "And tomorrow, the game is on. I'm going to crush you."

"It's not a game," I barked. "Stop being weird."

"This is going to be a great skit," Ava enthused, her blue eyes going to Landon, and her eyelashes batting. "I love when the leading man has a healthy appetite on top of everything else."

This was not how I saw this night going.

# Ten

I caught Aunt Tillie in the family living quarters after she quietly tried to duck out without engaging in the conversation I was desperate to have. Dinner had been boring—at least by Winchester standards—with most of the talk revolving around the pageant and who would be best for what parts. I was happy the discussion had gone that route because it allowed me to mentally check out.

"Oh, what do you want?" Aunt Tillie demanded when I cut her off from the hallway that led to her bedroom.

"You know what I want. Where is that grenade?"

"Don't worry about it."

"I am worried about it."

"Well, stop, because I'm not telling you." Aunt Tillie folded her arms across her chest. "Stop being you. Stop sticking your nose into other people's business. I can take care of myself."

"I'm not worried about you. I'm worried about what happens to everybody else if you drop that grenade." I narrowed my eyes. "What does it do?"

"All manner of things. It's a new weapon I've been developing the past year. I'm looking forward to testing it."

I froze. "You haven't tested it yet?"

"Like I want to waste it on a test. When I use it, you'll know."

"Aunt Tillie."

"You're not the boss of me. You worry about your stuff. I'll worry about mine." With that, she shoved me out of the way, and pranced—yes, pranced—down the hallway. I heard her laughing as she entered her room.

"That doesn't look like it went well," Landon noted as he joined me.

"I swear she actually gets more immature the older she gets," I groused.

"I can see that." He managed a smile. "Do you want to talk about it?"

"There's nothing to talk about. She's going to do what she wants. I can't stop her. She knows it. Somewhere out there, she's stowed a magical grenade, and even she doesn't know what it does."

Landon looked as if he was fighting off a burst of laughter.

"It's not funny," I growled.

"I know but ... she's Aunt Tillie." He held out his hand. "Let's walk home. I ate too much barbecue, and I need to digest. We can pick up the vehicles tomorrow morning."

I grudgingly slipped my hand into his. "Fine. But I want a massage when we get home."

"I think I can manage that."

**MY DREAMS WERE MUDDLED, A SERIES OF** scenes playing out with various dead-eyed prisoners as they threw magic at me from every direction. Despite that, I slept hard, and was smiling when I opened my eyes and found Landon watching me.

"It's creepy when you watch me sleep," I complained.

"I find it peaceful." He purred like a cat as he stretched. "How do you feel?"

"Pretty good. You?"

"Like I would be perfectly happy to spend the entire day in bed."

"I think that would be frowned upon given how many prisoners are still out there."

"Oh, I know. It's just wishful thinking at this point."

"The first big snowstorm," I promised. "When the weather people say it's coming, we'll stock up and hunker down."

"That'll only happen if we find all the prisoners. If they're still out there in a week..." He trailed off.

I knew what was worrying him. The longer the prisoners went without being captured, the more likely they would never be found. A law-and-order guy like Landon simply couldn't accept that. "We'll find them. Have a little faith."

"I have faith in you." He nuzzled my neck. "I have a plan for including you in today's searches if you're interested."

"What sort of plan?"

"I'm going to tell Chief Terry I want you with me. When that doesn't work, I'm going to tell him it's safer for you if you're with us, even if it does spark suspicion from the warden. His desire to keep you safe will outweigh his civic duty, and I'll win."

I barked out a laugh. "You sound like Aunt Tillie."

"I'm fine with that."

"Since when?"

"Since I realized she was going to win at life. Say what you want about her, she doesn't lose over the long haul. Maybe treating life as a competition is something we should all do."

I felt otherwise, but there was no sense arguing. "What time is it?"

"We have five minutes before we have to hit the shower."

"What do you want to do for those five minutes?"

"This." He hugged me tighter. His voice was a flirty whisper against my ear when he spoke again. "I want to check out that hot chocolate kissing booth when it opens. I have no idea what hot chocolate and kissing have to do with one another, but I'm game to find out."

"I think you just take your hot chocolate in there and kiss while you're drinking it."

"Sold."

He always made me laugh. That was one of his greatest strengths. "I love you, Landon."

"I love you, Bay. We're going to figure this out. One way or another, I'm getting that snow day. I want it more than you can possibly understand."

He was wrong. I did understand, and I wanted it too. "Then let's get to thinking. The fact that Aunt Tillie's locator spell misfired yesterday is a clue. I need to figure out what sort of clue. There's something there. I can feel it."

"Maybe take it to Emori," he suggested, referring to the voodoo queen who had set up shop on Main Street. "She's been helpful."

I wanted to kick myself for not thinking of that first. "Good idea."

"I'm full of them."

"You're full of something."

"I'm going to be full of bacon in an hour. That's my reward for the good idea."

I blew out a sigh. "We really need to talk about your eating habits. I don't want you to be unhappy, but I want you to live a long life."

"I plan to. Aunt Tillie and I have a deal. She's going to come up with a potion that will allow me to remain a glutton, and I'm going to look the other way on something big."

I pulled back far enough to eye him. "I see you've got this figured out."

"Yup."

"Well, when Aunt Tillie comes through with the potion, we'll talk."

His grin was so wide it almost swallowed his face when he leaned in for a kiss. "Finally, you're seeing things my way."

"Yeah, yeah, yeah."

**THE MORNING AIR WAS BRISK AS WE** walked to the inn. Our breath was visible in the gray solitude of the dawning day, and I frowned as we passed the barren trees and colorless ground.

"I know people like winter stuff—like skiing and snowmobiling—but the only thing that's good about winter if you ask me is that we can take snow days."

"I'm right there with you." Landon lifted his fist to bump mine. "Word, baby doll." He was playing it up to make me laugh, and it would've worked, but a whisper on the wind at that moment caused the trees to groan.

*Bay.*

Landon dropped all pretense of fun and stopped in the middle of the walkway. "What was that?"

I slowly turned to study the area surrounding us. We were halfway to the inn, and the only thing in close proximity was Aunt Tillie's pot field. The parcel of land was warded to the $n$th degree, and law enforcement couldn't get near it if they didn't want a serious case of the trots. Aunt Tillie designed it that way.

"I don't know," I replied. The hair on the back of my neck stood on end. I felt eyes on me, and yet there wasn't a soul to behold in any direction.

"The wind said your name, Bay," Landon growled. "That can't be normal."

I jerked up my eyes. "You heard that?"

"Yes."

"It was a warning," I said. "I thought it was just my witchy senses kicking into overdrive."

Landon reached over to grip my hand. "I think it's a sign that we should be heading to the inn."

"Or it's a sign that I should be checking out the pot field." I hadn't meant to say it, but one of the curses associated with being a Winchester was the inability to think something without saying it out loud.

"Are you kidding me?" Landon's eyebrows looked as if they were trying to make a break for the Canadian border. "We can't go into the pot field. It's been explained to me multiple times since before I even joined this family why that isn't allowed."

Aunt Tillie took her pot very seriously. "You don't have to go," I assured him in a soft voice. "I'm just going to give it a quick look." Aunt Tillie warded the field so you couldn't see the truth until you passed beyond the lie she wanted you to see. She was aces with a glamour when she put some effort into it.

"Bay, I'm putting my foot down." As if to prove it, Landon stomped his boot against the ground. "We're not going into that pot field."

"We're not," I agreed, taking an exaggerated step back when he reached out to snag me around the waist. "You wait here. In theory, nobody should be able to cross the wards and see that field. I'm just going to take a peek, and then we'll head up to the inn for breakfast."

"Bay!" Landon roared my name as he followed a few steps. The second he moved from the relative safety of the walkway and onto the grass, he bent at the waist and retched. "I think I'm going to be sick."

"Stay there," I ordered. I was almost to the ward line. "I'll be right back. I promise."

"This is not you operating with backup," he reminded me. He'd gone deathly pale, and the way he cradled his stomach told me things were about to go very bad for him. Aunt Tillie's wards were still working despite the fact that her plants had gone dormant for the season.

"Stay there," I barked when I reached the barrier. "I won't be more than a minute. Two at the most. Time me." I cast him one more look when he tried to take another step—why did he have to be so stubborn?—and then I crossed the threshold. Everything inside of me screamed that I had to look.

Stepping into Aunt Tillie's warded world was always a challenge. Somehow, she'd managed to keep her plants staked and green despite the weather, and they almost looked as if they were ready to start yielding product. I filed that away to question her on later—if she'd found a way to combat weather, my mother and aunts would be all over it so they could grow produce during the winter—and instead focused on the rows between the plants.

I moved forward, cringing when my footsteps sounded. My heart hammered with each step, and I was certain I was about to find something—or someone—important.

When I reached the fifth row, it happened.

A zing of magic whipped out from the right. I managed to contort so the blow only hit my shoulder, but it was strong enough to spin me. I went down hard. When I registered what I was feeling, it wasn't good. Pain the likes of which I hadn't felt in a long time—and didn't want to feel again—rocketed through me, bringing tears to my eyes.

"Oh, crap on a cracker," I groaned as I tried to force myself to a sitting position. It was only the knowledge that Landon was on the other side of the ward, that he was sick and wouldn't leave until I returned, that kept me focused.

The man heading in my direction had managed to get his hands on jeans and a sweatshirt.

"Son of a witch!" I threw out what little magic I could collect. It didn't even hit him. I was a good foot off, and I knew that even if I could gather another burst of magic, it might not do any good. I was in too much pain to focus. That's when I fell back on instinct.

"*Come*," I intoned. My voice didn't hold the power it normally did, but the necromancer magic was in my blood. I didn't have to pool it, I just had to want to use it.

Viola was the first ghost to appear. The annoyance on her face would've been funny under different circumstances. "Help." I waved at the approaching prisoner.

"Really, Bay," Viola tsked. "Why do you keep doing these things to yourself? Why not ask for my help beforehand instead of summoning me?"

"I had no idea I was going to run into a prisoner on my own property," I spat. "Do something!"

Viola turned to face the man, who was now only twenty feet away. He had what looked to be a hammer in his hand—now we knew where that tool had gone—and I knew he would use it as soon as he was on top of me. "You're going to owe me," she warned as she flew forward.

Now, in life, Viola wasn't known for her athletic ability. In death, however, she'd watched her fair share of shows with butt-kicking females—Buffy Summers and Sidney Bristow were her favorites—and she'd developed some moves. Unfortunately for both of us, those moves didn't prove useful when she started karate chopping at the escapee. If he felt the blows, he shrugged them off, and kept moving forward.

"Oh, crappity crap crap." I rolled to my knees, ignoring the pain clawing through me, and tried to push myself to a standing position. My legs were shaky. My head felt as if it was going to explode. My shoulder warned me that I was going to wish I was dead in about thirty seconds. It was obvious the magical blow came with some sort of debilitating physical ailment, like poison, but not of the ingestible variety.

"Get up!" I screamed at myself when I couldn't hold my footing and fell forward into one of Aunt Tillie's plants. There was no doubt in my mind now that escape was impossible. I couldn't run. Did I have the strength to fight? Especially when my best weapon had somehow been rendered useless?

And then I heard his voice.

"Freeze!" Landon sounded like he was yelling through a throat filled with broken glass. He'd somehow made it inside the wards. There was what looked like vomit on his shirt and his shoes. His hair stood up in a million different directions. He looked shaky, but his frame was locked as he pointed the gun at the prisoner. "One more step, and I'll shoot you."

The prisoner didn't hesitate, and I threw up an arm to protect my face from the hammer.

Landon fired, and instead of feeling the hammer hit me, I heard it hit the ground.

When I looked up, Landon had dropped to one knee, laboring for breath. The prisoner was down. I saw the rise and fall of his chest.

"Landon." His name was barely a whisper, and yet he heard it.

Sweat streamed down his face, and tears pooled in his eyes. "I'm going to kill Aunt Tillie," he growled.

All I could do was marvel at the strength it must have taken to get beyond the wards. Aunt Tillie had designed them to be pure torture for anybody in law enforcement. "You're going to have the trots all day," I said dumbly.

Landon was incredulous. "At least I still have my wife!"

Yes, there was that, but we had another problem. "How are we going to get help out here?"

Landon dug in his pocket for his phone. "I can only think of one way."

"Aunt Tillie won't drop the wards."

"Maybe not, but your mother won't let her keep them up when I tell her what's going on. You stay there."

I dropped back on the ground and threw an arm over my face. I was feeling sick to my stomach. "Have Aunt Tillie bring some of those hangover potions. I think I'm going to be sick."

Landon made a sound like he was going to puke ... or perhaps it was some other gastrointestinal problem I didn't want to know about. "You and me both, sweetie. You have no idea how badly I want to kill her right now."

He wasn't the only one. "I'm just going to close my eyes for a few minutes."

# Eleven

"What in the holy hell did I just step in?"

Chief Terry's lament woke me. The ground was surprisingly warm where I'd passed out, and when I felt a hand clasped around mine, I almost jolted out of my skin. Then I realized it was Landon. He'd managed to crawl to me, although he looked as if he was close to death's door.

"Get him out of here," I ordered Chief Terry in a voice so weak I almost didn't recognize it as my own. "He needs to be free of the wards, or he'll get worse."

"The wards are down," Mom volunteered as she dropped to her knees next to me. "We don't know what we're going to do about the pot plants just yet—Aunt Tillie refuses to destroy them—but the wards are down for now. Let me see your shoulder."

I whimpered when she tugged on my shirt.

"This looks like poison," Mom announced.

"Then we need to get her to the hospital," Chief Terry snapped. "Move. I'll carry her."

"Calm down, Esmerelda," Aunt Tillie chastised. "I've got this." Her face appeared over mine. "What did he hit you with?"

"I don't know." Aches I didn't even know were possible had started making themselves known, and shivering wracked my body. "I think I'm dying."

"No." Landon stirred next to me and rolled to his side. "You're not dying. Don't ever say that." His eyes were fierce. "Fix her," he barked at Aunt Tillie. "Right now."

Aunt Tillie gave Landon a "you're crazy" look and mouthed the word "wow" to me. "Here." She handed a potion to Mom. "Get that in her. Let's see if that fixes her. If not, I have some others to try."

Normally, I would've fought the idea of drinking one of Aunt Tillie's potions without knowing what was in it, but I didn't care at this point. Mom put the bottle to my lips.

"Small sips," she ordered. "Try not to spill it."

I followed her orders. The first swallow was difficult. The second was easier. I managed to sit up for the third and was almost feeling human by the time I finished the bottle. "What was that?" I asked, awestruck. I was still in pain, but I felt the potion running like wildfire through my veins, beating back the magical infection like a gladiator going to war.

"A little something I've been working on." Aunt Tillie winked, but now that I could take in her entire face, it was impossible to miss the worry lines creasing the corners of her eyes. "Better?"

"Yeah." I tried to rotate my shoulder and grimaced. "Not perfect yet."

"We'll get you there." Aunt Tillie managed a smile and then turned to Landon. "I'm not sure I should cure you."

"Cure him," I ordered.

"He crossed my wards."

"If he hadn't, I wouldn't be here." I gripped her wrist, squeezing as hard as I could. "He overcame the worst physical pain imaginable to get to me. He shot that prisoner, who would have beaten me to death. Fix him right now."

"Okay. Good grief." Aunt Tillie shook her head. "There's no need to be testy." She pulled a potion out of her bra and uncorked it. "Open that big mouth of yours."

Landon, still sickly and pale, did as instructed without complaint.

He swallowed the potion in two gulps and then closed his eyes. "You have a lot of explaining to do about this field."

"Gotta go." Aunt Tillie turned, but Mom snagged the back of her hoodie.

"Don't even think about it." Mom was grim as she turned to Chief Terry, who was kneeling next to the fallen prisoner. "Is he dead?" she asked.

"No," Chief Terry replied. "He's breathing, but he won't be for long if we don't get someone in here."

"Just move him out of the field," Aunt Tillie ordered. "The emergency responders can get him from the sidewalk."

"We need to document the scene," Chief Terry argued. "This, unfortunately, is the scene."

"This is my field." Aunt Tillie bordered on apoplectic. "You can't take over my field."

"This field has to be razed." Mom was firm. "No." She jabbed a finger in front of Aunt Tillie's face. "It's our only option. You need to disappear those pot plants. You can plant more in the spring. Although, I am curious why they're so green and this patch is so warm. What have you been doing out here?"

"Are you kidding me?" I thought steam was about to come out of Aunt Tillie's ears. "You want gardening tips when you're threatening to ruin my crop. Do you have any idea how long I've been cultivating those plants? I won't let you destroy them."

Sensing trouble—the sort that would blow up in all of our faces—I inserted myself in the conversation. "Can you hide them for about two hours? Like ... a special glamour. It needs to be powerful, but as soon as they're done here, you can have your field back."

Aunt Tillie looked momentarily thoughtful. "I can do that. They'd better be quick, though."

"Just get rid of the plants," Chief Terry barked. He had his phone out. "I'm getting help out here in the next ten minutes. If those plants are still here when the ambulance arrives, you're going to jail."

"Oh, don't threaten me with a good time, Terry." Aunt Tillie raised her hands. "You know, it seems that I'm being punished for something that isn't my fault. I was minding my own business when I got word that you invaded my field. You should be the ones punished this time, not me."

"I'm going to punish you into next year if you're not careful," Mom warned as she helped me sit up and hang my head between my knees. "Are you okay? Do you still feel poisoned?"

"I'm okay," I assured her. "My shoulder still hurts, but I'm okay." I turned my gaze to Landon, who was also sitting up. Puke ran down the front of his shirt, and he smelled like death, but I'd never loved him more. "You overcame a curse to get to me."

He blinked several times, confused. "Bay, there's nothing in this world that could've stopped me from getting to you. I'm just sorry I was too late."

"Too late? You saved my life."

"You were still hurt."

"Oh, look at the morose twosome," Aunt Tillie muttered. When I flicked my eyes to her again, the magic from her glamour had dissipated. She looked surly, which never bode well for our family. "We're going to have a talk about not touching other people's things. You both deserve punishment."

"Stuff it," Landon muttered. "Just ... don't even talk to me right now. If you hadn't erected those wards, I would've been able to go with Bay. She wouldn't have been hurt."

"I don't trust 'The Man' with my crop, and that's never going to change."

"I have a question," I interjected, hoping to stop their arguing. "How did the prisoner get past the wards? I thought they were meant to keep people out. Why didn't he get sick? Also, is Landon going to have the trots all day? That's going to really cut down on the loving I intend to give him for being a hero."

"Don't worry." She cast a disparaging look toward my husband. "Lover boy should be fine. The potion reversed everything from the wards. He just needs to shower and change because he looks like a drunk at Mardi Gras."

"I love you too," Landon threw back darkly.

Aunt Tillie continued as if she hadn't heard him. "As for how the other guy got past the wards, I'm not certain." She narrowed her eyes as she glanced around. "He shouldn't have even known anything was here."

"And yet he crossed the wards and was lying in wait," I pressed. "How did he manage that?"

"I honestly don't know."

"We need to find out."

"Yeah, that's probably for the best."

**WE LEFT CHIEF TERRY TO HANDLE THE** prisoner and ambulance and hoofed it back to the guesthouse to shower and change again. Despite the horror of the morning, we were both smiling when we set out for the inn.

"You're okay?" I asked, my hand in Landon's. "You don't feel sick?"

"Not so far, but I wouldn't put it past Aunt Tillie to curse me again just because it gives her a little thrill."

"She won't." Aunt Tillie was unpredictable, but I was certain she wouldn't go that route. "She feels bad about what happened."

"When was she feeling bad?"

"Through all of it. She just can't admit that she feels bad."

"Well, I'm still angry."

I didn't blame him. "I can't believe you made it into that field." I was still marveling at that development.

"Bay, nothing was going to stop me from getting to you. I would've died to do it." He meant that, which made his words all the sweeter.

"I'm going to give you a lot of sweaty sex as a reward tonight," I offered, causing him to snort. "You'd better hydrate today."

"I just want to be able to eat in peace this morning. No mention of cholesterol or heart attacks. If I want to eat an entire slab of bacon, you're going to sit there and smile."

"I think you've earned it."

"We both have." He slung his arm around my shoulders and kissed the side of my head. "You scared the crap out of me, Bay. Do you have any idea what I was feeling when I finally made it into that field and saw what was happening?"

"He knew I was coming." I'd been running what had happened

through my head since my brain started firing on all cylinders again. "He was waiting for me."

"What does that mean?"

We were back at the pot field, but it was empty, telling me Chief Terry had been quick in having the prisoner transported. The wards were back up, stronger than ever, suggesting Aunt Tillie hadn't wasted any time protecting her haul. There would be a reckoning there—Mom wasn't going to forget how different that parcel of land was from everything surrounding it—but it could wait.

"It means that whoever enchanted him did it with a purpose," I replied. "I thought it was weird enough that I stumbled across the one guy behind Hypnotic. It's a little too pointed for a second one to show up on our property."

"You think whoever arranged this is directing them to come at you."

"At least at my family," I agreed.

"Well, we can't allow that."

I had no idea how to combat it. "I'm going to visit Emori after breakfast. We need to start being proactive."

"Okay. Chief Terry and I will have to check in with the warden. I'm sure his questions will be real doozies. Once we're done there, we'll be in touch."

"That sounds like a plan to me."

**EMORI CLARK WAS ALL SMILES WHEN I LET** myself into her shop. The previous renter of the shop had been an evil witch bent on destroying my family at the behest of Mrs. Little—Goddess, that woman needed a good curse thrown at her—so I'd been naturally suspicious when she set up shop. Not only had I been wrong, but Emori had turned into a righteous ally. She seemed happy to see me when I sat in one of the puffy pink chairs at the center of her store.

"It's barely nine o'clock, and you look as if you're ready for bed," she noted, heading behind the counter for tea before joining me. "Here." She pushed a teacup into my hand when she returned. "You look like you need it."

I trusted her, so I sipped. "What is it?" I asked when my stomach sang a delighted refrain thanks to the golden liquid.

"It's supposed to help with nausea. No offense, but you've looked better. What happened?"

"Several things." I told her about the incident in the pot field. She'd only vaguely heard about the prisoner escape, so I filled her in on that too. When I finished, she looked flummoxed.

"Well, that's something." She cocked her head. "Do you have any idea what Landon must've gone through to overcome that curse and get to you?"

I wasn't surprised that she'd latched onto that tidbit. I couldn't keep myself from dwelling on it either. "He was pretty impressive. I was amazed when I saw him. Sure, he was covered in vomit—and maybe something else—but he made it through."

"He's a hero."

I smiled. "For the record, he's feeling pretty heroic today. He ate his weight in bacon, so he's in a good mood."

Emori chuckled. "What about you? How is your mood?"

"Surprisingly good given the circumstances. It's just ... I have questions."

"I bet."

"How did he get in that field? He shouldn't have been able to get anywhere near it. What sort of magic are these prisoners imbued with? I've never seen anything like it. How is someone sharing magic with them that way?"

"And, more importantly, whoever that someone is, how did they know to point the prisoners at you?"

I nodded. "I've been wondering that too. The whole thing is a mess."

"Well, let's think it through." She tapped her bottom lip, thoughtful, and encouraged me to keep drinking the tea.

"The first magically possessed inmate you found, you went into his head, right?" she asked.

"Yeah. I wanted to see what was going on in there."

"And you didn't see much of anything that made sense."

"Just fragments of memories."

"But, if someone else was in there, he or she might've gotten a look at you."

It was something I hadn't considered. "And whatever they saw was enough to mark me as an enemy," I deduced.

"Yes. That's why the most recent sightings have been in Hemlock Cove. They won't be the last."

"If we're right, the rest of the inmates will be directed at us. There are eight left."

"Actually seven, and someone controlling the rest."

"Whoever planned this had help from someone on the outside," I said. "I felt some strong magical remnants in Steve Mitchell's cell."

"He must be the central inmate."

"Yes, most likely, but I think the magic is coming from whoever is helping him."

"Hmm." Emori tapped her bottom lip again. "Sounds like an enchantress."

Her response threw me. "I don't know what an enchantress is." It was difficult to admit, but it was the truth. My magical knowledge had grown tremendously the last few years, but I didn't know everything. "That's basically a sexy witch, right?"

Emori's chuckle was low and largely devoid of humor. "Sort of. Enchantresses use sexual pheromones to their advantage. They entice individuals—usually men, although it depends on sexual preference—to do their bidding through these pheromones. Legend has it that enchantresses are largely interested in enticing men away from their noble paths."

I made a face. "We're dealing with prisoners. What noble paths?"

"That I can't answer. You did say the memories of the man in the alley didn't suggest he was an active participant. He was happy in prison. At least happier than he might've been under different circumstances. He wasn't yearning to escape, and yet he did."

I leaned back in the chair. "So what would an enchantress want with a bunch of prisoners? I mean ... what's the end game?"

"I have no idea. It might not be about all of the prisoners. It might be about one prisoner in particular."

"Steve Mitchell."

"You got a hit off him for a reason."

"I need more information on Mitchell. That's the only way we're going to find whoever is doing this, whether it's an enchantress or not."

"I can do some research if you want, see what I can find on enchantresses. They were en vogue a century ago but fell out of favor after an incident in California."

"I'll take whatever you can get." I rummaged in my pocket when my phone went off to signal I'd received an incoming text. When I read the message, everything that had begun to loosen inside of me tightened again. "Chief Terry wants me to meet him at the police station. I'm guessing things are about to go from bad to worse."

"Good luck." Emori looked sympathetic.

"Thanks. I think I'm going to need it."

# Twelve

Chief Terry was in his office, behind his desk, his head resting in his hands.

"What is it?" I demanded. "Is Landon okay?" My stomach twisted. "Is he in the bathroom?" The thought that he would be tortured all day because he saved me was almost too much to bear.

"Oh, don't be dramatic," Chief Terry replied, his gaze darkening. "He's fine. There's no reason to turn into Clove."

My mouth dropped open. "That right there is the meanest thing you've ever said to me."

He grinned and then inclined his head toward the door. Landon was walking through it, a huge box of doughnuts in his hands.

"There's my favorite person in the world." Landon dropped the doughnuts on Chief Terry's desk and swooped in to kiss me. He was clearly doing his best to pretend he was fine, but I saw the concern in his eyes as he swept back my hair and stared hard. "How are you feeling?"

"That was going to be my line. I thought maybe you were in the bathroom."

"Knock on wood, I feel pretty good, all things considered." Landon gave me a hug, ignoring Chief Terry's dramatic sigh, and then kissed my forehead before pulling back. "So, we have information."

"Me too." I settled in one of the chairs across from Chief Terry's desk. "I talked to Emori. She's going to do some research. She thinks we might be dealing with an enchantress. That's basically a sexy witch."

Landon's eyebrows hopped.

"Not me," I said quickly, shooting him a quelling look. "We're talking about the sort of witch who uses her feminine wiles to entice men to do her bidding. Emori said that in lore, enchantresses tried to pull men away from noble pursuits."

Chief Terry made a face. "We're talking about prisoners, Bay, not guys who made a tiny mistake and served a weekend in jail. This is prison, big boy crimes."

"I get that, but she pointed something out, and it's got me thinking. Jordan Fox, the prisoner I took down behind Hypnotic, didn't even want to be out of prison. He was perfectly happy there. Maybe 'noble deeds' can be stretched a bit in modern times."

Chief Terry rubbed his chin, considering. "It's interesting."

"What do you guys have?" I asked.

Landon sat next, seemingly more interested in the contents of the doughnut box. "I got something for you," he said.

When I glanced up, he handed me a cake doughnut with chocolate frosting and sprinkles, my favorite of all doughnuts. "We just ate breakfast two hours ago," I reminded him as I reached for the doughnut.

"Today is a day of celebration, Bay. We both survived a hairy situation. I do not have the trots—at least as of yet—and I will be eternally grateful for that. I believe doughnuts are in order."

"Admit it. You do this every single day, don't you?"

"No. It's a special occasion."

I looked at Chief Terry to see if he disagreed, but he seemed completely disinterested in the pastry conversation. "If you guys are going to keep throwing verbal foreplay at one another in my office, we're going to have a problem," he said dryly.

I bit into the doughnut—it was still slightly warm, which made it all the better—and then focused on Chief Terry. "I'm sorry this is hard for you." I meant it. Well, sort of. "We went through a trying ordeal. We're doing our best."

"I would've fallen for that six months ago. I know better now."

Chief Terry wrinkled his nose in disgust. "You two get off on it. You like terrorizing me."

"We do like terrorizing you," Landon agreed. He had a long john in his hand. "But it's time to get serious. Bay, you have to stop trying to lure me to bed with your eyes. Chief Terry doesn't like it. Show some decorum, please."

I giggled, as I was certain he'd intended, and all Chief Terry could do was roll his eyes.

"You're both the worst." Even as he said it, his lips curved up. Then he firmed them. "We have a new development. I don't know how this plays into your enchantress theory, but I'm guessing it might help the puzzle become clearer."

He had my attention.

"There's a missing guard," Landon said. "A woman."

Chief Terry held up a hand to silence Landon. "You just stole my thunder. I was going to tell her about the missing guard. You were going to spoil her with doughnuts, and I was going to wow her with the information. You just stole my moment."

Landon was blasé. "You were taking too long."

"Who cares who told me?" I snapped. "I want to know about this guard. How can they just be figuring out now that she's missing? This happened days ago."

"Yes, well, that's the wrinkle." Chief Terry was grim as he turned his computer screen so I could see the photo displayed on it. The guard was blond, although it was obviously from a bottle, and she looked to be closing in on fifty. She was dressed in a crisp brown uniform shirt. She wasn't smiling. There was a tenseness about her.

"Meet Natalie Bennett. She's forty-nine years old and has been a guard at Antrim for five years."

"Was she taken?" I asked.

"No." Chief Terry shook his head. "We believe she left the prison early that day—she claimed she had a headache and felt sick—and then waited one mile away for one of the inmates to get to her car before driving off with him."

My legs felt shaky, and I rested my half-eaten doughnut on a napkin on Chief Terry's desk. "I don't understand."

"Neither do we." Chief Terry rubbed his forehead. No wonder I'd assumed he was fighting off a headache when I entered. "Natalie was there the day of the prison break. She worked her usual shift in the morning, which consisted of overseeing inmate video court appearances. On a normal day, she might transport a few prisoners, but that didn't happen the day of the escape."

"Okay."

"Shortly before lunch, she approached the shift commander and complained of a brutal headache that was making her sick. She said she needed to go home and sleep. She was a good worker. She rarely called in sick. The shift commander told her to go home ... and they thought she had.

"She had the next two days scheduled off, so nobody was looking for her," Chief Terry explained. "Everybody thought she was taking it easy ... and then they started watching the security camera footage."

"You tell a story like Aunt Tillie," Landon groused. "This is why you should've let me handle it."

Chief Terry ignored him. "They've had people going through the interior footage," he said. "They're looking for visitors in the last two weeks or so. People who our escapees might've made arrangements with for transport."

"And they found something with this guard?" I asked.

Chief Terry was grim. "Natalie Bennett spent as much time as possible with an inmate named Carl Markham ... a lot of time."

"So much time that someone should've caught it and done something before the prison break," Landon added.

"Natalie put money in Carl's commissary," Chief Terry volunteered. "She brought him books. She helped him secure more time on the computer than he was allowed."

"How did nobody know about this?" I demanded. "You're suggesting she had some freaky relationship with this prisoner and helped him escape."

"Even more than that, she helped other inmates escape to serve as cover," Landon added.

"Nobody was paying close enough attention," Chief Terry said. "Things become commonplace in a prison because of the monotony, and you stop noticing things. The warden said most of the guards joked about Natalie's attachment to Markham. It was an ongoing thing. Nobody ever reported her to his office."

"It's one of those blue line things," Landon explained. "You don't rat on fellow officers. Every department has some version of it. Natalie did her job and rarely called in sick, so the other guards didn't want to give her grief. They thought it was a harmless crush."

"Doesn't seem so harmless now, does it?" I muttered.

"No, it doesn't," Chief Terry agreed. "It's a righteous mess. Natalie wasn't scheduled to return to work until today, so it's a miracle we even know about this."

"How do we know?"

"Because there's a traffic camera out on M-88 near that big curve. They had a bunch of accidents a few years ago. Remember?"

I nodded.

"Well, they put in a traffic camera, and somebody looked at it on a whim hoping for glimpses of the prisoners," he continued. "It showed Natalie waiting in a departmental-issued vehicle."

My mouth dropped open. "She knew nobody would stop her if she was in a prison van. They would assume she was part of the search team and let her go on her merry way."

"Yes." Chief Terry bobbed his head. "She shouldn't have been where she was. When they saw a man in an orange jumpsuit emerge from the woods and climb into the vehicle, they knew they had a big problem."

"The warden won't be able to keep his job after this, Bay," Landon supplied. "He'll go down for this. We're going to have to watch him."

I didn't have to ask why. Landon was worried about me. "Unbelievable," I muttered, shaking my head.

"It is indeed unbelievable," Chief Terry agreed. "There's more."

Of course there was.

"They went to Natalie's house last night," he said. "The prison transport was in the garage. Most of her stuff had been cleaned out. Come to find out, she'd actually sold the house three months ago and had worked into the agreement that she could continue to live there until next week."

I was dumbfounded. "If she sold the house months ago, she made the decision to sell the house even before that."

"A lot of planning went into it," Chief Terry confirmed. "If it were me, I would've fled the state through the Upper Peninsula right away. She could've been in Canada before anybody knew the prisoners were even missing."

"But?" I prodded.

"Unless she somehow procured documents for Markham—which isn't as easy as TV and movies make it out to be—she would've had issues trying to cross the border. She could've tried hiding him in the trunk of her car, but they have dogs at those crossings. It would've been a risky move."

"One she wasn't likely to make given how much planning went into this," I surmised. "So she's fleeing the state from the south."

"I think if she were to do that, they would've been gone the first day," Chief Terry replied. "By the time word spread south, they would've had the time they needed to get into Ohio."

"But you don't believe that's the case," I prodded.

"I think they're still here, and for one reason only," Chief Terry replied. "You keep getting magically attacked. We can pretend what happened in the alley behind Hypnotic was a coincidence—stranger things have happened, especially in this town—but what happened in the pot field this morning is something else entirely. Mick Wilcox was lying in wait for you."

I'd already come to that conclusion. "Emori has a theory on that too," I said. "She thinks that when I got inside James Barker's head at the machine shop, I wasn't careful enough. The enchantress was already there. She saw me inside Barker's head and recognized me as a threat."

"And now she's going to throw prisoners at you as a distraction," Chief Terry surmised. "Well, that's just great."

"There are eight still out there," Landon noted. He'd lost interest in the doughnuts—they were mostly for show anyway, so he could pretend he wasn't worked up by what had happened in the pot field—and was completely focused. "Markham is one of them. He's going to be kept separate from the other prisoners, but the rest of them are going to be a problem."

"Do you think they're all together?" I asked. "Like ... is she keeping them somewhere so she can send them out one at a time to wreak havoc?"

"I don't know." Landon held his hands palms out. "I'd like to say I understand what's going on, but I don't, Bay. It's a mess ... and I don't think it's going to be cleaned up anytime soon."

I nodded. It made sense, although I wished it didn't. To think that a guard had purposely put herself in this position, had let the other prisoners loose to cover for her freaky love story, made me distinctly uncomfortable.

"If we assume she's the enchantress, why did the magic spike in Steve Mitchell's cell instead of Carl Markham's that first day?" I asked. "Shouldn't it have been the opposite?"

"That's your area of expertise," Chief Terry said. "I don't know the hows and whys. The warden said Mitchell and Markham were friends. It's possible they were the brains behind this."

"But there's footage of Markham getting into Natalie Bennett's vehicle," I pointed out. "Was there any sign of Mitchell?"

"No."

"Then where is he?"

"I don't know, and given what happened in the pot field this morning, I'm afraid to find out," Chief Terry admitted. "You only picked up on magic in one cell, Bay, and yet two inmates who didn't spark magically have used magic to attack you. That seems like more than a coincidence."

I rolled my neck until it cracked. "They're like sleeper agents. I'm betting she embedded some sort of trigger in their minds. Now she can send them on magical missions, and there's nothing they can do about it."

"But why did you alert on Mitchell?" Landon asked. "What made him different?"

"When the final report is put together, I'm willing to bet that Mitchell did all the heavy lifting during the prison break," I replied. "That would be by design in case something bad happened and they were thwarted. If Mitchell was named as the guilty party, Markham would've been safe to try again. Natalie probably made sure he wouldn't be the focal point of the investigation."

Chief Terry bobbed his head. "Because even though the other guards weren't talking out of turn to the warden, the second Markham was brought up as a suspect, they wouldn't be able to stop themselves from volunteering information about her."

"And then it would be over," Landon added.

"She really was diabolical in the planning," Chief Terry said.

"And so far, she's getting away with it," Landon replied.

"Well, that's going to change." Chief Terry levered himself to a standing position. "The warden has asked that we conduct our own search of Natalie's house. He didn't come right out and say it, but I could read between the lines. And he wants Bay there. He thinks she'll be able to magically divine something."

"Do you want me to go with you?" I asked hopefully.

"I want you as far from danger as possible, but this morning proved that's not possible," Chief Terry replied. "It's best you come with us. If you pick up on something, we can act right away. The longer Natalie and Markham are out there together, the better chance they have of getting away."

His tone stirred me. "Okay." I grabbed my half-eaten doughnut. "You know Landon and I are going to be mushy for a few more hours. Do you want to drive separately?"

A long-suffering sigh escaped Chief Terry's upturned mouth. "No. I'll somehow get through it. We all need to stick together."

"Look at the martyr," Landon drawled. "And you think I'm good at feeling sorry for myself."

"Son, I've given you a pass this morning," Chief Terry warned. "You went through an ordeal, and because you put Bay's well-being above your own, she's safe. I appreciate what you did."

Landon puffed out his chest.

"I won't put up with this nonsense for much longer, though," Chief Terry said. "Stop with the mush. I can only take so much."

"We'll do our best," I promised, knowing it wouldn't be good enough.

Chief Terry, always my greatest champion, smiled. "That's all I ask, sweetheart."

# Thirteen

Natalie's house was on the outskirts of Hawthorne Hollow. It was a simple ranch, about five minutes from the downtown area, and set apart from most of the other houses. In fact, the nearest neighbor was a quarter of a mile away.

"She sold this place three months ago but arranged to stay until next week," I said as we hopped out of Chief Terry's vehicle. Landon seemed to be dragging a bit—perhaps the earlier adrenaline spike was catching up to him—and I made a mental note to keep an eye on him. A good night's sleep and he would likely be back to normal. Until then, he might have to fight to keep up.

"That's the information I got," Chief Terry confirmed. He stopped in front of the door, which had police tape across it. "Let's see what we find."

Inside, the house was stark, the furniture worn and ratty. The lone piece of art on a wall looked as if it had been stolen from a Holiday Inn. "I'm surprised she didn't try to sell this stuff," I said. "She'd need money while on the run."

"Just off the top of my head, if she was telling people she was moving to a new town, selling the furniture might look suspicious," Chief Terry replied. His upper lip curled. "Plus, she wasn't going to get much for this stuff. Maybe a couple hundred bucks. It might not have been worth it when she likely had other things on her mind."

We moved into the kitchen, and I immediately went to the refrigerator. Other than some old condiments, it was empty. "She planned well. She didn't spend money unnecessarily. She was biding her time between selling the house and waiting for him to get free."

"Pretty much," Chief Terry concurred. "I don't know if we're going to find anything here."

"We just started looking," I reminded him, my gaze snaking to Landon, who was resting his palms against the counter. "Maybe you should sit down," I prodded gently.

Landon immediately straightened. "I'm fine."

I wasn't convinced. "How is your stomach?" If I could've reached through time and space and strangled Aunt Tillie, I would've seriously considered it.

"Bay, don't worry about me." Landon's voice was low and full of warning. "We're here for a reason."

"I can't help being worried." I opted to tell him the whole truth. "Aunt Tillie's ward spells are really strong. Even if she did her best to cure you—and I believe she did—there might be lingering side effects that she wouldn't have wanted to own up to in the moment. If you're sick, don't be a martyr. Go to the bathroom and do ... whatever needs to be done." I didn't mean to make a face, but I obviously did, because Landon glared at me.

"I said I was fine," he barked.

"Okay." I held up my hands in supplication. "I was just checking."

"Worry about searching this place and finding some clues. Don't worry about me."

That was easier said than done, but I forced the concern away.

If Chief Terry was worried about Landon, he didn't show it. He ushered me into what was probably intended to be a child's bedroom, or maybe a guest bedroom. Natalie had clearly used it as an office. There was a huge metal desk in the middle of the room, the sort that would've been available at auction when a jail or prison was upgrading furniture. It has been painted multiple times, and notepads and pens were scattered across the top.

"I'm assuming she had a computer," I said as I moved to sit in the ratty desk chair. I immediately went for the drawers.

"She did, but it wasn't found on the premises," Chief Terry confirmed. "If I were her, I would've destroyed it and dumped the pieces. It's possible she took it with her. Her phone has either been shut off or destroyed. I'm guessing she bought burner phones in the days leading up to the escape."

I rummaged in the drawers. They didn't contain much. "There's no art on the walls in here," I noticed. "Well, except that." I inclined my head toward a map that had been tacked on the wall. "No marks on the map, though."

Chief Terry went to the map. He leaned close. "Looks like she marked something with tacks, but they've been removed. If we put tacks back in, maybe we can discern a pattern."

"There's an idea." I grabbed loose push pins from a drawer and joined him, casting a look to Landon, who was hovering in the doorway ... and who looked as if he wished he was anywhere else. "Landon—"

"Don't, Bay." His face twisted. "I'm going to kill Aunt Tillie."

"Don't be a hero," I said. "I'm so sorry, but ... you have to go through it. I really do think she did her best, but it's catching up to you. Once we're done here, I'll take you home and take care of you."

Landon made a horrified face. "I don't want you with me for this. It's embarrassing."

"You're still my hero," I assured him when I realized he was about to bolt down the hallway.

"I'm nobody's hero right now." With that, he broke into a run. I heard a door slam and realized he'd locked himself in the bathroom.

"I hope we don't need anything from in there," I offered. When I glanced at Chief Terry, I found him smirking. "This is not funny."

He blanked his face and acted gruff. "I didn't say it was."

"You're enjoying yourself." I was horrified. "Do you know that I was prepared to get that hammer in the head? I couldn't find the strength to fight him because of whatever curse was worked into that magic. There was no stopping him. The only reason I'm alive is because Landon managed to get through those wards."

Slowly, Chief Terry's lips curved down. "Bay, I'll always be grateful he managed to do what he did."

"But you still think it's funny," I said.

"It's his payback for all the mush I've had to sit through. Do you have any idea how painful that is for me?"

"You just like to complain." I handed him some of the pins. "Let's see what we find when we fill these holes."

I felt Chief Terry's eyes on me as I got to work. "Are you mad at me?" he asked after a moment.

"Mad is not the appropriate word. I'm not happy. I guess I'm disappointed."

"That's what I used to say to you when you got into trouble as a kid."

"Yes, and it crushed me every time."

"Oh, geez." He started adding tacks. When we finished, we both stepped back to study what we were dealing with.

"None of these tacks line up with anything that I can see," Chief Terry said after several seconds. "What do you think they mean?"

I'd managed to ascertain a pattern. "Hold on." I returned to the desk and grabbed the container of floss that I'd seen in the drawer moments earlier. I used it to wrap around the tacks. When I finished, my suspicions were confirmed.

"That's a pentagram," Chief Terry said grimly.

"Yup."

"So Natalie is definitely magical."

"I would say so, but I don't feel any remnants of magic here." I looked around. "She could've cleansed the property. That's what I would've done. She's near Scout, so if she managed to pick up on the magic that's being thrown around town, she might've been diligent about covering her tracks."

"But?" Chief Terry prodded.

"But why?" I held out my hands. "She wasn't on anybody's radar. Even if someone magical did come here to check after the fact, it wouldn't matter. It would only serve as confirmation."

"You're saying that if she was hiding something, it would have to be something good."

I nodded. "It's all very weird. Let's check the bedroom."

When we passed the bathroom door, there was no sound from the other side. I opened my mouth to yell out to Landon, make sure he was okay, but Chief Terry cut me off with a shake of his head.

"He's embarrassed," Chief Terry said as he prodded me into the second bedroom. "I don't blame him. He was feeling on top of the world, giddy because you were both okay, and now things have taken a turn. I would be just as surly."

"I'm going to kill Aunt Tillie," I muttered.

Chief Terry chuckled as he looked around the bedroom. There was little of interest that had been left behind. The closet and dresser were empty. Even the bed had been stripped. Like the rest of the house, there was no art. Only paperclips and an empty fast-food bag had been left behind.

"There's no television," I mused. "She took all the clothes." Something white caught my attention by the closet door, and I leaned over to pick it up. It was a price tag from an item of clothing. "This is for a man's flannel shirt." I held it up. "I bet she did some shopping for Markham."

"That would make sense." Chief Terry planted his hands on his hips as he looked around. "I don't think she brought him here."

"No, that would've been stupid, and all the planning she did proves she isn't stupid. She had another location in mind. The question is, why would she pick a location so close to home? I think she has to have done it because of the magical attacks that keep sprouting up, but why not flee?"

"I'll tell you why. Because the longer this goes on, the wider the search will spread," Chief Terry explained. "We assume that it makes sense for her to run, but what if it doesn't? If she managed to find a place where they can safely hole up for the winter, it's smarter to stick close."

"To what end?" I asked.

"People will stop searching this area sooner. They'll assume that a woman smart enough to pull this off would be far away by now. But what if she has a safe place nearby? She could've stocked it with enough food to get through the winter. She could've stocked it with clothes. If they hunker down there for months, they can change their appearance. When they emerge in spring, they'll look like different people.

"They'll probably both have lost weight," he continued. "Natalie is blond, so her hair will be brown or red when they emerge. Markham has brown hair, and it's short. It will either be longer, or he'll shave his head. They won't look anything like they do now."

It made sense. "Wherever they are, they're not as far as they want us to think," I said.

"And they still have seven inmates to throw at us. We need to figure out how to solve that little problem too."

I shifted my gaze to the doorway when Landon appeared. He looked like death warmed over. "I'm so sorry." I didn't know what else to say.

"Bay, you didn't do this." Landon sounded run down, and I definitely wanted to murder Aunt Tillie. "I don't regret it. I would put up with this the rest of my life to keep you."

"Yeah, but it's going to put a damper on my plans for you this evening." My smile was rueful when Chief Terry shot me a death glare. "We should get you home and put you to bed. The only thing that'll help is rest."

I thought he might argue, but Landon nodded. "Can you handle the rest of the day without me?" he asked Chief Terry.

"Sure." Chief Terry's lips twitched, as if he was fighting off a smile. "I think I can manage."

"Oh, stuff it," Landon growled. He was morose as we left the house, and when I went to help him into the truck, he pinned me with a dark look. "Are you trying to make this worse?"

"Stop being an alphahole, and let me help you," I ordered. "If you make this harder, it'll linger. Let me take care of you."

"Fine." Landon huffed as he let me load him into the back of the truck. "This is not how I saw this day going."

"I know." I reveled in our switched roles and brushed his hair back from his face. "I love you."

"I want to feel sorry for myself," Landon argued. "I can't feel sorry for myself when you say things like that."

"Duly noted." I closed the door and moved to hop into the

passenger seat, but a sizzling sensation rippled through me, and I froze with my hand on the door handle.

"What is it?" Chief Terry asked, instantly alert.

I only had time to act. "Get down!" I launched myself at him and dragged him down so the vehicle acted as a shield.

A sucking sound filled the air, and a ball of fire emerged from the house. Flames roared around us, and I threw up a shield to serve as protection. Just as quickly as the flames rushed out, they receded, and when I lifted my head, I found the house burning. There would be no saving it.

"What happened?" Chief Terry demanded as he lifted his head. He looked shell shocked.

"The house exploded," I replied dumbly.

"That wasn't a bomb. There was no noise to indicate it was a bomb."

Well, that was an interesting detail. "It was a magical bomb." I cocked my head as I studied the burning home. "It was aimed at me. Or I guess it was aimed at anyone magical who might come to the house looking for answers."

"How can you be sure?"

"Once she left this house, she wouldn't have come back." It was the only thing that made sense. "She set the spell before she left."

"That indicates she expected someone magical to come after her."

"Maybe. She could've thought that Scout would come after her. If she's as strong as we believe, and as smart, she would've known that Scout's group controls most of the magic in Hawthorne Hollow. She might've been preparing for them."

"Or?" Chief Terry prodded.

"Or she might've known I would end up on the case because of who I am to you and Landon," I conceded. "That feels like more of a long shot."

Chief Terry didn't look convinced. "Bay, I don't like this."

He wasn't the only one. "It doesn't matter why she set the trap. It only matters that she did. You need to call this in." I spared a glance for Landon, who was so pale he almost looked transparent. "And we need to get him home. Call Graham Stratton. He'll understand what we're dealing with."

Chief Terry nodded as he pulled his phone from his pocket to call the local police chief. "Bay, what would've happened if that bomb had gone off while we were still inside?" He looked almost as pale as Landon.

"You don't want to know," I replied as I crossed back to Landon's side of the truck. "We're okay," I reminded him. "There's no reason to get worked up."

"That's easy for you to say. From my perspective, that's two attacks in one day, and it's barely the middle of the afternoon."

I hadn't thought about it that way. "We're fine," I insisted. "I have everything under control."

"Now you sound like Tillie," he groused.

"That's definitely the meanest thing you've ever said to me."

He didn't smile. "Kid, you'd better have a plan. This is spiraling out of hand way too fast."

# Fourteen

Graham Stratton was less than impressed when he arrived at the remains of Natalie's house.

"You can't blow crap up in Hemlock Cove?" he demanded.

I kept quiet and let Chief Terry deal with the fallout.

"We believe a guard helped the inmates escape from Antrim Correctional Facility," he explained. "She lived here. The house exploded as we were leaving. It was not a bomb."

Graham blinked twice and then swung his gaze to me. "Is that why you're here?"

"We didn't know the house was going to explode," I offered sheepishly. "We're sorry."

Graham looked stern, but he couldn't keep his grimace intact. "I'll handle it. I'll say we're looking at it as a gas leak or something. Nobody was inside?"

"No." Chief Terry shook his head. "We really are sorry."

Graham's eyes flicked to Chief Terry's truck. Landon's head was just visible where he was sprawled in the backseat. "Is he okay?"

"That's a whole other thing," Chief Terry replied. "He'll be fine."

"Well, get him home. He looks as if he's dying."

"We're hopeful he'll be back to his normal self tomorrow morning," I said.

I hoped that wasn't just wishful thinking, because if Landon didn't get better soon, I really was going to kill Aunt Tillie.

**CHIEF TERRY DROPPED LANDON AND ME IN** town. He grumbled about having to help Landon to his Ford Explorer, but once Landon was fastened in his seatbelt, Chief Terry focused on me.

"Put him to bed. I don't want to see him again tonight."

"You could have a little bit of sympathy for his predicament," I complained.

"Yeah, I'm good."

I made a face but didn't offer another word in argument. "Fine. Just know that when you're sick, he gets to make fun of you as much as he wants."

"I'll keep that in mind."

I drove straight to the guesthouse. Landon was practically dead weight when I got him inside. I was going to suggest a bath, or maybe some tea, but instead he stripped out of his shirt, dropped his pants, and climbed into bed without a word.

I followed to tuck him in. He didn't have a fever, which was a good sign, but he was still too pale for my liking. I put a bottle of water next to the bed and left a note on my pillow so he wouldn't wonder where I'd gone, and then I headed to the inn.

It was growing dark when I passed the pot field, but nothing stirred as I passed. The area was a void, so Aunt Tillie must have stepped up her game with the wards. She was deadly serious about keeping her field from being invaded.

Aunt Tillie wasn't in her normal spot on the couch when I entered through the family living quarters. I didn't take that as a good sign. When I wandered into the kitchen and saw her easy chair empty, I was instantly suspicious. "Where is Aunt Tillie?" I asked my mother and aunts, who were preparing dinner.

"Who knows," Mom replied darkly. "She's been hiding all day. I want to talk to her about whatever spell she cast on that field—that pot has not gone dormant—but she's conveniently made herself scarce. She can't hide from me forever."

"I need to talk to her."

Slowly, Mom tracked her eyes to me. "Is something wrong? You smell like smoke."

I hadn't considered showering before I left the guesthouse, but now I regretted that choice. "We had a bit of a thing this afternoon." I glared at the empty recliner. "You'll have to get in line behind me when she does show up. I need another potion for Landon."

"Why?" Mom asked. "He was fine earlier."

"It didn't last. He's sick as a dog right now. I put him in bed. He's going to be so sad about missing the pot roast."

"Does that mean Aunt Tillie's spell hit him later in the day?" Marnie asked.

"It hit him while we were searching a house, and it wasn't pretty. He's embarrassed, and that doesn't seem fair given what he went through to get to me this morning."

"It doesn't seem fair," Mom agreed. "As for the pot roast, we'll set some aside. You can take it home, and he can eat it later if he wakes up feeling better."

"I'm not sure I want him to wake up," I admitted. "I think it might be best if he sleeps until morning."

"We'll have pancakes for breakfast," Mom offered. "Blueberry, with lots of bacon on the side. That should perk him up."

"That doesn't fix the problem right now." I planted my hands on my hips. "Do you think she knew that potion wasn't going to get him through the entire day? She said he would be fine, and I believed her."

"That's entirely possible," Mom conceded. "I don't want to cast aspersions on her—oh, who am I kidding? I totally want to kill her myself right now—but I think she was trying to help. She might have known there was no way to fully beat back his body's response to those wards, and she just tried to mitigate the problem until she was out of sight."

"Well, it's not fair." I couldn't let it go. "He saved me, Mom. If he hadn't overcome those wards, I would've had my head bashed in with a hammer this morning."

"Really, Bay," Mom scolded. "Must you put those pictures in my head?"

"If they're in mine, they have to be in yours. Landon feels like he's dying."

"I'm assuming you left him in bed."

"Yes. I thought I'd try to get another potion from Aunt Tillie, but if that just delays the torture, I'd rather him get it out of his system now."

Mom's hand was warm when it landed on my shoulder. "I'm sure he'll be fine."

I wasn't convinced. "He'd better be." I rolled my neck. "How's life with the Happy Holidays Players?"

"They seem fine." Mom's smile was legit when it returned to her face. "I think they'll be very happy with the audition I've prepared."

"Not nearly as happy as they'll be with my audition," Twila barked from her spot across the kitchen island. Her eyes were narrowed. "I thought you were focused on the pie-baking contest. Why are you trying to steal my glory when you should be striving for your own?"

"Who says I can't have glory in more than one thing?" Mom shot back.

"Me!" Twila thumped her chest. "Acting is my thing. You know I was passed over for that part in that movie. This is my second chance."

I perked up. "What movie were you passed over for?"

"It was the role I was born to play." Twila looked momentarily forlorn. "It would've launched me to stardom."

"What role is she talking about?" I asked Mom.

A half smile played out over Mom's face. "I think you should hear it from her."

"The year was 1996," Twila began. "I was a young lass barely on the cusp of adulthood."

"You were twenty-eight," Marnie muttered.

"I had it in the bag," Twila insisted. "That role was meant for me. And then that upstart, that British thief, came in and stole what should've been mine."

"I can't decide if I want to keep listening or if I'm done," I admitted to Mom in a low voice.

"Keep listening." Mom's smile told me she was holding back raucous laughter.

"Her name was Kate Winslet." Twila said the words with a soupçon of venom. "She didn't even apologize. She just swooped in and stole my glory."

"Is she saying she auditioned for *Titanic*?" I asked.

"She's saying she saw the movie after the fact and thought she was born to play Rose," Mom clarified.

"Oh, well, sure." I managed a smile that quickly turned into a laugh powerful enough to have me bending at the waist. "Thanks for that, Twila," I offered as I straightened, wiping an errant tear from my cheek. "I was in a terrible mood when I got here, but you made me feel better."

"I don't feel better." Twila vehemently shook her head. "I lost out on the role of a lifetime and the love of my life."

"Leonardo DiCaprio?" I guessed.

"Of course not." She made a face. "Billy Zane."

"Yup, that fits." I moved past Mom and headed toward the dining room. "I'm going to find Aunt Tillie. If she's difficult, I might need you to help me hide the body."

"That's fine, Bay, but I'm guessing she won't show herself until dinner is served because she knows that we won't cause a scene in front of the guests."

"I'm still going to kill her," I warned. "Mark it down."

"I'll set pot roast aside," Mom promised. "I have some leftover chicken noodle soup in the fridge I can send back with you too. If he can't eat the pot roast, the soup might be okay."

"I'll take both. I can't stand seeing him sick."

"He'll be fine tomorrow."

"He'd better be."

A couple members of the Happy Holidays Players were in the dining room. I scanned their faces. The Sam Elliot lookalike was present, so I thought there was a possibility that Aunt Tillie would be hanging around. She was nowhere to be found, though.

"You haven't seen Aunt Tillie, have you?" I kept my voice breezy, but it took effort.

"No," Ava replied. She had a glass of wine in her hand and a flush to her cheeks, suggesting this wasn't her first serving. "She was downtown this afternoon. She was on a scooter and wearing a combat helmet. I think she might've also been wearing a cape. We thought she was coming to audition for the pageant, but she just kept riding the scooter up and down Main Street."

"She had a really hot guy with her," Robin added. "Like ... *really* hot. Is he a cousin we don't know about?" She looked hopeful.

I didn't have to ask who the hot guy was. "He's a family friend. We utilize him as a babysitter of sorts sometimes. Aunt Tillie is old and has dementia." I said it loud enough that my voice carried, knowing Aunt Tillie wouldn't be able to stop herself from racing in to punish me if she was close enough to hear. Evan wouldn't be happy about being relegated to babysitter status, but he would survive.

"So, not a relative." Robin looked sad. "We shouldn't expect him for dinner?"

"Probably not," I conceded. "Sorry."

"What about the yummy FBI agent?" Ava asked. "I wouldn't mind seeing him again."

I was already agitated, so her question was enough to send me spiraling close to the edge. "You mean my husband?" I challenged.

Ava either didn't recognize my tone or didn't care. "Oh, is he your husband? I wasn't certain."

I met Robin's gaze over the blonde's shoulder. She looked amused.

"Ignore her," Robin admonished. "She's hot to trot in every town we visit. No offense to this area, but there aren't many really hot guys in this part of the country. Unless you like lumberjacks. This town seems to have a lot of them."

Ava started ticking them off on her fingers. "There's the hot FBI agent. There's the hot guy who babysits your great-aunt. There's the hot guy who runs the petting zoo."

"Also taken," I gritted out.

"So the only guy who isn't taken is your aunt's babysitter," Robin mused. "I guess it's good I called dibs on him."

As if on cue, Evan appeared in the dining room, his hair swept back from his face, looking healthy and happy. Well, for him. He smiled at me, but the expression didn't last when he caught me peering around his shoulder.

"What?" he asked.

"Where is she?" I demanded, moving toward him. "Where is your partner in crime?"

"I really wish you wouldn't call her that." Evan looked pained.

"Where is she?" I was in no mood for his "aw shucks" charm.

"She was right behind me? Why?" Alarm rippled over Evan's features.

"Because I'm going to kill her." I jumped past him—he had vampire reflexes, so if he really wanted to stop me, he could have—and raced down the hallway. The sound of the front door slamming told me she was outside. "Oh, that's not happening, old lady."

Aunt Tillie was spry for her age, but I was determined. I flew through the door, went left instead of right because that route was shorter, and caught her just as she was about to make the final turn at the rear of the inn.

"You're dead!" I snapped.

Aunt Tillie knew when she was beaten. She stopped running—shuffling in place—and turned to face me with a defiant look. "It's not my fault."

Of course she would say that. "You knew when you gave him that potion that it wouldn't last." I took a threatening step toward her. "Why didn't you tell us?"

"I didn't want to ruin your day," she sniffed. "Really, I was doing you a kindness. I gave him a few hours to bask in his hero status. He wouldn't have had that without me."

"And he wouldn't be in bed right now missing one of his favorite meals without you." I moved closer. "I want you to fix him right now."

"I can't. There's no cure. He has to go through it." She didn't look apologetic. "Is he puking, or is it the other stuff?"

"He's going to puke too?" I was horrified. "What is wrong with you?"

"That's my field," Aunt Tillie fired back. "He wasn't supposed to be in there."

"He was saving me."

"Like I knew that was going to happen. The other guy shouldn't have been in there either. I'm still trying to figure out how that happened." She took a breath. "Just out of curiosity, you didn't catch any more convicts today, did you? I'm still behind, and it's bugging me."

I was about to bug her a whole lot more, but when I threw myself at her, intent on tackling her to the ground and making her cry, a strong arm caught me from behind. Evan hauled me back before I could get my hands on her.

"You'll break her hip if you're not careful," Evan chided. "You'll regret that if she's stuck in the hospital with nothing to do but plot her payback."

Aunt Tillie jabbed a finger at Evan. "Listen to him. He's smart. That's why I chose him as my sidekick."

"Knock that off," Evan warned. "I'm not your sidekick. I hate when you call me that. I'll let her kill you if you're not careful."

I kicked back at him, knowing even if I managed to hit my target that it wouldn't hurt him. "You'd better start running now, Aunt Tillie!" I screeched. "If I get my hands on you, it's all over."

"Chill out." Evan refused to release me. "What's all this about?"

I told him, and when I got to the part about Landon having to race to the bathroom in Natalie's house, he looked as if he was fighting a fit of the giggles.

"It's not funny," I shouted. "He's sick, and it's not fair."

"Well, Bay, life isn't fair." Evan used his most reasonable tone. It only served to infuriate me further. "He'll be fine in the morning. He glanced over my shoulder and frowned.

Aunt Tillie had disappeared. "You let her get away." I gave him a shove.

"I was trying to keep you from doing something you'd regret." He rubbed the back of his neck. "She's freaking wily."

"I'm going to hurt her when I find her," I warned.

"You won't. You know as well as I do that she would save Landon from this if she could. She might not want to coddle him, but she hasn't stopped talking about the sheer force of will he had to exert to get to you this morning. She's proud."

"That doesn't save him tonight."

"He has to endure it."

That didn't make me feel better. "I'm going to make her cry before it's all said and done. Mark my words!" I jabbed my finger in the air.

The sound of applause from a distance drew my attention. The Happy Holidays Players were gathered around the dining room window, clapping and whooping.

"Well, look at that," Evan drawled. "Maybe you'll get a part in the pageant."

That was the last thing I wanted. "This day has sucked."

"Yes, well, it can always get worse."

# Fifteen

Dinner was a tense affair. Without Landon there to serve as a buffer, there was an open chair between Aunt Tillie and me. Evan ultimately took the spot—perhaps afraid of what I might do—but that didn't cut down on the silent vitriol I cast in her direction every five minutes.

Whenever she opened her mouth, I made a slashing motion across my throat. My mother sent me a series of quelling looks, but it didn't matter. I was worked up, and as everybody knew, there was no calming an excited Winchester.

When dinner was done, Mom handed me a bag of food and then politely asked me to leave the inn. She knew I wasn't going to calm down as long as I was under the same roof with Aunt Tillie.

"Evan will go with you," she volunteered, causing the vampire sitting at the counter to jerk up his head.

"Oh, I will, will I?" Evan's expression was impossible to read.

"He doesn't have to walk with me," I countered. "I think I can handle a five-minute walk on my own."

"I'm sure you thought that this morning too and look what happened." Mom's tone brooked no nonsense. "I don't want her alone,

Evan. I should've asked and not just assumed you would do it, but it's been a trying evening."

Rather than argue, or tease her, Evan nodded. "It's fine. I want to get away from that Robin chick anyway. She makes me uneasy."

"That's because she wants to climb you like a tree," I said.

Evan smirked. "I'm hot. What can I say?" He gestured to the door that led into the family living quarters. "Let's leave that way. It will be safer for all concerned."

"If you see Aunt Tillie, don't start something, Bay," Mom warned. "She can't fix this. I'm sorry for Landon—I really am—but he has to get through it."

I hated how reasonable she sounded. "If it was Chief Terry, would you sit back and let him go through it?"

She gripped her hands together, perturbed. "I wouldn't like it, but I hope I would realize that there was no way around it. Go home. Go to bed. When you wake up, things will be back to normal."

"You'd better hope that's true," I shot back. "If he's still sick tomorrow, I'm coming for Aunt Tillie."

"You'll have to get in line," Mom muttered.

The living room was empty. I searched every corner for a sign of Aunt Tillie. She'd wisely retired for the evening.

The night air was brisk, and Evan wasted no time launching into his lecture.

"I know she drives you crazy," he started.

"She drives you crazy too."

"She does, but she also makes me laugh. I went a long time without laughing. Tillie might not be perfect—she's a pain in the ass most of the time—but she has a good heart. I think she feels really bad about what happened to Landon."

"She should feel bad. I asked her months ago to make an exception for him and that field. Did she? No. If she had, he wouldn't be suffering."

"Something tells me she's made that exception now."

"That doesn't change the fact that he's sick."

"No, it doesn't. I'm sorry for him. He wouldn't have changed what happened regardless. Even knowing he would have to go through this, how bad it is, he'd do it again. For you."

I was surprised when tears pricked the back of my eyes. I'd thought myself too angry to cry. "I'm just tired," I complained. "I'm tense ... and tired ... and I feel guilty."

Evan's lips curved. "You'll feel better in the morning too."

I cast a look at the pathway that led to the bluff, the heart of our magic, then sighed. "I've been thinking that maybe Emori is right. If this enchantress thing is real, I could use my magic to call her to me. I could end this, and then all we'd have to do is round up the prisoners."

Evan followed my gaze. "You want to call her out there?"

"I can surround myself with ghosts. They'll protect me. I think it's worth a try."

Evan didn't look convinced. "Maybe you should have some magical backup."

"I don't trust Aunt Tillie right now."

"She wouldn't screw up something like this."

"I don't care. I don't want to see her." I knew I was being petulant, but I couldn't stop myself.

"What about Scout?" Evan was practical by nature, so I wasn't surprised he brought up his best friend. "She's been spoiling for a fight the last few weeks."

I considered it, and then almost immediately discarded the notion. "She has her own stuff to deal with right now, and it's far graver than what I'm dealing with. Between finding her parents and the other issues ... losing Bonnie, I don't want to bother her."

Evan sounded exasperated when he sighed. "You're going to make me go with you."

"No." I shook my head. "I can do it myself."

"Right, because I'm going to let you call an evil enchantress to you when your husband—who I happen to like a great deal—is down for the count. That sounds just like me."

"I don't know that it's going to work," I cautioned. "If I could end it tonight, though, and tell Landon the good news in the morning..."

"Bay, you're blaming yourself, but it's not your fault," Evan insisted. "You couldn't have known what would happen."

"He didn't want me to go in there. I did anyway."

"He won't hold it against you."

Landon wouldn't hold it against me, but I was a bit of a whiner. I would blame myself for a long time. "I just want to get it out of the way if I can."

"Then let's do it." Evan was decisive. "Let's drop the food off, check on Landon—because I know that's what you want to do—and then get it out of the way."

A smile rose to my lips. "I can see why Aunt Tillie wants you for her sidekick. You're loyal and you always do the right thing."

"Not always," Evan countered. "I spent years doing terrible things. Maybe I'm just trying to atone."

"You can't be held accountable for what you did when you were without a soul."

"Can't I? Perhaps I'm a martyr like you."

He made me laugh. "Then you can atone with me. We'll know fairly quickly if the spell will work."

"Then let's get it done."

**I PUT THE FOOD IN THE FRIDGE, CHECKED** on Landon, then left him to sleep. He was down for the count, and I didn't want to risk waking him. If he could sleep through the entire night, it would be best for all concerned. Sure, he'd be angry when he learned what I'd done, but taking Evan with me fulfilled my promise to him.

Besides, now that I had the idea in my head, there was no backtracking.

Evan had been to the bluff with us before. He lifted his nose as we approached, scenting the air, and then shook his head at my unasked question. "I don't think that prisoner ended up out here."

That was good. At least I thought it was. "I still don't understand how he ended up in the field."

"Neither do I," Evan admitted. "It feels pointed, doesn't it?"

"Yeah." I let loose a sigh and then grabbed the bag of ingredients I'd taken from the guesthouse. "Stand there." I directed him to a specific spot as I used the ingredients to draw a circle.

"I'm going to call the ghosts first," I explained. "They'll stand guard. Then I'm going to try to call the enchantress in. When she comes—if she comes—she'll have to arrive in this circle. It should trap her here."

"Should?" He arched an eyebrow.

"Should," I repeated. "I've never dealt with an enchantress. I don't know much about them."

"Which suggests we shouldn't be doing this, but whatever." Evan held up his hands. "We're here now. Let's see what happens."

He was gung ho. I liked that about him. "At the very least we'll learn something," I agreed.

Once the bag was emptied, I shoved it in my pocket and threw out my magic to enhance the circle. Then I called the ghosts. It was second nature now. I'd always been able to talk to them. Necromancy was a unique power, though. It caused more than one witch to lose her mind. Was I worried I might follow suit? A little, but as I'd grown more comfortable with my powers, that fear had taken a backseat.

"*Come*," I intoned, magic blowing through me as I watched with satisfaction as a number of ghosts popped into existence beyond the circle, Viola among them.

"You're just a regular Bossy McBossypants these days, aren't you?" the ghost complained bitterly. "I was watching *Grey's Anatomy*. It's nowhere near as good these days, but some of those doctors are still hot."

"I won't keep you long," I promised. "I'm trying to see if I can lure an enchantress. I need protection before I start."

"I could say no," Viola sniffed.

She could, but we both knew my magic could overpower her. "I promise it won't take long."

"Fine." Viola folded her arms across her chest and waited.

The other ghosts were all new faces. I'd cast a wide net. "Thank you all for coming," I said. "I won't keep you long."

None of them responded. They weren't familiar with me, and some were probably adjusting to new realities.

"Here we go," I muttered, casting Evan another look before closing my eyes. "I call upon the powers of the north," I started. The chant was a familiar one. Normally, I would have my cousins or mothers with me to help—almost always Aunt Tillie—but I was the one anchoring all four directions this evening.

When the fourth line snapped into place, I watched with determination as the magic began to coalesce. There was a hum beneath the magic, and Evan appeared intrigued as he moved to the circle boundary to touch it. He pulled his fingers back almost immediately when a spark appeared.

"That's pretty impressive," he noted. "You clearly mean business."

I did mean business, but the spell didn't appear to be working. "She should've been forced here almost immediately," I complained as I looked around. It was dark beyond the ghosts as I scanned the trees. There was no magic hiding there, just darkness.

"Scout sometimes needs a piece of the individual she's trying to summon when working a spell like this," Evan noted. "Something the individual has touched is often required."

I rolled my neck. "I don't have anything of hers."

"Maybe you can get something from the guard's house and try again tomorrow."

"Her house blew up."

Evan cocked his head, considering. "What about her locker at the prison? I bet she left something there, a hairbrush or something."

That was a solid suggestion, but it didn't help me now.

"Come on!" Frustration reared up, causing me to stomp my foot. The magical circle flared bright, and a thin scream filled the air, causing me to straighten.

"She's here," I whispered.

Evan circled and stared. "I don't see anyone."

"She's in the ether." I pointed up, frowning. "She won't come into the circle. She's fighting it."

"That means she's strong, because this spell is freaking powerful."

*You can't summon me, girl.*

The words weren't spoken out loud, and yet they boomed over the bluff.

"We'll see about that," I grunted as I unloaded more magic into the circle. It wasn't the smartest move I'd ever made—apparently, today at least, I was acting on instinct and leaving strategic thought out of the mix—but nobody could say I wasn't putting in my full effort.

*You can't control me.* The voice sounded strained, telling me that I was at least causing this creature to work to keep out of the circle. *I don't answer to anyone.*

"Natalie?" I kept tugging on the magic, trying to draw her in. The voice was sexless, but it had to be her. "I think it's best we put an end to this now."

*The only thing ending will be your life. You should've stayed out of this.*

"And you should've stayed away from my family," I barked. "You can't keep doing this. You're not strong enough to fight us all."

*And you're not strong enough to stop me.*

"Maybe not alone," I conceded. I was starting to feel the drain of expending so much magic. "But I'm not alone. This isn't over."

*No, it's not over. Tomorrow is a new day. The day you'll fall.*

"Maybe it's the day you'll fall," I shot back.

*I've been preparing for this moment for years. You'll not be the one who takes me.*

"Yeah, we'll just see about that." She was gone. I felt her sever the final tie to the spell. The magic flared bright and then died, plunging the bluff into darkness.

"Well, that was a bit of a letdown," Viola noted. She sounded bored. "Can we go now?"

I nodded, my hand pressed to my side as I fought to catch my breath. "Sorry to interrupt *Grey's Anatomy*."

"That's fine." Viola waved off the apology. "It's been boring ever since Alex left anyway. I just watch out of habit now."

When they were gone, and it was just Evan and me, I turned a rueful smile toward him. "Sorry to have wasted your time."

"It wasn't a waste," Evan insisted. "In fact, it was illuminating. You almost had her, Bay. If we'd brought Tillie with us, you could've taken her."

"I'm not talking to that woman."

He chuckled. "Your family is a trip. I love how the prospect of winning isn't enough. You need to win without Tillie's help."

"I'm mad at her."

"Well, you need to get un-mad at her. You're going to need a bit of witchy help before this is over. This enchantress is strong, but not strong enough for multiple Winchesters."

I hated that he was likely right. "Let's get out of here." I took a step toward the path that led back to the inn and frowned when a niggling sense of dread brushed the back of my neck. "Did you feel that?" I asked, straightening. I searched the darkness. "There's something—or someone—out there."

Evan's forehead creased, and he stepped in front of me. The way he squared his shoulders and held out his arms told me he was ready for a fight. After a few seconds he shook his head. "I don't hear anything."

"I swear someone was there."

He gave me one more look, and then we started down the hill. About three hundred feet from where I'd cast the spell, he moved between me and a stand of trees. His eyes scanned the ground. "There are footprints," he said in a low voice. "Smaller ones."

"Like a child?"

"More like a woman."

"Can you tell where she went?"

He shook his head. "I think your spell brought her even closer than we realized."

"So she was here, and now she's gone."

"That's my guess. Either that or someone from the inn followed us and attempted to cover their tracks. If that's the case, they weren't entirely successful."

"Aunt Tillie?" Anger bubbled up.

"No, she smells like Bengay and whiskey. With a hint of pickled beets. It wasn't her."

"The enchantress," I surmised.

"I think it had to be. She didn't stay long."

"At least we know she was here."

"Now we just have to figure out how to get her back."

"Yeah, I'll get right on that ... after I get some sleep."

"Sounds like a plan."

# Sixteen

I had enough mental bandwidth to lock the doors and check on Landon before falling into bed next to him. He still wasn't running a fever, was still dead to the world, so I allowed myself to follow him into dreamland.

I woke the next morning to him wrapped around me, his nose in my hair and his hands wandering.

"Good morning," I murmured as I shifted to look at him.

His color was back. His eyes were bright. His smile was at the ready.

"How are you feeling?" I asked, the roar of guilt returning with a vengeance.

"Like a new man." His nose immediately went back into my hair as he pulled me tight. "Or maybe like an old man but with some added energy. I think I slept sixteen hours."

"It was about that," I agreed, frowning when he inhaled so deeply, he snorted. "What's up?"

"You smell like a maple bacon breakfast sandwich."

I laughed ... and then scowled. "Aunt Tillie."

"Shh." I swear it felt like he had eight hands as he felt me up. How he managed to grope me front and back given the way our bodies were twined together was beyond me. "Don't ruin the moment."

I remained still, even though I was annoyed, and managed a laugh when he bit my earlobe. "You really are feeling better. I'm glad." I pulled back far enough to stare into his eyes. "I'm so sorry."

"Shut it." He shook his head. "You didn't do it, Bay. I knew the ramifications of going into that field. I knew what would happen. I'd do it again ... especially when this is my reward."

Evan's words from the previous evening roared back with a vengeance. Aunt Tillie really did feel guilty. This was her gift to Landon for what he'd gone through. The bacon curse was his absolute favorite. It was one of my least favorite because it meant every man in town was going to be all over me as soon as we left our cocoon. I didn't complain, though. I wanted Landon to be happy.

"Go ahead and be an animal." I gave in. There was no stopping him at this point.

His eyes gleamed with flirty delight. "Don't mind if I do." When he jumped into the deep end of the pool, it was headfirst. My giggles mingled with his for a delightful morning.

**BY THE TIME WE WERE SHOWERED AND HEADING** to the inn, Landon was in great spirits.

"I hope your mother understands that I'm eating for two this morning," he said, my hand firmly clasped in his.

"Is there something you want to tell me?" I asked. We were in front of the pot field—Landon giving it the evil eye and a wide berth—but the morning was quiet. Nothing jumped out at us. Nothing tried to entice me into the field. It was just us.

"I'm not pregnant, if that's what you're worried about." He scuffed his shoes against the path. "But I did miss dinner."

"There's leftover pot roast in the fridge."

He looked wounded. "You ate pot roast without me?"

"I didn't. I spent the entire night trying to kill Aunt Tillie. I even chased her along the side of the house when she thought she could outrun me. The only reason I didn't catch her is Evan stopped me. He said I was going to break one of her hips."

Landon laughed, and it warmed me. "I'm sorry I missed that."

"He said I was being unreasonable." I scowled at the memory.

"I don't want to cause a fight, but I kind of agree with him."

I was caught off guard. "You spent the majority of yesterday wishing you were dead."

"It was a small price to pay for what I got in exchange." He leaned in and gave me a friendly kiss. "That's you, Bay, in case you're wondering. I wasn't lying about not regretting it."

"And that's the reason I wanted to hurt her."

He sighed. "I don't think there was anything she could've done once I was cursed."

"She could've told us."

"To what end? I still wouldn't have remained behind and let you run off with Chief Terry. It is what it is, Bay."

"Ugh." I was disgusted. "Since when are you on her side?"

"Have you smelled yourself?"

"So you can be bribed."

"Exactly." He beamed at me, only letting his smile slip when I refused to match his grin. "I'm okay. Actually, I'm better than okay. I would totally go through what I did yesterday once a month if it meant you smelled like Heaven in a pretty blond package the following day."

"Oh, geez."

I let him paw me the entire way to the inn. He was still frisky when we let ourselves in through the back door. There was no sign of Aunt Tillie in her normal spot—she liked mocking the morning news commentators before breakfast—and when we walked into the kitchen, her easy chair was vacant.

"Where is she?" I demanded.

"She's in the dining room with the Happy Holidays Players," Mom replied. Her gaze was on Landon. "You're not to cause a scene this morning, Bay. I'm putting my foot down."

My lower lip came out to play. "What is it with everybody protecting her?"

"She's in a bit of a mood," Landon volunteered for my mother's benefit. He was already on his way to the other side of the counter, where Twila was patting the bacon with a paper towel to absorb the grease. "Pancakes and bacon?" He cast my mother a look over his shoulder. "Who is your favorite son-in-law?"

Mom's grin was lightning quick. "You don't seem any worse for wear."

"I feel reborn," Landon agreed.

Mom was haughty when she turned back to me. "See. You were acting like a baby for no good reason."

I narrowed my eyes. "Just because the rest of you are willing to let her rule the roost doesn't mean I'm going to sit back and do nothing. Landon felt like he was at death's door most of yesterday. And why? Because he saved me."

"Oh, listen to you." Mom's eye roll was pronounced. "Good grief, Bay. It's not as if he died. He's obviously happy." She wrinkled her nose. "And you smell like breakfast."

"Why do you think I'm happy?" Landon winked at Mom before holding out his hands for the bacon tray. "I'll take that for you," he said to Twila.

Mom chuckled as she shook her head. "I take it your appetite is back."

"It is," Landon agreed. "I'm eating for two today."

Mom opened her mouth to ask the obvious question, but I shook my head to cut her off. "It's not that," I said.

"I didn't think it was." She patted my arm. "You should head out. Mary mentioned over coffee this morning that she wanted to talk to you."

"Why would she want to talk to me? I've already finished the first article on her group. It's too late to change it."

"I have no idea. She asked about you."

I grumbled. Landon had already disappeared with the bacon—and was no doubt already in his chair digging in—so I followed him, resigned to my fate.

Aunt Tillie looked up from her spot at the head of the table, squaring her shoulders in preparation for a fight.

"Everybody sit down," Mom ordered from behind me as she slid into the room with a platter of pancakes. Marnie followed with a second platter. "We have a big day." Her eyes sparkled as she looked at Mary. "It's audition day."

Oh, well, that explained that. I kept my gaze on Aunt Tillie as I passed behind her. Landon snagged the belt loop on my jeans and steered me to my usual chair as I moved in close enough to breathe down Aunt Tillie's neck.

"Enough," Landon ordered as he poured me a glass of juice "Let it go."

"I'm glad to see you back on your feet," Chief Terry noted. "That's good because we've been summoned to the prison. We're expected there in an hour, so eat fast."

"You don't have to tell me twice." Landon doused his pancakes with syrup and shot me a coy look. "Eat, Bay," he ordered. "The war is over."

The war was pretty far from over, but I decided to let it go ... for now. "Why does Childs want you at the prison?" I asked as I put one pancake and two slices of bacon on my plate.

Landon frowned at my meager haul and added two more pancakes and three more slices of bacon. "I want my woman carbed up," he said to my unasked question.

"Eat your breakfast," I ordered. His adorableness was wearing off quickly. "What does Childs want?"

"I'm not sure," Chief Terry said. "He's feeling the pressure."

"You're talking about the prisoners?" Mary asked from the other end of the table. She sat between Lenny and Ava, who was making cow eyes at Landon. Unfortunately for her, Landon was much too in love with his breakfast to even cast her a passing glance. "We've been following that story. Wasn't one caught here yesterday?"

I paused with a forkful of pancakes halfway to my mouth. I hadn't considered what story my mother and aunts had spread when the emergency vehicles arrived. I'd been too caught up in my own issues.

"That was a minor incident," Mom replied primly. "Bay and Landon caught him right away. No muss, no fuss."

"Why would a prisoner come to where a police chief and FBI agent live?" Lenny asked in his Sam Elliot voice. Seriously, if I was a couple decades older and single, I would be all over him. "That doesn't speak to a smart criminal."

"It doesn't," Chief Terry agreed, "but it's possible he didn't know. He's not saying much. He was knocked out during the capture—the good news for you folks is that lightning won't strike twice here, so you're safe—and hasn't been talkative. His lawyer probably told him to keep his mouth shut."

"Then you're not worried that they'll show up here again?" Mary asked.

"It's not impossible," Chief Terry hedged, "but it's very unlikely. There are still a significant number of prisoners out there. It makes no sense for them to end up here."

"Well, that's good." Mary smiled. "I would hate to have the pageant ruined. We're really looking forward to the auditions today. Tomorrow is rehearsal day. After that, it's magic." She wiggled her fingers and giggled. "It's going to be delightful."

"We're looking forward to the auditions today," Mom supplied. "They start at ten o'clock?"

"They do." Mary beamed at her. "I'm so glad you're looking forward to it." I was midchew when her eyes landed on me. "You're auditioning?"

Was she joking? "Um ... I don't think so." It felt necessary to explain why I wasn't interested. "Acting isn't really my thing."

"And yet the performance you put on last night was breathtaking," Mary insisted.

"It was," Robin said solemnly. "You and that hot guy had crackling chemistry. When he wrapped his arms around you, I felt the sexual tension through the window."

Landon stilled, his eyes moving to Robin. "What's that?"

Perhaps sensing she had an opening to talk to him, Ava inserted herself into the conversation with bubbly gusto. "Oh, they were all over each other," she said. "It's great that you build romantic relationships into the dinner theater. That only enriches the story. We've found that out ourselves."

"There was sexual tension?" Landon demanded.

"There was no sexual tension," I fired back. "He was there to protect Aunt Tillie." I looked at the woman. "Tell them."

I felt Aunt Tillie owed me and expected her to immediately take up for me. Evidently, she felt otherwise. "The sexual tension was something," she agreed. "I was worried for poor Landon for a few minutes."

"I'm going to kill you," I growled as I gripped my butter knife so tightly my knuckles turned white.

"I think you missed a few details when you were telling me the story of your exploits last night," Landon said to me.

I practically exploded. "Are you kidding me? There was no sexual tension."

It was only then that I noticed the twinkle in Landon's eyes. He was having a good time. "You're messing with me," I deduced. "You think this is funny."

"Sweetie, I don't think it's funny that you're having a bad day," he said, tapping the side of my plate to get me to refocus on my food. "You need to take it down a notch. You're wound a little tight." His head tilted as he regarded me. "You told me everything that happened last night?"

I hadn't. I'd left out the trip to the bluff. I couldn't lie to him now that he'd asked. "We'll talk about that later," I said as I avoided his steady gaze.

"Oh, geez." Landon shoveled more pancake into his mouth and waited until he'd swallowed to speak again. "Eat up, Bay. I need ten minutes of your time before we go, and we're on the clock."

His tone told me I didn't have a choice.

**LANDON DRAGGED ME TO THE LOBBY** before leaving with Chief Terry.

"Spill," he ordered. All traces of mirth were gone from his face, and I hated that I'd ruined his good mood.

"I went for a walk with Evan last night," I admitted.

He was quiet as I told him the rest. When I finished, instead of exploding, he pursed his lips. "Well, at least you didn't go alone."

I waited for him to expand. When he didn't, my eyebrows practically flew off my forehead. "That's it? You're not going to yell?"

"I'm not your keeper, Bay." He was serious. "You took Evan with you. You called in the ghosts to protect you. Would I have preferred you called in Scout to help? Yes. But I get why you didn't."

"But ... if you're the reasonable one, that means I'm the unreasonable one," I whined.

His face split into a wide grin as he tapped the end of my nose. "Perhaps there's a lesson in that for you." He pulled me in for a hug, inhaling deeply when his face disappeared into my hair. "You are my favorite person in the world, and all I want is to take you back to bed."

"Oh, man." Chief Terry picked that moment to stroll into the lobby. I was surprised he didn't turn around and stalk right back out. "Are you trying to kill me?"

"Sorry." Landon didn't look or sound sorry as he pulled back. "I'm ready to head out." He flicked his eyes back to me. "You're going to keep us updated if you do anything today." He sounded stern.

"I'm going to inform you of my plans before I even leave." If he wanted me to be open and honest, he was going to get a huge dose of it. "I'm going to Hawthorne Hollow this morning. I did some research when you were in the shower. Carl Markham's ex-wife lives there. I thought I might ask her some questions."

Landon darted his eyes to Chief Terry to gauge his response.

"Don't look at me," Chief Terry said. "You're her husband."

"It will be fine," I insisted. "Markham is with Natalie Bennett. It's not as if he's going to drop in on his ex-wife. I just want to know if she has any idea where he might hole up."

"I'm sure the state police have already been there," Landon said.

"Then the worst she can do is send me away."

He seemed to consider it for several seconds and then nodded. "Okay. Just be careful."

"I'm always careful."

"Be way more careful than that. I'd suggest taking Evan, but I don't want you exploring more of that sexual tension you seem to be suffering from."

The glare I shot him was withering. "Don't make things worse."

He gave me a hard kiss and then turned for the door. "We'll be in touch."

"Me too. Count on it."

# Seventeen

Ann Markham lived in a cute Cape Cod about two blocks from Hawthorne Hollow's downtown. Much like Hemlock Cove, Hawthorne Hollow was tiny. The center consisted of a town square, a hardware store, a coffee shop, a pizza place, and a cute diner. Across the street, the police station was housed directly next door to the library. That was it. Even the lone gas station was located farther outside town.

I parked on the street instead of in the narrow driveway. There was a small-sized SUV parked there, but it didn't look as if it had been driven in a few days if the crusted snow on top was any indication.

I knocked on the door, waited for someone to answer, and then moved to the bay window on the porch to see if I could make out any movement inside.

There was movement, furtive, and the size of the person who slipped from the living room and disappeared down a hallway had my heart rate picking up a notch.

I glanced around, debating, and then pulled out my phone. Landon might've believed I was prone to thinking I was unstoppable, but I didn't believe so. I'd grown braver in the last year or so—having ghosts to use as backup whenever the mood struck was enticing—but this felt off.

Scout picked up on the second ring. "If you're looking for Tillie, she's not here yet," she said by way of greeting. "On top of that, if you try to murder her here, Graham will be mad."

I took a moment to digest her words. "How do you even know about that?"

"Evan is with me," she replied. She sounded as if she was outdoors. "We're running Doc through a drill. He's terrible in the field."

I reconsidered asking her for help for a second, but then bit the bullet. "Can you spare a few minutes to serve as backup?"

"Sure. I'm looking for any reason to abandon this job. Where are you?"

"On Sycamore Street."

She was quiet a moment. "Here in Hawthorne Hollow?"

"Yeah. The ex-wife of one of our escaped prisoners lives here. I'm on the front porch now, and there's someone inside."

"Someone other than the ex-wife?"

"I haven't seen her. There's a man here. I saw his shadow. He didn't answer when I knocked. I have a weird feeling."

"Say no more. Text me the address. We'll be there in five minutes."

"Thanks." I disconnected and did as she asked. Rather than wait for her, I moved to the side of the house to peek through another window. It was dark inside, no hint of movement, and yet I felt a presence closing in. Someone was inside, and if I wasn't mistaken, that someone was magical.

I considered going to the backyard but thought better of it. I remained in my spot, the window directly in front of me, and waited. Scout arrived with her boyfriend Gunner Stratton and Evan within five minutes, as promised.

"Where?" she asked when they found me.

"I'm not sure." I cast her a wary look. "Has Evan kept you up to date?"

"I've told her everything," Evan confirmed. "I like to gossip as much as the next person."

"We're disappointed we missed you chasing Tillie outside the inn," Gunner said. "I would've loved to have seen that."

I glared at Evan.

"I would've loved the pot roast too," Gunner added. "Thanks for not inviting me."

"Hey, the inn is full," I countered. "Do you want to hang out with the Happy Holidays Players?"

"For your mother's pot roast, I'll hang out with just about anybody," Gunner replied. "What are the Happy Holidays Players?"

"An acting troupe. They used to be the Merry Christmas Troubadours but changed their name."

"The war on Christmas?" Scout asked, eliciting a smile from me.

"The leader—her name is Mary—says no, but I have my doubts. Mrs. Little sent out a flyer making sure everybody in town knew she wasn't responsible for the name change."

"Ah, you've got to love her," Scout said. "She's always consistent." She turned her eyes back to the house. "Somebody in there is magical."

I nodded. "Yeah, and it feels like the same sort of magic I felt taking on the possessed prisoners."

"Think it's the ex-husband?"

"It's possible. It's also possible that Natalie guessed I would come out here to talk to the ex-wife and sent one of the other escapees as a welcoming committee."

"Where is the ex-wife?" Scout rolled up to her toes and peered inside the window. "Do you think she's being held hostage?"

"She's dead," Gunner replied matter-of-factly.

I jerked my eyes to him. "What makes you say that?"

"Because there's a dead body inside," Evan replied. "I can smell it too."

"It's not a fresh kill," Gunner added. "There's blood. It's dried now. The body has been in there at least forty-eight hours."

I frowned. "You can't be sure it's Ann Markham," I said.

"No, but she makes the most sense."

I growled. "I wanted her to be alive."

"Well, I don't think she is." Gunner reached in his pocket for his phone.

"What are you doing?" Scout asked.

"Calling my father. He needs to know about the body."

"Shouldn't we capture the inmate first?" I demanded. "I mean ... there's still a dangerous guy in there."

Gunner snorted. "There's one of him and four of us. Even if he puts up a fight—which I'm hoping he'll do—we'll have him well in hand before my father arrives."

I wanted to argue, but there was no point. "Let's just get it over with." I was resigned.

"You guys go in through the front," Gunner ordered. "I'm guessing he'll try to flee through the back door. We'll be waiting for him there."

"Shouldn't we be waiting in the backyard? We're magical."

"Yes, but we're more his speed size wise." Gunner didn't back down despite my obviously frayed nerves. "Isn't the goal to get him on the ground so you can deprogram him? We should be able to do that before he even has a chance to use his magic on us."

"Yeah, but ... he's probably inside listening," I pointed out.

"Then you can take him out inside. Either way, we win."

I made a face and glanced at Scout. She looked more amused than aghast. "You're okay with them stealing the win from us?"

"I don't really consider it a win either way," Scout replied. "Why does it matter who takes him down?"

I thought of Aunt Tillie but didn't respond.

Evan chuckled, as if reading my mind. "Tillie has concocted a competition. If we take down the escapee, it won't count in Bay's win column."

"Who's winning?" Gunner asked.

"That would be Bay," Evan replied.

"Aunt Tillie hasn't caught a single escapee." My smile took over my face with a vengeance. "Not a single one."

"And she's bitter about it," Evan confirmed. "She feels she should've realized there was one in her field yesterday. As guilty as she feels about Landon getting the trots, she's angrier that she didn't get credit for the catch."

"We'll give you credit no matter what," Gunner volunteered. "It doesn't matter to me."

"Well, it does to me," I snapped. I had no idea when I'd gotten so competitive, but I blamed Aunt Tillie.

"Fine." Gunner let loose an exasperated sigh. "We'll let him pummel us until you arrive. Does that make you happy?"

"Not really."

"Let's just do this," Scout insisted. Her patience appeared to be running on fumes. "We'll go to the front. You guys wait in the back. Either way, one of us will crush him."

I pouted as I followed Scout to the front of the house. "I would've thought for sure that you'd get my need to win," I admitted.

"Maybe on another day," she replied. "Right now, little things like this competition don't really have the power to blow up my skirt."

Embarrassment coursed through me. "How are things with your parents?"

She didn't make eye contact. "Fine."

"How are they really?"

"Fine."

"Scout."

"I haven't seen them." When she finally met my gaze, there was guilt there. "I haven't shifted them back from the other plane yet. I can't. There's no immediate danger, at least that we know of, but I haven't done it yet."

I didn't know what to say. She finally had a chance to get to know the family that had abandoned her, and I was trying to emotionally crush the great-aunt that had spent oodles of time with me. In my case, I knew my family too well. Scout struggled with abandonment issues and a hard outer shell that she didn't want to risk cracking.

"Well, I'm sure you'll figure it out," I said. I was contrite. "Sorry my competitive spirit has gotten out of hand today. I'm in a mood."

Scout chuckled. "I'm the last person to comment on someone's competitive spirit. I've lost my head more than once. Don't worry about it."

I couldn't help but worry. "I think I'm losing perspective. This entire thing ... there's something off about it."

"When isn't there something off about magical Armageddon?"

Ah, another point. "I feel as if I'm missing something important."

"Well, then we'll figure it out." She flashed a smile. "For now, let's get you another win in the inmate column. After that, we'll talk."

Just having her on my side, saying she understood my whininess even if she didn't, calmed me. "Let's do this."

Scout grabbed the door handle and twisted. She entered before I could, her hands catching fire. In the darkness of the room, I caught the shape of the hulking figure as he rushed us.

I turned at the same moment as Scout. She slammed her magic into him just as I pushed back with mine. The result was a man caught in limbo. His eyes were wide, his mouth hanging open, and magic pinged around him so quickly it seemed like an optical illusion.

"Huh," Scout said as she took in the scene. "Did you plan for that to happen? His feet are hovering over the floor. He was midleap."

"I was trying to freeze him," I said.

"Me too."

"I might've been trying to push him back at the same time."

She smirked. "Me too." She leaned forward and studied the spell. "I have no idea what we've done. It almost looks as if he's suspended in time or something. I can't hear his thoughts."

"Maybe he doesn't have any," Gunner suggested as he swaggered into the room from the hallway. "What happened to you guys chasing him toward us?"

"He was lying in wait in here," Scout replied. "We had no choice."

"I think you had a choice," Gunner countered. "You just didn't want to cede the glory."

"Oh, right." Scout shook her head. "There's no glory here. Although ... what's that in his head?"

I'd already picked up on the flashing images. They were faint echoes, just strong enough to overcome the spell we'd cast, but they grew in strength. Within seconds, they were much more prominent.

"It's the same thing I saw with the others, maybe a little more intense," I said. "It's a shrouded figure. I think it's a woman. She somehow implanted a trigger into the escapees and taps them when she needs them."

"Do you think she did it with all the escapees?" Gunner asked.

"Two of the first three we came across—we're talking within hours of the escape—weren't magical. Since then, all of them have been."

"Maybe she got caught unaware that first day," Scout said. "Now she's prepared."

The sound of footsteps on the porch had us all turning in tandem. Graham appeared in the open doorway.

"What is this?" he demanded.

"Right now, he's frozen," Scout replied. Graham was used to people deferring to him, but Scout wasn't just anybody. She wasn't cowed by his blustery persona, and Graham was tickled by her surliness. They had a unique relationship, and I loved watching it unfold.

"He's magical?" Graham asked, wrinkling his nose. "What's that smell?"

"There's a body in here somewhere," Gunner replied.

Graham moved away from us and took in the mess that had been left in the living room. It was fast food wrappers mostly. There was also a bright orange article of clothing tucked between the couch arm and the end table. "And this?" He held it up.

"That's a prison jumpsuit," I replied.

"Is this guy Carl Markham?" Gunner asked. "Did he come home to be with his ex-wife?"

"This isn't Carl," I replied. It wasn't difficult to pick his name out of his head. "This is Donald Logan."

"I remember his name from the list," Graham confirmed. "He was locked up ten years ago or so for robbing a bank. A security guard was shot."

"Okay, well, he's here now," Evan said. "But why was he sent to this particular house?"

"Especially when he has no obvious ties to the victim," Gunner added.

"We don't know that the ex-wife is the victim," I argued. "For all we know, Carl Markham is dead in the next room, and the ex-wife took off with Natalie."

Evan gave me an improbable head tilt before heading toward the source of the smell. I remained behind—I would take his word for whatever he saw—and my stomach heaved when he returned less than a minute later.

"It's a woman, and she looks a lot like the woman in the photos on that table." Evan pointed to the end table. "I'm sorry, Bay, but it's the ex-wife, and she's definitely dead. She was stabbed ... probably strangled too."

"At least two days," Gunner confirmed. "I think they came here not long after carrying out the escape. Although I can't fathom why."

"I can," Graham replied. "It was payback. Carl Markham was only caught because his ex-wife turned him in. He killed the neighbor, and she refused to lie to the police for him. The state police stopped here right after Markham was confirmed as one of the escapees. She was fine. Maybe a little afraid, but otherwise fine. She turned down protection. She said there was no way he would come for her."

"She was obviously wrong about that," I mused.

"She was," Graham agreed. "From the looks of this place, I think that more than one person was staying here. This is just a guess, but I think it was Natalie, Markham, and this guy." He jerked his thumb toward Donald Logan, who was still frozen.

"How can you be sure it was Natalie?" I asked.

"I guess I can't be certain, but it makes sense." Graham folded his arms across his chest. "Natalie and Carl are the couple. Maybe she agreed to appease him by bringing him here to quench his bloodlust. It's also a good place to hide if they didn't come in until after she'd already been questioned."

I felt sick to my stomach. "So where are they now?"

"In the wind." Graham held his hands palms out. "I would've assumed they had a place locked down—one close by—to hole up in. Maybe they have something else planned. Maybe they only needed to stay a night because the rest of their plan kicked in the following day."

"And they left this guy behind as a gift because they knew either the police or someone magical would turn up to check on Ann Markham," Scout surmised.

"It fits," Graham said.

I pressed the heel of my hand to my forehead. "If Natalie is the enchantress, she's still around. We got a gander at her last night."

"It makes sense she's the enchantress," Scout said. "As for sticking around, that seems stupid on the face of it."

"And yet she's here."

"I think you were right before." Scout was rueful. "There's something to this story that we're missing."

"Well, we had better figure it out," Graham said. "A bulletin just came across the radio a few minutes before I got the call to come here. One of the other prisoners has been found in the woods. He's dead. He had injuries that suggest he cut himself on the razor wire and bled out before making it very far."

"So five prisoners left?" I said, doing the math in my head. Landon had mentioned another prisoner was caught overnight sleeping in a rest area.

"I believe that's right." A muscle worked in Graham's jaw. "Five escapees is enough to still do some damage. Let's get this guy into handcuffs and in my truck. I need to transfer him to the prison ASAP."

Something occurred to me. "Can you do me a favor and leave out my part of capturing him?" I didn't need Childs more suspicious than he already was.

"I think that can be arranged," Graham said.

"I appreciate it."

"Just end this, and we'll call it even."

# Eighteen

News had spread about the Hawthorne Hollow incident by the time I got back to town. Mrs. Little, who was holding court in front of her store, flagged me down to spread gossip she didn't think I'd heard about. She wanted to act like a big shot, even when it wasn't necessary.

"Did you hear the news?" Her eyes sparkled. "They caught another prisoner in Hawthorne Hollow. With the one they found dead, they're saying that there are only five left."

She was far too excited for my comfort level. "There are still five of them free," I pointed out. "We're not in the clear yet."

"But the one found in Hawthorne Hollow committed a murder," Mrs. Little insisted. "That's way worse than what happened on your property yesterday. Don't think I don't know why it happened at the inn."

I narrowed my eyes. Years before I might've taken her abuse because I was taught to respect my elders. Sure, Aunt Tillie taught us that Mrs. Little was the exception to that rule, but when we weren't with Aunt Tillie, we always deferred to Mrs. Little. Those years were long gone.

"Why don't you share with the class why it happened?" I suggested.

Surprised, Mrs. Little blinked.

"She's talking to you, Margaret," Clara Rutledge prodded when the silence had stretched on so long it was uncomfortable for the small group gathered around Mrs. Little.

"I don't remember what was said," Mrs. Little hedged.

"You said you knew why a prisoner was found on our property," I pressed. I wasn't going to let her get away with this. "You acted as if we were somehow to blame. I was attacked walking from the guesthouse to the inn. Landon saved me from having my head caved in with a hammer." My tone was icy enough to freeze water. "So, why don't you tell me why we deserved that?" I challenged.

"Uh-oh," Clara muttered as she took a step back.

"I told you that she was going to be the new Tillie," Jenna Gibbons whispered as she eased away from the street corner. "I need to run to the bakery. I'll leave you two to ... do whatever comes naturally."

Jenna bolted across the street, Clara giving chase. That left only Mrs. Little and me to glare at one another.

"I see you managed to clear out my friends in record time," Mrs. Little drawled.

"What friends?" I shot back. "We both know they were only over here because you provide them with gossip. And you'll make their lives difficult if they don't at least feign interest. There's nothing genuine about the relationships."

Mrs. Little's eyes narrowed. "What did you just say?"

"The truth," I fired back. This woman had plagued my family for years, and there was no turning back now. I couldn't forgive, and I could no longer forget. It was war from now on. Not only would I encourage Aunt Tillie to go after her, I would go after her when the opportunity arose.

"What's the truth?"

"You think you're superior. You think we somehow deserved what happened yesterday. You're a terrible person." I heard footsteps on the street behind me. Landon's familiar presence washed over me like a soothing balm as he came to stand behind me.

"I am superior to you," Mrs. Little fired back. "Give me a break, Bay. Your family has been a blight on this town for as long as I can remember. Even now, you're bringing criminals into town to put the residents at risk. That says nothing for what you're doing to the tourists, the people we need to survive."

"What's going on?" Landon asked.

"Mrs. Little was just explaining how what happened in Hawthorne Hollow was a good thing because the prisoner attack at our place yesterday was somehow a black mark for the town. And it's all because of us."

"That's a succinct way of putting it." Mrs. Little preened. "I speak the truth, Bay. I don't know why you're so worked up. If you're asking if I wanted you to get your head beat in with a hammer, the answer is no, but you brought it on yourself. All of you. Everybody in town knows it."

I wanted to hurt her. Landon snagged me around the waist before I could wrap my hands around her turkey neck.

"Mrs. Little, you might want to be careful who you throw stones at," Landon warned as he pressed me tight against his chest. "You brought a djinn to town. You caused an FBI agent to be killed. For you to cast stones at my wife, well, that's a little hypocritical, don't you think?"

Rather than concede her part in some of our troubles, Mrs. Little shook her head. "Good luck proving any of that. I used to think that your family getting away with so much was a burden on me. Now I realize that it's a blessing because I can get away with things too."

A huge smile stretched across her face, and she taunted us with a finger wave before stepping back into her shop.

"I'm going to kill her," I growled as I fought Landon's grip. Was I really going to give chase? Probably not, but I wouldn't have minded watching her scurry like a rat to safety.

"Yeah, you're not doing anything." Landon kept his grip on me as we walked across the street. He didn't release me until we were in front of the festival grounds. His gaze was searching as it wandered my face. "What's up, sweetie?"

He was so calm, so earnest, my resolve crumbled. "I've had a bad day," I admitted, my breath hitching.

"I know." He opened his arms. "Let me hold you."

If I let him hold me, I would cry. That wasn't what I wanted, and yet I needed the release. "Carl Markham's ex-wife is dead." I burst into tears as he wrapped himself around me. His hand wandered up to the back of my head.

"I know. Graham called. He's covering your part in all of this—and I'm grateful—but he was worried about you. I'm glad you waited for Scout to get there. That was a smart move."

Was he just placating me? The statement seemed more pointed. "I saw movement. Believe it or not, I'm not an idiot."

"I know you're not. The thing is, if you'd thought the ex-wife was still inside and there was a chance she was alive, you would've put yourself at risk for her. You didn't do that. I know that was hard for you, but I appreciate the restraint you showed."

That struck me as funny. "I want a reward."

"A reward?" Landon looked bewildered.

"For doing the right thing."

"Okay." He dragged out the two syllables. "What reward do you want?"

"I want festival food and time in the kissing booth."

His eyes gleamed with delight. "That's what I want. We're a perfect match." This time when he pulled me in for a hug, he was playful. "We should probably talk about a few things first. Let's get some hot chocolate and take it in the kissing booth. We need to discuss a few things."

He wouldn't let it go. "I'm going to want a big pile of festival food when we're done."

"Baby, you don't ever have to beg for festival food. I will gladly give it ... as long as I get to eat it too."

"I guess we're a good match."

He winked. "The best ever."

**MOST PEOPLE WOULD FIND THE HOKEY OFFERINGS** of Hemlock Cove to be too much. Landon had embraced them right from the get-go. Sure, the first time he'd seen the kissing booth, he'd been confused. Now it was his favorite place to visit—well, other than the food trucks—during a festival.

"Lay it on me." We settled on the cutesy couch in the booth, hot chocolate clutched in our hands, and Landon slid me a serious look.

"You want to hear what happened at Ann Markham's house," I surmised.

"I was actually talking about this." He leaned in and gave me a serious kiss. I'm talking a soul sucker. He was thorough to the point of leaving me breathless, and I had no idea what I'd been about to say.

"Oh, um, oh." I was a bit dazed.

He laughed. "Did you think I came in here for serious stuff?"

"Yes."

"I did." He brushed my hair from my face. "I wanted to get that out of the way first."

"That was really nice."

He was smug as I rested my cheek against his shoulder. "Now tell me the other stuff."

I ran it down for him. He listened, and when I finished, he shook his head.

"None of this makes sense. Why go to his ex-wife's house? Why not have a different location already plotted out?" he asked.

"I don't know. Gunner said he thought she'd been dead for days, since the night of the escape probably."

"Obviously, we'll have to wait for the autopsy report," Landon mused. "Even when we get it, all that does is give us a timeline. Why wouldn't they have a different spot to hide out in? Why go someplace the police would ultimately check?"

"Would it make sense if they planned to bolt that night? Maybe they only needed a few hours to hide. Maybe Carl wanted some payback and they thought they had a way out of town afterward."

"And it fell through?"

"That's possible. Maybe Natalie thought she had a deal with someone, but that person backed out at the last moment. It's one thing to talk about helping with a prison break; it's another to actually do it."

"It still feels off. I don't get it."

"Me either." I sipped my cocoa. "They'd obviously gotten fast food while they were there. I'm guessing they spent at least one night. I didn't hang around. Once Graham showed up, I thought it was best to make my escape."

"He told me." Landon slipped his left arm around me and tugged me in tight at his side.

"Was he upset about lying?" I felt bad. "Maybe I shouldn't have asked him to do it."

"He wasn't upset at all, and that was the best thing you could've done." Landon was firm. "Childs is already suspicious of you. We couldn't lie about the guy in the alley because too many people saw you head in that direction. There was no lying about the one in the pot field. Well, other than the obvious lying we had to do to keep Aunt Tillie out of jail."

He grinned. "This time there was no way to pin it on you," he continued. "The house was set back from the action. Nobody saw you. Gunner and Scout can obviously take the heat. There's no way for Childs to connect them to you."

"Unless he really decides to dig," I countered. "If he were to come to town and ask around—say, ask Mrs. Little—he would find out relatively quickly that I have a relationship with Scout."

"That's true, but he can't prove it," Landon argued. "Besides, there's no proof you were in Hawthorne Hollow. Childs has bigger problems than proving you're a real witch."

"Do you think he'll lose his job?" I asked.

"Without a doubt." Landon was grim now. "Ann Markham is dead. That changes the game. He should've already been fired, but nobody made the push because nobody had been seriously hurt until now. Well, except you." A muscle worked in his jaw. "We couldn't exactly be forthcoming about the extent of your injuries."

"I'm fine," I reminded him. "You ended up worse than me."

"And you're feeling guilty about that, and I wish you wouldn't." His eyes twinkled as they locked with mine. "There are worse things than what happened to me. Yes, I know I'm a baby when I'm not feeling well, but ... that was a small price to pay to keep you."

I blinked back tears I didn't even know were coming. "I really want to take those days off we've been talking about," I said. "Just some time for us."

"So do I, but we need to finish this first."

"I have no idea where to look."

He smiled. "I guess we should do some brainstorming over dinner."

I didn't have to ask where he wanted to eat. "Some of your favorite food trucks are here. They also have the heat lamps by the tables so we can stay toasty."

"That proves we are perfect for one another," he said on a grin. "You know the way to my heart."

"Yes, I'm a true mind reader," I confirmed.

"What am I thinking now?" he demanded, wiggling his eyebrows.

"You want to finish the hot chocolate and make out some more before we get dinner."

"Ah, perfection." He leaned in for a kiss. Sure, we had serious issues to deal with, but life had to be lived.

**FIFTEEN MINUTES LATER WE EMERGED FROM** the kissing booth, cups empty and cheeks flushed. Mrs. Little stood with her cronies twenty feet away, and she did a double take when she saw us. I practically dared her to say anything with a glare, and after several seconds, she tore her eyes from us and focused on Clara.

"Well, that was bracing," Landon muttered as he slid his arm around my back. "You two seem to be getting along splendidly these days."

"Aunt Tillie wants to play a grand prank on her for Christmas," I said. "I was going to beg off, but I think I'm all in this year."

Landon chuckled. "Sounds like fun."

"It will be. For us."

We made our way to the food trucks to debate what we wanted for dinner, but my attention was drawn to three morose looking figures as they emerged from the outdoor theater area. Mom, Marnie, and Twila seemed dejected as they shuffled toward the parking area on Main Street.

"How did the auditions go?" I asked.

The look my mother shot me was withering. "Do I look as if I'm ready to dance naked in the street, Bay?"

I pressed closer to Landon. Her disapproval was akin to a blast of freezing air. "I guess not."

"None of us got parts," Marnie complained as she planted her hands on her hips. "Can you believe that?"

"What happened?" I was legitimately sympathetic. Well, maybe only kind of sympathetic. Still, they'd all wanted parts. For none of them to get them had to be a blow.

"They said we weren't natural enough," Twila replied. "Can you believe that? Us? Not natural enough?" She threw her hands into the air. "Why, Goddess, why?"

"I think we might've gotten a preview of the unnatural part," Landon muttered.

Mom pinned him with a murderous look. "We're not all over the top. Some of us can act with nuance. They painted us all with the same brush."

"Mary said that Winnie lacked energy and asked if Twila had smoked meth before the audition."

I had to bite back a laugh. "And what did they say about you, Aunt Marnie?" I asked.

"They said that I had the misfortune of being sandwiched between two bad actors."

"They said she led with her boobs," Mom said. "Apparently, she kept feeling herself up during the audition, and it distracted the men."

"I didn't even realize I was doing it," Marnie complained. "If they'd told me, I would've stopped."

"So the Winchesters are just too much for the Happy Holidays Players," I surmised.

"Yes, and we're not happy about it," Twila said. "We're not even going to go all out for dinner we're so unhappy about it. It's hamburgers for them."

"We're going to eat here," I said. "Landon wants festival food."

"Whatever." Mom waved us off. "Do what you want. We're going home to drink away our feelings. Just keep an eye on Aunt Tillie. She's been making noise about doing something to Margaret, and I'd like her to wait until closer to Christmas so we can all enjoy it."

"I'll keep an eye out for her, but I'm not her keeper," I warned.

Mom put her head down as she headed for her car. "What a waste of a day."

"It was," Marnie agreed. "What do you say we put out some cheese and crackers, and get drunk instead of worrying about the Happy Holidays Players? That will teach them."

"That's a fabulous idea."

# Nineteen

Festival food was a favorite for both of us, so we didn't skimp. By the time we needed to look for a table, most of them were filled. We found Chief Terry eating alone at one and joined him.

"Why are you here?" I asked. "I thought you'd be with Mom. Her ego took a beating today."

"That's why I'm not with her." Chief Terry said. "She plans on drowning her sorrows with your aunts, and that always goes off the rails."

"But you could tell her how great she is and how all that matters is you think she's amazing," I argued. "That's what Landon does when I'm feeling down." I smiled at my husband, who returned the expression.

"I don't want to be like the two of you," Chief Terry groused. "We're adults. She needs to suck it up."

"You're just afraid they're going to get naked and start dancing. Admit it."

"Fine. I'm afraid they're going to get naked and start dancing." Chief Terry's mouth was a flat line. "I figure I'll give them a few hours, and by the time I get back, your mother will have gone from feeling sorry for herself to wanting romance."

Now it was my turn to frown. "I didn't need to hear that."

"But I have to listen to you two coo like irritating little doves while petting each other on a daily basis? I think that's a double standard that I'm not ready to settle for."

"Whatever." He was ruining my appetite. "Let's talk about something else. Any news on the prisoners?"

"We're down to five on the loose. We caught most of them, which hasn't gone unnoticed. Childs is still in charge—but I don't expect that to last much longer—and he placed an official call asking for me to bring you to the prison tomorrow."

I froze with my shawarma halfway to my mouth.

"That's not happening," Landon interjected. He had ketchup on his face from his hot dog, but the intensity in his eyes told me he was more interested in the conversation than the food for a change.

"I said the same," Chief Terry acknowledged. "I was nice about it but said Bay had other things going on. I also pointed out that Bay had nothing to do with what happened in Hawthorne Hollow. I almost thought he knew I was lying."

"I know you think it's not possible that he tied me to Hawthorne Hollow, but it's not completely out of the realm of possibility," I pointed out. "A few calls and he could've figured out I'm tight with Scout. Heck, if he got one of Graham's men on the phone instead of Graham himself, one simple question would've led him to the truth."

Chief Terry was grim. "We've told the lie. We need to stick to it."

"What do you think?" I asked Landon, who had a mouth full of hot dog.

Landon chewed and swallowed before responding. "I think we have to stick to the lie too. There's no way around it."

His response didn't make me happy, but I nodded. "Well, what's next?"

"I wouldn't mind using that locator spell again tomorrow," Chief Terry said. "The faster we track down the rest of the escapees, the better. I want Childs focused on his own problems, not you."

"Okay, but Aunt Tillie tried the locator spell, and it didn't work."

"Maybe it didn't work because she's Tillie. She could've been doing something weird instead of what she said she was going to do."

"She knows how to cast a locator spell. Who do you think taught me?"

"She's still Tillie."

"Yeah, but she's obsessed with winning. She wants to catch some of the prisoners. She's not just screwing around for the sake of screwing around."

"Says you."

He was in a mood. "I have no problem trying, but I think this enchantress has figured out a way to roil the atmosphere. I don't expect a spell to work."

"Well, there's no harm in trying." Chief Terry's chin jutted out stubbornly. "Just give it a shot."

I didn't want to argue. "We'll do it tomorrow." Before I could turn the conversation to something else, I caught a furtive movement out of the corner of my eye and turned. There, Aunt Tillie stood dressed in a pair of camouflage pants, her combat helmet firmly in place, Evan at her side. Their attention was fixated on Mrs. Little. "Crap," I moaned as I shoved a huge bite of shawarma in my mouth.

Landon followed my gaze, amusement lighting his features when he saw the duo. "What do you think she's going to do?"

I was still chewing and didn't answer.

"I hope she does something horrible to her," Chief Terry said, shaking his head. "She's been a real pill all week regarding these prisoners. She actually suggested we somehow erect an electric fence to keep the prisoners out."

I almost choked. "That seems a tall order," I said when I could speak without sputtering. "How does she think you're magically going to manage that?"

"She doesn't think. That's her problem. She likes to issue edicts and then whines when things don't go her way."

"She definitely needs to be taken down a notch," I agreed, narrowing my eyes when she stood and carried her plate to the trash receptacle. She hadn't yet seen Aunt Tillie, and the way my great-aunt slid behind a tree with Evan following told me that was by design. "Oh, she's definitely up to something."

For the next few minutes, we ate in silence and watched. Mrs. Little left her minions at the table and started across the street to her store. Aunt Tillie and Evan remained out of view for almost a full minute after she passed their hiding spot. When they emerged, Aunt Tillie had a mischievous look on her face. Evan looked resigned.

"Do you think we should stop whatever she has planned?" Landon asked. He didn't look thrilled with the idea, mostly because he still had half a plate of food to finish.

"Nope." There was no hesitation when I answered. "We should let Aunt Tillie torture her any way she wants."

"I don't see that grenade on her belt," Chief Terry noted. "I would really like to know what happened to that thing."

He wasn't the only one. The grenade was my only cause for concern when it came to Aunt Tillie these days. "She won't use that grenade on Mrs. Little," I said. "There's no reason to. She can torture Mrs. Little without having to unleash the big guns."

"What do you think she's up to?" Chief Terry asked when Aunt Tillie and Evan started across the street. They still hadn't seen us as far as I could tell.

I couldn't muster the energy to care. "If she's still not back by the time I'm done eating, I'll check on her. Evan is with her. She'll be fine."

"I'm not worried about her; I'm worried about Margaret."

"Margaret has earned what's coming to her." It was rare that I would think that, let alone say it out loud, but I felt it to my bones. "Whatever Aunt Tillie is up to, I'm sure it will be fine. It's not as if Mrs. Little hasn't earned every drop of vitriol we throw her way."

Chief Terry was quiet a long time, and when I shifted my gaze to him, I found him watching me with wary eyes. "What?" I demanded. "You can't think Mrs. Little is the wronged party here."

"I don't think that, Bay," Chief Terry replied evenly. "I just ... don't like that you're so angry. I want you to be happy. I know Margaret deserves it. But you've never been one to focus on the negative."

"Well, maybe the murderous djinn she conjured to hurt my family was the tipping point."

"She's not a good person, Bay. I would never say otherwise, but you're better than her and better than that."

I flicked my eyes to Landon and found him following the conversation with rapt attention, French fries hanging out of his mouth. He remained silent.

"I don't want to be a negative person," I said after several seconds. "Margaret Little is constantly trying to hurt my family. Giving her a pass isn't working. I don't want her to die or anything, but I have no problem watching Aunt Tillie torture her. She's earned it."

"Just don't let your need for vengeance change you. That's not who you are. You can be a realist without losing that streak of optimism I love so much. That's always been your source of strength, Bay. Don't change because Margaret is a horrible person."

His words threw me. "I won't change," I said after a moment. "It's okay. You don't have to worry about me."

"I'll always worry about you. You're my source of optimism."

I let out a sigh. "Let me finish my food, and then I'll check on Aunt Tillie. But if she's doing something harmless, I have no intention of stopping her."

Chief Terry beamed. "I can live with that."

**LANDON STAYED WITH CHIEF TERRY.** I could tell by the look on his face he wanted to argue with his pseudo father-in-law. He smiled, but there was an edge to his eyes. He was annoyed that Chief Terry had given me grief. Landon didn't see me through the lens of my childhood. He was okay with me being negative regarding Mrs. Little. I could see things from both of their perspectives and left them to hash it out.

I'd lost sight of Aunt Tillie when she crossed the street, but I didn't have to look very far to find her. She was in the alley behind Mrs. Little's store, her hands raised. Evan looked on from behind her as he leaned against the brick wall, arms crossed.

"What are you doing?" I called out.

Aunt Tillie froze at the sound of my voice. Then she glared at Evan. "What did I say about serving as backup? You're a freaking vampire. There's no way she should be able to sneak up on you. She's a heavy stepper."

I was fairly certain there was an insult buried in there. "I am not a heavy stepper." I was almost positive that was true. "What does that even mean?"

"You're not dainty when you walk," Evan replied. "Some people are fleet of foot, like Tillie here. Despite her age and the amount of shuffling she does, she can be quiet. You're not all that graceful."

Yup. I'd definitely been insulted.

"Why didn't you warn me she was coming?" Aunt Tillie demanded. "I could've finished the spell before she got here. You dragged out the conversation. Why?"

"Yes, that sounds just like me," Evan drawled. "There's nothing I love more than conversation."

His wit had me grinning, but only briefly. "Seriously, what are you guys doing?"

"I'm just ... sending Margaret a little message," Aunt Tillie replied, averting her eyes. "Don't worry about it."

"What message?"

"I said not to worry about it." Aunt Tillie's eyes flashed. "Can't you just trust me for once in your life? You'll like this one."

My mind flashed back to what Chief Terry had said about my need for vengeance coloring me. I focused on Evan. "If you're okay with it, that tells me I should be okay with it."

"You're putting a lot of faith in me," Evan replied. His lips twitched. "You'll be fine with it, Bay. It's inspired."

That was enough for me. "Do it."

Aunt Tillie's mouth spread into a sly grin, and her hands sparked with red and green energy. She'd obviously done all the work to build the spell, because the second she waved her hands, a cacophony of song exploded from the other side of the wall.

It was a Christmas song—but not one that anybody could call wholesome. It was the *Jingle Bells* rhyme kids used when I was growing up, the one about Batman smelling and Robin laying an egg. But there were more lyrics than I remembered, and they were dirty. There was mention about playing with his batarang and a couple profanities. It was all set to the familiar tune ... and it was loud.

Slowly, I tracked my eyes to Aunt Tillie. "Are those the unicorns singing?" I asked.

Aunt Tillie's smile was smug. "It is, and it's going to happen every half hour until Christmas. There will also be some farting tinsel to liven things up every six hours."

I didn't know whether to laugh or scold her. Oh, wait, I did. "What a great way to pay her back." I folded my arms across my chest as the song mentioned a foursome on the couch. "Ah, the gift that keeps on giving." Just as I was about to leave the alley to watch the unicorns dance from Main Street, a figure appeared at the end of the alley ... and it wasn't Mrs. Little looking to scream at us.

Evan, who had been relaxed up until that point, straightened at the same moment I did. His eyes narrowed when he realized the person had started in my direction.

"That guy is teeming with magic," I announced as Evan moved in front of us, his fangs extending.

"He's mine!" Aunt Tillie lost interest in her unicorn spell when she saw the escaped prisoner. "Don't you dare touch him!"

Evan ignored her and raced along the alley. The prisoner, seeing that he was coming, extended his hands. I knew a magical blast was coming and waved my hand to deflect it. The move turned out to be a waste of energy because Evan's reflexes were the stuff of cinematic gold. He jumped to the right, planted his foot on the brick wall, and spun to land behind the prisoner. His arm wrapped around the prisoner's neck, his other hand serving as a brace, when I caught up to them.

"What do you want?" Evan rasped.

"I want you to let him go," Aunt Tillie yelled from behind us. "He's mine. I called dibs."

We ignored her. "Let me see." I froze the prisoner so he couldn't fight back and slapped my hand against his forehead. The name that swam to the forefront of his brain was a welcome one.

"Steven Mitchell," I gritted out. We'd been waiting for news on him, and we'd finally gotten it. "Good grief. I can't believe the amount of magic coursing through him."

"Can you get it out?"

I exhaled heavily and closed my eyes. "*Solvo.*"

The magic began leaking from Mitchell like a deflating balloon, and as it seeped out, the magic edged away from Evan and me and down the alley. It was almost as if it was a sentient being bent on escaping.

"That's new," Evan noted.

I nodded. The magic was disappearing into the ground. Was it returning to the woman who had cast the spell?

Mitchell bled all the magic within thirty seconds.

"We need Landon and Chief Terry," I said, glancing over my shoulder at Aunt Tillie. "We need this kept quiet too."

Aunt Tillie's glare was the stuff of nightmares. "Oh, right. Like I'm going to act as your errand girl. You totally stole my takedown."

"It doesn't matter who takes who down," I shot back, reaching for my phone. "All that matters is that we get them off the street." I glanced at Mitchell's face. "We're down to four."

I was surprised Aunt Tillie could even see given how narrow her eyes were slitted. "I called dibs!"

I ignored her and pressed Landon's name on my contact list.

"What's up, baby?" Landon sounded as if he was mid laugh. "I take it you didn't get to Aunt Tillie in time to stop this. Don't worry. Even Terry is laughing. It's okay."

"I did get here in time to stop her. That's not why I'm calling."

Landon must've picked up on the edge to my voice because he shook off all traces of mirth in an instant. "What is it?"

"Remain calm and do not react," I ordered him. "I have Steve Mitchell. He's free of magic now, and we're in the alley behind Mrs. Little's shop. Evan caught him. Don't make a big scene when you come."

"Holy…" Landon viciously swore. "Why is every single prisoner attracted to you?"

"That's something we should talk about later. We need to get this guy out of the alley without anybody noticing. Do you have any ideas on that front?"

Landon was quiet for a beat. "I've got it. I'll borrow Marcus's truck. Can you hold on for five minutes?"

"We're not going anywhere."

"Keep safe. I'm coming for you."

# Twenty

We loaded Mitchell into the back seat of Marcus's truck. Aunt Tillie was still miffed—enough so that she refused to go with us—and Evan promised to keep an eye on her. He cajoled her with a reminder that Mrs. Little was likely melting down over the singing unicorns, and that propelled her to leave the alley.

"You're definitely on my list," Aunt Tillie warned.

"You know what would serve as great payback?" Landon asked from the driver's seat. "If you kind of ramped up that maple bacon smell. It's been fading throughout the day. I bet she would hate it if you did that."

"That was a reward for you," Aunt Tillie shot back. "She's due for punishment from me."

"I promise to spank her later if you ramp up that smell."

Aunt Tillie scowled. "This day sucks! When am I going to win?"

"I think you already have," I replied as I hopped in the passenger seat. "The Batman *Jingle Bells* song is an amazing curse. You beat Mrs. Little. Isn't that all that matters?"

"It's as if you don't even know me," Aunt Tillie muttered.

"I've got her," Evan promised. "You guys handle your problem. I'll take care of her."

I smiled. "You're becoming one of my favorite people ever, Evan."

He winked as he slid an arm around Aunt Tillie's hunched shoulders. "Come on, fireball. I'll get you a drink, and you can rant to your heart's content."

Aunt Tillie muttered something under her breath.

"Let's hold off on cursing family until you've cooled down some. Some doctored hot chocolate and a full showing of the singing unicorns will perk you right up."

I watched them go, shaking my head. "They're the oddest couple ever."

"He's my new hero," Landon replied. "He keeps her in line like nobody else."

"He is pretty special."

"As special as me?"

"Of course not. Nobody can touch your halo."

"Good answer, Bay."

**CHIEF TERRY WAS WAITING FOR US AT MARCUS'S** barn. We pulled to the back, transported Mitchell to Chief Terry's waiting vehicle, and then tackled the obvious problem.

"They're all coming after Bay, and I don't like it," Landon complained.

"Join the club." Chief Terry scratched his chin. "I don't get why this witch is sending all the prisoners after her."

"The only reason I can think is what Emori said," I volunteered. "When I got in Barker's head, the enchantress was already there. She saw me and marked me as a threat."

"How do we fight that?"

I didn't have an answer. "I'm not sure. I need to think about it."

"Well, start thinking fast. We're down to four prisoners. I'm taking this one to the prison right now. When this enchantress—we're still assuming it's Natalie Bennett, right?—realizes she's losing soldiers, she's either going to create more or solidify her forces and attack en masse. I don't like either option."

He wasn't the only one. "We'll strategize over breakfast tomorrow," I promised. "For now, I just want to go home and get some sleep."

"Or finish what we started in the kissing booth," Landon countered.

"Or that." I smiled at him. He beamed at me. Chief Terry scowled. "Are you sure you can transport him alone?" I asked Chief Terry. "We can go with you if you want."

"I've got it," Chief Terry assured us. "I'll head home as soon as I make the transfer. I want Landon to stick with you just in case."

"You don't think she'd actually send another prisoner so soon after this one failed?" I asked.

"That's exactly what I think. I want you locked away safe for the night. Then I need to deal with your mother—that's going to be a drunken mess, mark my words. And then I need some sleep. Tomorrow is soon enough to start strategizing."

"Text us when you make the transfer," Landon ordered. "We want to know you're safe."

"Won't you be elbow deep in kisses and cuddling by that point?" Chief Terry shot back.

"Yes, but we can still monitor our phones."

"Fine." Chief Terry wrinkled his nose. "Why do I smell pancakes?"

Landon leaned closer to me and then happily clapped his hands. "Because Aunt Tillie loves me. You smell like every dirty dream I've ever had, Bay. It's amazing."

"Kill me now," Chief Terry lamented.

Landon waved him off and kept his eyes on me. "Let's go home, my little pancake whisperer. I have some things I want to talk to you about." There was no mistaking the intent in his eyes.

"You'd better never call me the 'pancake whisperer' again," I muttered as we headed to his truck in front of the police station. "That's a one-time thing."

"We'll see."

"Oh, you're going to turn this into a thing, aren't you?" I whined.

"Very likely."

**I SLEPT HARD, WHICH SHOULDN'T HAVE BEEN** possible given the events of the day. Two attacks by magical prisoners had wiped me out, though, and when I opened my eyes the next morning, Landon was already up and reading on his phone.

"Anything?" I murmured as I shifted closer to him, my cheek coming to rest on his chest.

Landon slid his arm around my back and anchored me at his side, his eyes still on his phone. "Childs knows you were involved in the takedown yesterday."

"Why wouldn't he jump to that conclusion?"

"Chief Terry tried to direct him away from that assumption, but he couldn't outright lie in case someone saw us. It wasn't out of the realm of possibility, and if we get caught in a lie given our positions, that won't be good."

I couldn't get worked up about it. Not like Landon. This would always be a concern for him, but not for me. "If he tells someone I'm magical, and that's how I'm doing it, he'll look like an idiot."

"There are people who live on conspiracy theories," Landon pointed out. "I don't want those conspiracies following you."

"I don't see that we have much choice. Besides, conspiracy theories have followed my family for as long as I can remember. Aunt Tillie's reputation as a magical nut job has made it beyond the boundaries of Hemlock Cove. I'll be fine."

Landon stroked my hair. "I don't like feeling that you're in danger."

"I'll be fine." I meant it. "He can't hurt us as long as you're not embarrassed by the things he says."

"I hate when you insinuate I would ever be embarrassed by you."

"I know. That's why I do it."

Landon growled and buried his face in my hair. The way he inhaled told me I still smelled like maple bacon.

"I'm going to kill Aunt Tillie," I muttered.

"She's my current hero." His hands began to wander. "How do you feel about a repeat of last night?" The way he waggled his eyebrows told me he was joking—mostly.

"Sure. But I have a request first."

His eyes gleamed. "Name it, and I'll make it happen."

"I want to talk to Natalie Bennett's mother."

His smile flattened. "You want to track down Natalie Bennett's mother?"

"I do."

"Bay, they've already talked to her. The second Natalie was tied to this case, the Michigan State Police sent a unit to question her. She claims she doesn't know anything."

"And that's entirely possible," I conceded.

"But you think it's unlikely."

"Witch powers often pass from female to female," I replied. "I mean ... look at me."

"I'm trying to look at you, but you're making odd requests." Landon's hands moved over my rib cage. "What happens if the mother is magical?"

"I can ask her the sort of questions the state police wouldn't know to ask."

"Like what?"

I exhaled heavily. "I'm not really familiar with this enchantress stuff," I admitted. "I've done a little reading."

"Lay it on me." Landon relaxed against the pillows. The flirty intent he'd greeted me with had died when I told him what I wanted. Part of me regretted it. The other part was resigned.

"Well, for starters, enchantresses can only be women," I started. "That became apparent right from the get-go when I started digging. There are no enchantress men."

"Why do you think that is?"

"It's the sexual component. Since the enchantress—at least more often than not—directs her magic toward men, it comes down to sex. How many times a day do you think about sex?"

"Are you looking for an exact figure or should I ballpark it?"

I narrowed my eyes. "According to a study I read, men think about sex nineteen times a day."

"If you mean actively thinking about it, I'd say that number is high. If you're talking about passive thoughts, I can see that."

"What would passive thoughts entail?" I was honestly curious.

"Like ... when I go to lunch and have a burger, I always forego the onions, even though I like onions. I just don't want to torture you later.

I don't actively picture what I want to do with you. I just think, in the back of my head, that I don't want to repel you."

"I guess that makes sense. The study said women think about sex ten times a day."

"Do you?"

"I think it's a passive thing too. Like ... I'll passingly wonder if I need to shave my legs for you in the morning."

"You don't have to if you don't want to."

I made a face. "Yeah, that's one of those things I can't just ignore. And trust me, there are times in the winter I want to let it grow like fur for an added layer of warmth."

Landon's laugh was warm as it washed over me. "I don't care about that stuff," he promised as he recovered. "I'll love you regardless."

"It's just the way my mind works."

"And this enchantress takes advantage of the fact that men think about sex more than women," Landon prodded.

"Her preferred weapon is sexual control," I confirmed. "It could work on lesbians too, I think, but this is one of those times when stereotypes turn out to be true. Men are often portrayed as sexual simpletons who can be led around by the nose. That's what the enchantress uses to her advantage."

Landon pursed his lips. "Just out of curiosity, why wouldn't she go after me? I mean ... I get why she used the other prisoners as fodder, but if she really wants to get you, why not try to enchant me?"

I hadn't considered the possibility, and I took a moment to think about it. "Maybe she doesn't think she can get close to you. So far, she's only sent prisoners after me. To my knowledge, the only time she's been close is when I tried to summon her to the bluff. She was in the ether that night but never touched the ground."

"I don't want to talk about that. I'm still annoyed I was passed out in bed then."

"Evan was with me."

"Another reason I'm grateful to him, but I would've preferred to be with you."

"But ... what if you would've been in danger due to that proximity?"

I asked. "You said it yourself. It makes sense for her to try to enchant you. She hasn't—yet."

I shifted to my side and looked directly into his eyes. "Consider this: Natalie Bennett was a guard at the prison. Her bond was with Carl Markham. We've already figured out this plan was in the works for months. If she took the time to implant a trigger into the other prisoners' heads, she can use them as weapons whenever she wants, even from afar.

"Enchantresses are masters at mind magic. Sexual attraction is often a chemical thing, but it's still controlled by the mind. She saw me when I was in Barker's head. I wasn't anticipating that. Now she's fixed me as her enemy. I guarantee part of that is going to include her sending the rest of the prisoners after me."

"Including Markham?"

I hesitated and then lifted one shoulder. "I'm not sure," I admitted. "There was nothing in her house to indicate either way. It could be love. Maybe it's something else."

"You have an idea," Landon prodded.

"What if she was always a witch but somehow falling in love with Markham turned her into an enchantress?"

"I have no idea how that would work."

"Love changes people."

"It does. I'm nowhere near the same man I was the day we met in front of that corn maze. I like to think I've grown as a man and a person."

"You have, but I'm pretty sure you were a good man right from the start. You barely knew me, but you put yourself on the line to save my family."

"I put myself on the line because I already couldn't stand the idea of something happening to you," he clarified. "The other guys in that group I was with didn't feel the same way about women. I'm not talking about you specifically. I'm talking about women in general. They didn't believe in love."

"And you think Markham is the same," I surmised.

Landon hesitated. "I'm not sure how I feel about any of that," he admitted. "It's possible for people who have broken the law to love.

Sometimes I think that's why they break the law in the first place. Love made them do it.

"But when you've become hardened to the world in certain respects, you come to see love as a burden, or something for saps," he continued. "Carl Markham was a murderer looking down the barrel of a life sentence with no parole. Isn't it possible that romancing the guard was a way to get favorable treatment, and not a result of actual love?"

"We're assuming that Natalie was lonely and fell for whatever story Carl was selling. She has real feelings for him, but he's feigning his for her. Isn't that stereotypical?"

"Maybe, but Markham has been in prison almost two decades. He would've learned a long time ago that there's only one way to survive the system, and that's to do things a specific way."

"Does that mean he'll stay with Natalie?" A bevy of ideas had popped into my head, none of them pleasant.

Landon rested his cheek against my forehead. "Not everybody loves the same, Bay. I look at you and can't imagine a day I don't itch to hold you, or that I won't desperately need to hear that laugh of yours. Markham is a user."

"What happens if Natalie believes what he's selling, and he shows his true colors?"

"It won't be good." Landon moved his fingers to the back of my neck and started rubbing. "Markham will keep up his ruse for the foreseeable future. He'll understand that he has to keep her close to make his ultimate escape."

"And then?" I prodded.

"Markham may have a side plan he's waiting to spring. He may have someone else waiting in the wings to steal him away. I can see him leaving Natalie holding the bag, but her magic is the wild card. I'm guessing she won't just sit back and let him leave her in the dust."

"No way." I shook my head. "If she learns he's not as into the relationship as she is, she'll do whatever it takes to keep his interest."

"Does that include enslaving him with her magic?"

"I think so."

"What does that mean over the long haul? You once told me you can't force someone to love you with magic."

"You can't. It's all an illusion. Over time, the illusion will break down."

"We need to get a feel for what Natalie felt before she disappeared," Landon said. "That means a trip to visit her mother." He sounded resigned.

"Are you okay with that?"

"I want this behind us, Bay. You're the knowledgeable one. You have to lead. I'm more than willing to arrange a sit-down."

"Thank you."

"No thanks are required." He rolled on top of me, and the devilish intent was back in his eyes. "But I do have two requirements."

"Oh, here we go." I braced myself.

"One, we have to eat breakfast before we go out. I'm starving."

"What else is new?"

He pretended he hadn't heard me. "Second, I want to bask in that delicious smell that's wafting off of you."

"Oh, geez." I closed my eyes. "You and the bacon scent. It's like a sickness."

"It really is. I can't help myself. She knows exactly what my weak points are."

"And I'm betting Natalie knows the same of Carl," I mused.

"I wish you wouldn't compare them to us."

"I'm not." I forced my full focus to him. "Do your worst. If you want to act like an animal, knock yourself out."

He lowered his mouth to mine. "Don't mind if I do."

# Twenty-One

We drove to the inn so we could leave for Natalie's mother's house right after breakfast. Aunt Tillie was pouting in the living room, the morning news on the television. She had a knife—a huge one meant for hunting—and a stick. She was using the knife to sharpen the end of the stick into a point.

"Do I even want to know?" Landon asked.

Aunt Tillie didn't look to be in the mood to be interrogated. "Probably not."

Landon seemed to consider it for a moment before saying, "Don't stab anybody if you can help it."

"We'll see what the day brings."

We left her to her whittling and walked into the kitchen. Mom, Marnie, and Twila bustled about. At the sound of our footsteps, Mom glanced up and looked Landon up and down.

"How are you feeling?" she asked.

Landon shifted from one foot to the other, uncomfortable. It was two mornings since the incident, but people were still curious. "I've been worse."

"He doesn't want to talk about it," I explained. "He's embarrassed."

"Hey! I was a hero." Landon sent me a severe look. "I have nothing to be embarrassed about."

"I agree," I said as I reached out to take his hand. "I believe that was my stance the day it happened."

Landon eyed me. Seemingly satisfied, he clasped my hand tightly. "I feel so good I'd like a big breakfast."

Mom's smile was quick. "In ten minutes. We're running a bit behind this morning."

"Someone thought it would be a good idea to open a fourth bottle of wine last night," Marnie said, shooting Mom a dark look. "Now we're dragging."

I'd forgotten about their disappointment with the Happy Holidays Players auditions. "Have you voiced your opinion to Mary?"

Mom lifted her nose and sniffed. "We haven't seen her since yesterday."

"We would kick her out if we could," Twila added. "I mean ... this is worse than Kate Winslet stealing *Titanic* from me."

Landon straightened.

I'd forgotten he wasn't present for that conversation. "I'll tell you over coffee and juice." I tugged him toward the swinging doors. "I would offer to help but ... you seem to have everything in hand despite your hangovers."

"And you're a menace in the kitchen," Mom added.

"There is that."

The far end of the dining room table was filled with members of the acting troupe. Mary sat looking at a sheet of paper, Lenny looking over her shoulder, speaking to one another in low voices. I smiled in greeting when Renee and Robin waved at me, and then scowled when Ava hopped up from her seat and scurried toward Landon. She was starting to annoy me.

"We missed you at dinner the last two nights," she purred as Landon grabbed the orange juice carafe. "I was starting to think you weren't coming back."

"Oh, I always come back," Landon replied easily as I poured myself some tomato juice. "The food is too good."

"Have you ever considered a life on the road?" Ava asked. "You have leading man good looks. You're not so old that you couldn't make your mark given the right role. Samuel L. Jackson didn't break out until *Jungle Fever* in 1991. He was forty-two."

Landon stilled. "Do I look forty-two to you?" he demanded.

"Of course not," Ava replied. "You don't look a day over thirty."

Landon slid his eyes to me. "You told me I was still young and hot."

"Lay off the bacon, and maybe you'll go back to being young and hot," I suggested.

"You're sleeping on the couch tonight." He made a big show of sweeping away from me, and almost ran into Chief Terry, who was entering the room. "Bay says I'm no longer young and hot."

"I never thought you were," Chief Terry replied. He sidled closer to me. "How are you feeling?"

The question caught me off guard. "I'm fine. Why wouldn't I be?"

"Just checking." He smiled, but there was a wariness in his eyes I didn't like.

Even Landon, determined to be a prima donna this morning, seemed to catch on almost immediately. "What's on the agenda this morning?" he asked pointedly.

"I have a meeting with several people at the prison," Chief Terry replied as he sat in his usual chair and poured himself a mug of coffee. "It seems some decisions might be made today."

It wasn't hard to read between the lines of what he was getting at. "Childs is out?"

"If he's not ousted today, it's only because they don't have his replacement lined up yet. It's coming. He seems resigned to it, and yet still I swear the guy has some weird form of hope. He keeps suggesting that if we can find the rest of the prisoners within the next few days, he'll get off light, and things will get back to the way they were."

"Tell that to Ann Markham," I muttered.

"Yes, well, Childs doesn't seem to have a firm grasp on reality. He was thrilled with the return of Mitchell, though. Given Mitchell's past, there was worry he would hurt someone."

"Another prisoner was captured?" Mary asked from the far end of the table. She looked enamored. "That's good."

Chief Terry bobbed his head. "We only have a few more out there."

"I heard it was an inside job," Thomas offered. "That's what they're saying on the news. Some lovelorn guard set everything up, so she could escape with a prisoner. The guy is an actual murderer, and she thought it was okay to run away with him."

"That sounds sad," Ava lamented. She sat in Aunt Tillie's usual chair, the only seat open near Landon. "I can see how you would want to believe that someone loved you, even if it was a bad guy. She probably just wants to be loved." She batted her eyelashes at Landon, who looked perplexed.

"You know I'm married, right?" Landon asked, taking me by surprise. Normally, he tried to charm his way out of uncomfortable conversations.

"What?" Ava's face was blank.

"Unbelievable." Landon shook his head. "That's Aunt Tillie's chair."

"I'm sure she won't mind giving it up for one meal," Ava said with a laugh.

"Good luck with the gaping hole she's going to leave in your skull." Landon turned back to Chief Terry. "Do you want me at the prison with you? I'll go if you think it will make things easier."

Chief Terry shook his head. "It's best you steer clear of the prison today. Childs is already interested in ... certain things." He flashed a smile for my benefit, but it didn't touch his eyes.

"Bay and I are going on our own mission today," Landon volunteered. "We're going to talk to Natalie Bennett's mother."

Shock reverberated across Chief Terry's face. "Why?"

"Who knows their offspring better than a mother?"

Landon was trying to be coy, but I saw the realization dawn on Chief Terry's face. He nodded in understanding. "I guess that makes sense."

"I'm hopeful she'll be able to give us some leads," I said as the swinging door opened for Aunt Tillie and Peg.

Aunt Tillie pulled up short. "Has the world started spinning backward on its axis?" she demanded as she glared at Ava.

It took everything I had not to burst out laughing.

*Snort. Snort.*

"There's my girl." Landon abandoned the table and crawled under it. "How is my favorite girl?"

*Snort. Snort.*

Peg hopped on him and started giving the pig version of kisses.

"Is he talking to the pig?" Ava asked.

"Yes," I replied. "He loves Peg above all else."

"Oh, don't be jealous, sweetie," Landon countered as he stroked a wriggling Peg. "You know I love you best. Peg is a close second."

"Whatever." I was over being jealous of the pig.

Ava was another story. "Seriously, I've been trying to get his attention for days, and now he's all about the pig?" She looked frustrated and flummoxed.

"He's always been in love with the pig," I replied. "He can't help himself. He's even covert when eating bacon so he doesn't hurt her feelings."

Aunt Tillie, still standing, picked that moment to make her move. She boldly stepped up to Ava and rapped her knuckles against the woman's head, as if knocking on a door.

"Ow!" Ava's eyes were full of accusation when she fixed them on Aunt Tillie. "What do you think you're doing?"

"You're in my chair," Aunt Tillie shot back. "I was knocking to see if there's an echo in there."

"There are other chairs," Ava shot back.

Aunt Tillie blinked, flicked her eyes up to me, then blinked again. "What did she just say?"

I sensed trouble but couldn't decide if I wanted to stop it. "She said you should sit somewhere else because she can't flirt with my husband unless she's in your chair."

"That's what I thought she said."

*Snort. Snort.*

"I only care about sitting next to you, sweetie," Landon called out from under the table, where he was still playing kissing games with Peg.

"Get out of my chair," Aunt Tillie ordered.

Ava was either stupid or stubborn. It could've been a mixture of both, but her stubbornness made her even more stupid than should've been humanly possible. "Sit somewhere else."

"That did it!" Aunt Tillie turned on her heel and stormed through the swinging kitchen door.

Mom, carrying a platter of French toast, entered the room as Aunt Tillie fled. "What's her problem?" Mom asked as she placed the platter on the table. "She says she's getting her stick."

"Ava won't get out of her chair," I replied.

"I see." Mom shot Ava an unreadable look.

*Snort. Snort.*

"I don't smell bacon yet," Landon called out from under the table.

"It's coming," Mom replied. She pasted what she likely thought would pass as a sweet smile on her face as she regarded the blonde sitting in the wrong seat. "Ava, dear, I don't think you understand. That's Aunt Tillie's chair."

"There are other chairs," Ava persisted. "Agent Michaels wants me to sit next to him." She pushed back far enough to look under the table. "Isn't that right?" she asked Landon, who was busy being mauled by Peg.

"No," Landon replied. "I prefer Aunt Tillie."

Something occurred to me. "Stick? Is she getting her old stick or the new one?"

Mom blinked. "I didn't know there was a new one."

"She said you took the old one."

"I did." Mom frowned. "Wait ... she doesn't know where the old stick is."

I was on my feet in an instant and ran to the other side of the swinging door. Aunt Tillie flew through the door with a vengeance on her return, her new spear clutched in her hand. I was in the perfect spot to snag it from her when she tried to swing it at Ava's head.

"Hey!" Aunt Tillie's nostrils flared, and she looked as if steam should be pouring from her ears. "That's my stick!"

"That's a deadly weapon," Chief Terry countered. "Why do you have that?"

"Ask your love muffin," Aunt Tillie hissed.

Chief Terry's cheeks filled with color. "Love muffin?" He looked distinctly uncomfortable.

"I heard the two of you after the wine fest last night," Aunt Tillie sneered. "She's your love muffin, and you're her cuddlekins. The whole thing makes me want to puke. In fact, it's so gross I want to start a puke club."

I wanted to become vice president of that club. "Love muffin?"

"I've heard Landon call you far more disgusting names," Chief Terry fired back. "Wine puts your mother in a good mood. It's not my fault we got carried away last night."

I wanted to die. Before I could respond, however, Twila appeared with the bacon.

"Hello," she said in icy fashion as her eyes landed on Mary.

The troupe leader looked confused. "Hello."

"I just want to know one thing," Twila said primly as she placed the platter in the center of the table. "How did she get to you?"

Mary looked baffled. "Who?"

"You know who." Twila's tone was deadly.

"Actually, I don't," Mary replied. Her eyes skipped to me. "Do you know who she's talking about?"

I had a feeling I did. Unfortunately for Mary, I couldn't get worked up over Twila's verbal meltdown when Aunt Tillie was trying to wrestle a deadly spear from me. "Give her the other stick," I ordered my mother. "She's going to put someone's eye out with this one."

"I really don't know who you're referring to," Mary insisted from the other end of the table. "Nobody got to me."

"How else do you explain none of us getting parts in the pageant?" Twila demanded.

Mary looked caught. "I ... you ... just weren't right for anything this time. I apologized yesterday. I didn't think it was a big deal."

"I know it was Kate Winslet," Twila wailed. "She's been out to get me since we were the final two auditioning for *Titanic*."

Thomas's eyes almost popped out of his head. "You auditioned for *Titanic*?"

Twila nodded and sniffed. "It was the role of a lifetime, and it was stolen from me. I thought that would be the worst moment of my life." Slowly, she tracked her eyes back to Mary. "I was wrong."

"Give me that!" Aunt Tillie tried to kick me in the shins in an effort to recapture her spear. "That's mine!"

"Are you going to help me?" I demanded of Landon. He'd abandoned Peg under the table and was in his chair, a slice of bacon in each hand.

"You look like you've got everything under control, sweetie," he replied. His eyes were on Chief Terry. "Now, Cuddlekins here, he's a different story."

"You're not going to let me live this down," Chief Terry complained.

"Nope." Landon bit into his bacon and flicked his eyes back to me. "Bay, you're bigger and stronger. Don't be afraid to throw your hips around. Aunt Tillie won't know what's coming."

Was there an insult in there? "Are you saying my hips are wide?"

"I love your hips, baby."

"I swear it was nothing personal," Mary insisted to Twila. "You just weren't right for the part. You kept yelling 'line' every three seconds. You only had two lines."

"I'm method!" Twila howled.

"How did you hear us last night?" Mom demanded of Aunt Tillie. "You took a bottle of wine into your room when you got home. You were pouting and ready for bed. There's no way you heard us."

"I'm middle-aged, not deaf, Winnie," Aunt Tillie fired back. "Bay, if you don't give me my stick, I'll curse you to smell like Margaret Little's thong!"

"Ugh." Landon blurted. "How do you know she wears a thong?"

"I know things," Aunt Tillie sneered. "Give me my stick. I'm going to reclaim my chair through whatever means necessary."

"You can't stab her because she's sitting in your chair," I argued.

"How about because she's trying to steal your husband?"

"That's a different story."

"Bay, nobody can steal me from you," Landon called out around a mouthful of French toast. "I'm yours forever."

"This day pretty much sucks," Ava lamented. "Why are the only good-looking guys in this town taken?"

"Dibs on the babysitter," Robin announced from the far end of the table, her hand shooting into the air. "He's mine."

"The guy at the petting zoo won't even look at me," Renee complained. "I think he might be gay."

"Or have a live-in girlfriend he adores even though she's snarky and mean," I said.

"*So* snarky and mean," Landon intoned.

"Get out of my chair!" Aunt Tillie roared, wheeling on Ava. "Do you want me to curse you to smell like toe gunk the rest of your life?"

Ava jutted out her lower lip. "You're really mean."

"I can get meaner." Aunt Tillie's hands landed on her hips. "Get. Out. Of. My. Chair."

Ava held her gaze for a moment longer and then sniffled as she rose. "This family is really horrible."

"And another thing," Twila snapped. She was halfway across the table and invading Mary's personal space. "I could've totally saved the *Titanic* from going down, and that's another reason I should've been cast in the movie. I would've made room on the door for Leonardo DiCaprio."

I let loose a breath as I leaned against the wall. "It's going to be a long day," I said when Landon snagged my gaze. "A really long day."

"You'd better eat up, sweetie," Landon said. "That day starts in forty-five minutes. You need to fortify yourself, or you'll be dragging before lunch."

I handed the spear to Mom. "Give her back the other stick. She could kill someone with this one."

"Maybe I'll confiscate both," Mom replied.

"You're on my list," Aunt Tillie warned Mom.

"Yeah, yeah, yeah."

# Twenty-Two

The Happy Holidays Players looked shell-shocked after breakfast. I wanted to laugh at the way Mary shrank from Twila, but I had other things to worry about.

"I'll handle Childs," Chief Terry said in front of the inn. "You guys do whatever it is you need to do."

"Bay is convinced the mother has to be magical because the daughter is," Landon volunteered. "It's worth a shot. Bay will know better what questions to ask."

"Just be careful." Chief Terry sent me a fond look. "You're still my little sweetheart."

"Yes, and I will forever picture you being my mother's cuddlekins," I said dryly.

Chief Terry's gaze turned challenging. "Given how you and this fool fall all over each other on a daily basis, I'm pretty sure you should get over it." Chief Terry jerked his thumb in Landon's direction.

"It's not the same," I insisted. "But you do you, I guess."

"Don't mind if I do." Chief Terry squeezed my shoulder as Landon and I started across the parking lot.

Mary emerged from the hotel with Lenny and Ava flanking her. I felt her gaze on me as I hopped into Landon's truck.

"I'm pretty sure they're regretting not coming up with roles for your mother and aunts," Landon offered as he started the Explorer.

"I'm sure they are too." I smirked at the memory of Twila accusing Mary of conspiring with Kate Winslet. "Sometimes I just love my family."

"They were an absolute delight this morning," Landon agreed. He paused before pulling out of the parking spot. "What did you do with that spear?"

"I gave it to my mother. She said she would handle it."

"The spear is worse than the stick."

"Mom won't let her leave the house with it," I promised. "Besides, I'm betting Aunt Tillie only made the spear so she can watch where Mom hides it. Then she'll reclaim her stick, and everything will be back to normal."

"Here's hoping." Landon plugged a Shadow Hills address into his GPS.

"What's her name?" I asked as I got comfortable for the drive.

"Carolyn. She's been married three times and has one child, from her second marriage."

"Anything interesting on her record?"

"There have been a surprising number of disturbing the peace calls to her address. Apparently, she also likes to get drunk downtown and accuse the other women of trying to steal whatever man she's currently bedding."

"Lovely." I made a face. "Did you ask Hunter about her?"

Hunter Ryan was a police officer in Shadow Hills. Chief Terry had taken him under his wing years ago because Hunter's father, also a policeman, was an abusive jerk. Hunter's father was long gone from the department. When Hunter had questions, he went to Chief Terry.

"I did," Landon confirmed. "He said that she's a rowdy partier but mostly harmless. He didn't have any idea she was Natalie's mother. He didn't know anything about Natalie, and Carolyn moved to Shadow Hills about ten years ago."

"Natalie would've long since been an adult," I mused.

"Yeah." Landon rolled his neck as he pulled onto the highway.

"Hunter said that Carolyn hangs at the senior center during the day and carouses at night."

"Shadow Hills doesn't strike me as the sort of town you can do much carousing in," I noted.

"I'm pretty sure she's happy as long as she can get a drink."

"She self-medicates," I said. "I wonder if that has something to do with her daughter."

"I'm guessing that the relationship is strained," Landon replied. "It's likely Carolyn was a rowdy mother and passed along her bad decision-making skills to Natalie. What I don't get is how the magic figures into this."

"It's not really that hard to figure out," I replied. "Carolyn likely has magic in her genes. She probably used it to get her way through the years and passed on what she knew to Natalie."

"But Natalie is somehow imbuing prisoners with magic they shouldn't have access to," Landon pointed out.

"I'm still trying to figure that part out. The enchantress stuff, especially after learning that her mother has been married three times and constantly changes boyfriends, isn't that hard to figure out. Natalie has a warped view of what love is."

"Not everybody can have a perfect husband like you, Bay."

I smirked. "I'm just saying that it sounds like Carolyn bases her self-worth on whether or not a man is in her life. Perhaps she passed that on to Natalie, who likely struggled following the path her mother laid out. That's why she fell for a captive participant. Carl Markham had no choice but to love her if he wanted special perks."

Landon made a face. "I thought we both agreed that it was unlikely Carl has true feelings for her."

"We do agree on that. Natalie is the one who disagrees. She either can't or won't see the truth about him. If she won't, she'll do whatever she deems necessary to keep him in line. If she can't see the truth about him, it's going to be messier."

"Because his ultimate betrayal will come as a shock to her," Landon surmised.

I nodded. "If Natalie is smart—and she can't have been an idiot to have pulled this off—then the death of Ann Markham will have gotten her thinking. There's no way that was her idea."

"Carl was still bitter about his ex and set that in motion," Landon surmised. "Carl's ex lived in the same town as Natalie. Do you think that was a coincidence?"

I frowned. "I don't know. How long was Natalie a guard at the prison?"

"Five years. Before that she was a guard in the county jail. She only worked with females when she worked for the county."

"Do you think that was the reason she went to work at the prison?"

Landon opened his mouth, then shut it, considering the question. "I wouldn't assume that," he said finally. "The prison job pays better. The thing with Markham might've simply been a coincidence."

I pressed my lips together as I stared out the window. "Was Markham already at the prison when Natalie started there?"

"If I remember Markham's file correctly, he's been at Antrim two years."

"Then she was there first."

"But he's a master at reading a room," Landon pointed out. "Even if he was the new prisoner on the block, he might've figured out she was an easy mark early on."

"So they start talking," I said. "They would've started interacting slowly. Markham would've taken his time luring her in."

"And at some point, it turned romantic. He would've seen her weakness, that she wanted to be loved, and used it."

"Could they have found a way to hook up in the prison without anybody noticing?" I asked.

"I would like to say there are safeguards in place, but the guards would've grown complacent. And even if the other guards found out, they might have figured that was her business and ignored the situation."

"Which means they're partly to blame for what's happened," I groused.

"I'm sure there was no malice involved, Bay. It was just laziness."

"Tell that to Ann Markham."

"I'm not saying it's okay." His voice was low. "I've seen it happen before. The whole thing isn't quite as nefarious as you imagine in your mind."

"It's still a mess, and we're the ones who have to clean it up."

"There is that." He let loose a sigh. "We're heading for a reckoning, Bay. I think we can all agree on that. Markham will show his true colors at some point. Either Natalie is going to realize that she made a mistake, or double down."

"Which do you think it will be?"

"I'm hoping for the former but bracing for the latter."

I was right there with him. "It's going to get ugly."

"We need to figure out a way to stop it from happening."

"Hopefully, Carolyn can help us."

**IF CAROLYN'S ATTITUDE WHEN SHE OPENED** the door to us was any indication, Natalie was going to be an absolute nightmare when we finally caught up with her.

"Oh, geez." She looked Landon up and down. "I already told the state boys I don't know anything. Did they send the pretty boy intern because they thought it would loosen me up? If so, they made a bad mistake."

Landon, his training kicking in, remained calm. "I'm not an intern, ma'am." He flashed his badge. "I'm with the FBI, and I have a few more questions."

"The FBI, huh?" Carolyn didn't look impressed. When her gaze landed on me, there was a darkness that left me distinctly uncomfortable. "Is she your secretary?"

"She's a consultant," Landon replied. He introduced us, giving our full names, and watched Carolyn closely for a reaction. She didn't show any interest in either of us.

"Well, come in I guess." Carolyn left the door open as she trekked into the house. "You're not going to leave until you get what you want. That's typical of a man ... and 'The Man,' I guess." She laughed at her own joke. "What happened now?"

"You're aware that Carl Markham's ex-wife is dead?" Landon asked as we sat at a round kitchen table with her.

"I'm not sure who Carl Markham is." Carolyn feigned confusion. She wasn't a very good actress. Anybody—trained or not—could tell she was lying. "You'll have to give me a refresher."

"He's an inmate at Antrim Correctional," Landon replied patiently. Before he could launch into his spiel, I rested my hand on his forearm. He would jump through as many hoops as it took to get information from Carolyn. It was unnecessary.

"Don't bother," I said to his questioning look. "She knows who Carl is. In fact, she's probably heard more than a few stories about him. She knows all of it."

"*All* of it?" Landon pressed.

I nodded. "What sort of witch are you?" I asked her.

Carolyn cackled like a mad woman. "What sort of witch are you?" she shot back.

"I'm a necromancer. I don't fall into one of the four elemental designations. Back in the day, before my powers took full shape, I fell into the air witch category."

Carolyn looked momentarily impressed. "You're one of the Hemlock Cove Winchesters," she said. She already knew my last name from when Landon had introduced us, so it wasn't much of a leap for her to get to the next part.

"I am," I agreed.

"I've met two of them. Twila and Winnie. Twila was nicer than Winnie."

"Twila has a good heart," I replied. "I'm guessing you got close to them because you wanted to learn from them."

"I thought they would let me into their coven."

"Our coven was forged in blood. That's familial blood. We don't accept outsiders."

"Hmm." Carolyn pursed her lips. All of the scattered energy she'd been putting on display at the door was gone. "What do you want?"

"The truth," I replied. "Where did Natalie get her magic? You're nowhere near powerful enough to pull off what she's doing, so there has to be an angle we're missing."

Carolyn's eyes narrowed. "Is that so?"

"Yes. That's true."

Carolyn threw out a jolt of magic. It wobbled, indicating she was either out of practice or so weak she couldn't muster anything other than a tiny display. I easily deflected it, and when it hit the wall it knocked a framed photograph of Captain Morgan—autographed—from the wall.

Carolyn's eyes went momentarily wide, but she shuttered her surprise quickly.

"You can't take me," I warned her in a low voice. "In fact, you know what? I'm done with this." I got to my feet faster than she—or Landon for that matter—could've foreseen and slapped my hands on either side of her head. "*Ostendo*," I hissed.

Carolyn went immediately still. There were no barriers in her mind, which made taking a look around easy.

"Well, that was less than diplomatic," Landon complained as he moved next to me.

"She wasn't ever going to voluntarily help us," I replied. "This will be quicker."

"You could've warned me."

"I would've been warning her too. She's no threat. She has a bit of air magic. It's weak, which indicates that whatever she got was inherited through her father's line."

"I can't help thinking there's an insult buried in there," Landon muttered.

"Not an insult, just truth. The reason my line is so powerful is because we nurtured it through the females. That's not what happened with her line." I cocked my head as a series of images became apparent. "She was an even crappier mother than we thought."

"Don't tell me you're suddenly feeling sorry for Natalie," Landon said.

"I can feel sorry for her and know we have to beat her at the same time," I said. I frowned when another image pushed to the forefront. "She went to Hollow Creek. They both did."

Hollow Creek had been teeming with magical shards thanks to our constant battles in the area. We'd cleaned it up, and it was no longer a threat. Yet Carolyn and Natalie had visited more than once.

"I think she stole Hollow Creek magic to put the triggers in the prisoners' heads," I said. "That doesn't explain how she's been fueling them. I can't get a clear picture of that."

"She wouldn't tell me either," Carolyn said dully. "She was suddenly way more powerful than she should've been. She was selfish and kept the reason to herself."

That fit given the family dynamics. Carolyn hadn't nurtured Natalie, so there was no way the daughter would help the mother.

"Natalie cut ties with her right before the prison break," I told Landon. "Carolyn didn't know the specifics. She was aware her daughter had something in mind—even asked her about it—but Natalie wouldn't tell. She didn't trust her mother."

"That's because I'm a truth teller," Carolyn sputtered. She was caught in my spell and couldn't move, but speaking was a different story. Apparently, there was no shutting her up. "She told me she was in love with a prisoner, and I told her how stupid that was. Love doesn't get you anywhere. If she's going to rely on a relationship, the man has to be able to give her something. What could a prisoner give her?"

"Apparently, more than you," I shot back. "Even fake love from Carl Markham was better than the nothing burger you gave her."

"Another weak one," Carolyn trilled. "You think love is the answer to everything."

"I do. Now, shut up." I rolled my neck and looked deeper, but there wasn't much to glean. "Natalie came to say goodbye two days before the prison break. She told her mother she would be seeing her in the news and asked that her mother keep her mouth shut. There's nothing else."

I released Carolyn and took a step back. When the woman tried to slap me, a bit of magic added for some oomph, I pushed back her hand, so she slapped herself. She was dazed when she spun and stumbled into the next room and fell on the couch.

"Well, *that* was different," Landon said. He looked Carolyn up and down and then flicked his eyes to me. "Do you want me to take her in?"

I shook my head. "There's no point. You can't charge her with magically trying to slap me, or with being a crappy mother. She doesn't have anything in her head that can help us."

"What do you want to do now?"

There was only one thing I could think to do. "I want to check around Hollow Creek."

"Why? The magic fragments are gone."

"Yes, but if they spent enough time there to figure out how to use the magical fragments, maybe they found a little something else too. Like a place to hole up for a few weeks."

Understanding dawned on Landon's face. "Nobody goes there now that the weather is turning."

"There's that woman living on the other side of Hollow Creek, the one Scout is in contact with, but she wouldn't have anything to do with Carl and Natalie. We need to at least check it out."

Landon nodded. "Okay. At least it's somewhere to look."

# Twenty-Three

Hollow Creek was quiet and felt desolate since so many trees had shed their leaves. When we were kids, we hung out in the area to avoid our mothers and gossip about how annoying our parents were. As we grew older, it became a party spot. In recent years, it had become a battle site. And the way my hair stood up on the back of my neck told me that perhaps it would be the location of a battle yet again today.

"What are you thinking?" Landon asked as we met in front of his Explorer. It was an overcast day, no sun in sight, and it did little to ease the tension pooling in my stomach.

"I'm not sure," I replied, glancing around. Something felt off.

"Maybe we should turn around and head back to town," he suggested. "We can get backup."

I shot him an amused smile. "You don't think we can handle them?"

"I'd prefer to have more firepower than we need. We could grab Thistle, Evan, and Aunt Tillie. Even with the nonstop sniping, I'd feel better if they were with us."

He had a point, but it was too late. "They know we're here," I whispered.

Landon frowned.

"I feel their magic."

Landon worked his jaw. "What happens if we run?"

"It will be the magical equivalent of them shooting us in the back."

Grimly, Landon unhooked the strap that kept his gun holstered and drew it. The creek itself looked empty, but we'd both learned through the years that looks could be deceiving. "Bay, don't do anything heroic. Just do enough to create a window for us to escape."

"I have no idea what I'm going to do yet, but I'll try to keep us from dying." I stepped to my right, eyed a stand of trees on the other side of the creek and made up my mind. "Stand back."

"Stand back?" Landon sounded shrill. "What are you going to do?"

I threw a burst of magic strong enough to shake the trees that had drawn my attention. Branches fell.

At first, I thought I'd failed. Then there was movement.

Natalie stepped to the forefront, as if emerging from behind a glamour. Her eyes were slits of disgust as she regarded me. "The witch," she intoned.

"The guard who made a very big mistake judging her romantic partner," I shot back.

Landon leveled his gun on Natalie. "Link your hands together on top of your head."

Natalie smirked. "I think not." She focused on Landon for a moment before turning her eyes to me. "How did you even get involved in this?"

"I was about to ask you the same thing," I replied. "Where is Carl Markham?"

"Don't worry about it."

"I am going to worry about it," I replied. "He's dangerous. He's a killer."

"Some people are forced to kill. They have no choice."

"I don't think that was the case with Carl," Landon replied. "Was he forced to kill his ex-wife when you escaped? Wasn't that an unnecessary risk? Why put you through that after all the planning you did?"

Annoyance flashed across Natalie's face. "She lied to the police. She said he beat her. She said he was always talking about the things he wanted to do to the neighbor. She made all of it up."

"Or is Carl lying to you?" Landon challenged. "I've read his file. They had physical evidence. DNA. He had blood on his shirt."

"She attacked him!" Natalie's eyes flashed. "He was protecting himself."

"He let himself into the neighbor's house after dark, when her husband was out of town, and she's to blame," Landon said. "You've been sold a bill of goods."

"You don't know what you're talking about," Natalie shot back. "It was all a setup. The police lied. Carl's wife lied because she was jealous. She deserved what she got for stealing so many years of his life."

"You need help." Landon was matter of fact. "Put your hands up."

Natalie snorted. "How are you going to even get to me?" she demanded from the other side of the creek.

"I could put you down," I offered. "Then it wouldn't matter how long it took us to cross to you."

"You don't have the strength. Carl told me."

It was an odd thing to say. Like, *really* odd. "Carl told you I don't have the strength to put you down?" It was a struggle to wrap my head around the statement. "I've taken out all the soldiers you've sent for me."

"They were just a test," Natalie insisted. "He wanted to see what you could do. We still have more out there. Each one deadlier. Carl will see to that."

I slowly slid my eyes to Landon. Did he understand what she was insinuating?

"Carl is the one with the magic," he said under his breath.

I nodded. It was something we hadn't considered. "She's not an enchantress. She's a woman with minimal magic. Carl understood that and took advantage of her."

"What do we do?" Landon asked.

I could think of only one thing. "Hold on." I blew out a breath and glanced around, my heart fluttering and stomach twisting. "*Come*," I intoned.

Two ghosts hung around Hollow Creek. They were dormant, essentially keeping separate from the land of the living, but they had no choice when I called them.

"Restrain her," I ordered when the now familiar faces popped into view.

The ghosts flew across the creek and were on Natalie in an instant.

"What's happening?" Panic contorted Natalie's features, and she ducked her head to avoid the ghosts. Could she see them? I couldn't tell, but she could feel them, the power they still possessed even though there was very little humanity left in them. "Stop!"

The woods to our right exploded when she screamed. Carl Markham, his eyes glowing yellow, was on me before I could erect a shield.

"I don't think so," he rasped as he shoved at Landon with his magic.

Landon wasn't ready for the magic, which flung him into the air and spun him into the creek. He hit with a terrific splash, his gun flying free and landing in the sand of the creek bank. "Now it's just you and me." Carl looked hungry as he stared down into my face.

"What are you?" Even though I was in trouble, my curiosity couldn't be contained. "You're not human."

"Oh, but I am. I'm a better human than you."

I shoved my hands into his chest, throwing magic into the effort, and managed to dislodge him. It was only thanks to the ghosts rushing in and pulling him the rest of the way off that I managed to slide back.

His eyes were on fire—yellow fire—when he glared at me and puffed himself out, managing to blow the ghosts back with minimal effort. "It's cheating to call in others to fight your battles."

I glanced across the creek. Natalie was down, unmoving. I had only Carl to worry about. "I assumed you guys were using her magic. She doesn't have much, but she stole some from this place. It was all in her mother's head. That's how we found you."

"I know about the stolen magic." The way Carl held himself reminded me of an animal. He was on the ground, rocking back and forth on his hands and knees, no doubt he was preparing to strike. "Who do you think told her to start collecting it?"

"But..." I had so many questions. The sound of Landon sloshing in the creek behind me had me starting to swivel, but I caught myself as Carl lashed out with a hand that had grown claws. I yelped as I fell backward, protecting my arm and internally screaming at the red-hot pain shooting through me.

"Bay!" Landon stormed to the spot behind me.

I didn't move my eyes from Carl's face even though I felt blood pouring down my forearm. "What are you?"

"It doesn't matter." Carl's lips curved. "You're not in charge of this situation, girl. I warned you about that the other night. You wouldn't listen."

I frowned. "You were the presence I called to the bluff."

"You didn't have the strength to hold me. Now that I'm free and powered up, nobody does. You need to understand that."

"Baby, let me see that arm." Landon was on his knees behind me, his chest pressed to my back. He was soaking wet, but I felt warmth emanating from him.

I kept my arm cradled in front of me. "You don't know who you're messing with," I warned. The ghosts that had come to my rescue flanked us, listlessly floating and staring at nothing.

"You don't know who you're messing with," Carl replied. "Don't!" He raised his finger and wagged it at Landon. "Your gun is all the way over there, and if you go for it, I'll tear your wife limb from limb."

Landon growled. "You're not going anywhere near my wife."

"Think again." Carl was unbelievably calm. "You can both escape if you sit there and do nothing. If you move on me, it will be over. Your wife knows it. I see the resignation in her eyes. You only have one move here."

I felt sick to my stomach. Anger I didn't know I was capable of coursed through me. "Are you going to leave Natalie behind?"

Carl cast a weary glance to the other side of the creek. "She served her purpose. By letting her believe she was in charge, I allowed her to feel important. That was something she was never capable of in life. She should be grateful I gave her that time."

"She'll wake, and you'll be gone."

"That's on her. The idiot believed me." Carl's hands looked normal as he stood. The claws that had left the burning rips in my arm, were gone. His eyes had gone back to normal too. "I commend you for being able to find us. The truth is, I wasn't keen on living in a cave all winter. I made ... alternative ... arrangements. I was going to spring it on her today. You saved me a very uncomfortable conversation."

"You're going to wreck her," I said. "You don't even care."

"I never cared. She was a means to an end." He glanced at Natalie's still form again. "I was going to kill her. I had it all planned out. She should be grateful I don't have the time."

"I'm sure that's what she'll feel," I shot back. "Grateful."

"Nobody forced her to do this." Carl sounded utterly reasonable, and it made me want to punch him in his special place. "She made the decision. She chose to believe every lie I told her. She knew better. Deep down, she had to realize that I was never going to be the man I pretended to be. She deluded herself."

He was preparing to leave. My inability to stop him didn't stop me from digging for information. "If you had this power at your disposal all this time, why didn't you use it to escape earlier?"

"Power is only part of it, girl. I needed a plan. I needed to consolidate my magic. I needed someone on the outside to provide me with money so I could run. All of that had to be organized."

"You have Natalie's money," I realized.

"She really is an idiot." Carl made a tsking sound as he shook his head. "Tell her I appreciate all the work she did. I am grateful, believe it or not. Make sure she understands what will happen if she tries to find me again." He was grim as he held my gaze. "This is the end of the tale for her."

I narrowed my eyes.

"It had better be the end of the tale for you too if you want to survive," he continued. "I'll be out of here by nightfall tomorrow. I'll have to kill you if you get in my way." He straightened and focused on Landon. "If you love your wife, you'll keep her at home. Problems arise in relationships when the wife thinks she knows better. Remember that."

He turned to walk away.

"Is that why you killed Ann?" I yelled at his back. "Did she get too big for her britches?"

"Ann ruined my life. I told her what would happen if she didn't come up with an alibi for me. She thought she knew better. Everything that happened to her she earned. If she'd just kept her mouth shut, she'd still be alive."

"Did Natalie realize what you were going to do to Ann?" I was desperate to keep Carl close, even though I had no idea what to do with him. The look he shot me from halfway up the embankment told me he knew.

"Natalie believed whatever I told her," Carl replied. "She was a sad, sad woman. She had no self-esteem. She just wanted to be loved. I used that to my advantage. Even when I told her that I just wanted to talk to Ann and get the money I'd hidden under the house, a ridiculous lie, she believed me. It wasn't because I was such a good liar. It was because she needed me to be telling the truth. She was just that pathetic."

"You don't have a soul." I felt sick to my stomach. "You're a sociopath."

"What I am is none of your concern. I'd get that arm looked at. There are nasty germs out here, and an infection can be worse than the initial wound." He was quiet until he got to the top of the hill. "Let it go, girl. If you don't, I won't be as nice the second time around."

With that, he was gone, and I closed my eyes to ward off the pain.

"Let me see your arm," Landon barked, tears streaming down his cheeks. "Bay, this is really bad. You need stitches."

It was rare that human medicine could be of any help, but in this case, he was right. "We should head to the urgent care." I tried to use my good arm to push myself to a standing position but slipped. The resounding cry that escaped had Landon losing the rest of his color.

"Let me." As Landon helped me to my feet, his hands were shaking with rage. "Just ... stay right there." He moved to the side of the water, to where his gun had fallen when he'd been thrown into the creek. He checked it and then shoved it in the holster before moving back to me. "Up," he ordered, sliding his arms around my waist to lift me.

"I'll get blood all over you," I said.

"I don't care, Bay. Clothes can be replaced. I want you stitched up as soon as possible." He wouldn't meet my gaze. Was his anger directed at me?

"Landon."

"Sweetie, no." He brushed his lips against my forehead as he started up the hill. "It's okay. I'm going to get you to an urgent care. It's going to be fine." He was shaking.

"I should've called in backup," I said

"That doesn't matter now." He didn't speak again until we were at the Explorer. He put me inside, not caring about the blood, and then pulled out his phone to call Chief Terry. "Natalie Bennett is on the ground on the south side of Hollow Creek. She's alive—at least I think she is—but Bay has been hurt, and I have to get her to an urgent care for stitches. You have to collect Natalie because I can't waste the time."

He was quiet for a beat. "I don't know everything," he said. "I only know that Carl Markham is the true power, and he beat us today. The rest of it, well, it's a mess. We'll have to talk about it later. I need Bay stitched up, or I'll have a coronary."

Another pause.

"Yeah, I'll see you there." With that, he shoved his phone in his pocket. "Chief Terry will take care of Natalie and meet us at the urgent care. I'll have you there in fifteen minutes."

"Landon, I'm okay," I promised him.

"Only because Markham didn't care enough to kill us."

"We'll figure it out," I promised.

He grunted in response. Really, what else was there to say?

# Twenty-Four

The gash was long enough that I needed fifteen stitches. The doctor offered me pain meds, which I politely declined. Aunt Tillie had better stuff at home, and Mom brought it when she arrived at the urgent care, Thistle in tow. Apparently, they didn't bring Clove because she was whining and carrying on as if the world had ended.

She handed the ointment to me when the doctor excused himself to answer a call. I dabbed it on quickly and then took the clothes she'd brought for Landon and me to change into. I quickly stripped out of my shirt and jeans and dumped the ruined items in the trash before tugging on a flannel to cover the injury.

Landon stripped out of his shirt and tugged on a new one before dropping his blood-soaked button-down in the trash. He'd washed his face while waiting for me to be stitched up. I had things I wanted to say to him, but he didn't look open to that just yet.

"Terry called me because you're not picking up your phone," Mom said to Landon. "He's worried Bay's injury is worse than you let on."

"I'm fine," I volunteered, drawing Mom's eyes to me. "It doesn't even hurt now thanks to Aunt Tillie's ointment."

"It's a nasty wound, Bay." Mom looked as if she was searching for the right words. "What happened?"

"We were caught off guard," I replied. "Natalie wasn't the true threat. It was always Carl. He's some sort of monster. His hands turn into claws, which is how I got this."

Mom turned her attention back to Landon. "You're not hurt?"

Landon finally spoke. "I'm fine. I wasn't even involved. I got thrown in the water and lost my gun."

"Is that what's bothering you?" I asked.

Landon's eyes were dark when they locked with mine. "You could've been killed, and there wasn't a thing I could do."

I felt bad for him, but only to an extent. "You wanted to call in backup. I didn't listen, and it almost backfired on us. You shouldn't be blaming yourself. You should be blaming me."

He let loose a little hiss but otherwise didn't respond.

"I get it," I said. I really did. "You felt helpless in the moment. So did I. Carl could've killed you, and there was nothing I could do. He seemed impervious to the ghosts. Even when I tried to order them to go after him, they didn't. I got us into that mess."

"You're hurt," Landon said. "I'm the FBI agent. I'm the one who was supposed to have control of that situation."

"We couldn't have known how it would go. Everything we knew suggested Natalie had the magic. It was a mistake. If you want to say we both made mistakes, fine, but don't sit there and wallow. We have to put it behind us."

Landon made a face. "I'm not wallowing."

"You are," Mom interjected. "You're being a big baby. I understand you're upset—we all are—but this really is on Bay."

"Thanks, Mom," I said dryly.

"Don't take that tone with me, young lady," Mom snapped. "If this was a one-time error, it wouldn't be such a big deal. Everybody makes mistakes. This is the second time in a week that your ego has gotten you into trouble. The first was the pot field. Why didn't you come to the house to get backup? You knew there was someone out there."

My mouth went dry.

"Landon wanted to get backup today, but you brushed him off," she continued. "I know you're more powerful than you used to be—you truly are the power in this family now, Bay—but you're not invincible. No more running off to face trouble without taking someone with you. Enough is enough."

I couldn't believe she was turning on me. I expected it from Aunt Tillie and Thistle, but Mom was supposed to be on my side. Despite my bitterness, I knew she was right. My ego had been growing the last couple of months. It started with the birth of Calvin, when I practically blew the top off the house unleashing magic to protect Clove and her baby.

"I'm sorry." Being contrite after the fact wouldn't erase what had happened, but it was all I had to offer. "I made a mistake. I'd taken down so many prisoners that my head got too big. I'm better now." I held up my injured arm. "I guess this was a wakeup call of sorts."

"Good." Mom didn't back down. "We're a family, and we're stronger together. As for you," she swiveled to face Landon head on. "You couldn't have known what would happen. Even if you'd had your gun, you don't know that you could've taken out this Markham fellow. You might just have made him angry and something worse could've happened. You misread the situation and paid the price. No further pouting is allowed."

To my surprise, Landon managed a wan smile. "Fine. I'm done pouting." He dragged a hand through his hair. "What did Chief Terry say?"

"He has Natalie at our jail and wants you there to question her before she's transported to the prison. He's keeping things silent for now because he wants to get everything that he can out of Natalie before relinquishing her to the higher-ups."

I perked up. "Natalie might know something that can help us find Carl."

"Even if we find him, can we beat him?" Landon didn't look convinced.

"There's only one way to find out." I held out my hand to him. "Don't be mad at me. Don't be mad at yourself. We survived. We'll know better next time."

"What if there's no next time?"

I was grim. "Oh, there's going to be a next time. There's no way we're letting that douche canoe win."

"And here we go," Thistle muttered. "It's about to get ugly."

"You have no idea," I replied. "That guy has earned a butt kicking. We're going to deliver it."

**THISTLE MADE ME PROMISE WE WOULDN'T** go after Markham without calling her. She was annoyed, but there were no histrionics for a change. Apparently, my meltdown, coupled with Landon's self-doubt, kept her levelheaded.

At least for now.

Chief Terry had Natalie in an interrogation room. He was in the hallway, watching her through the glass, and did a double take when he saw us.

"I'm angry," he announced as we closed the distance. "So angry." He cuffed the back of Landon's head before gently reaching for my arm. "When I call, you pick up. Do you understand?"

Landon nodded. "Sorry. I was having a moment."

Chief Terry tugged up the arm of my flannel. "That doesn't look good."

"It's fine," I assured him. "I put some of Aunt Tillie's magic ointment on it. I can't even feel it now. I'll be able to keep it numb until we're through this, and by the time it starts itching Landon will be in full dote mode, and we'll be putting this behind us."

"You're both in trouble," Chief Terry growled. "I can't believe this happened."

"Well, believe it." I was over feeling sorry for myself. "We got caught with our pants down. I was so fixated on Natalie, it didn't occur to me that Carl could be the mastermind. I knew he was involved, but all of this was beyond Natalie. It was him, through and through."

"We won't be able to keep the fact that we have her under wraps very long. I was alone when I went there to get her, and nobody saw me bring her in, but we have a narrow window. Then I have to notify the others that we have her."

"I only need a bit of time with her," I promised. "I'll be able to figure out right away what she does and doesn't know."

Chief Terry let loose a hefty sigh and nodded. "Do you want us with you?"

I shook my head. "It's better we talk woman to woman to start."

"I'm willing to let you take the lead." Chief Terry kissed my forehead. "If I feel that things are getting out of hand, I'll join the party."

"It won't get out of hand." I felt that to my bones. "I'm about to break her into a million pieces. We were wrong all along about her. She's not a threat."

"She still helped him escape."

"Because she's a sad and lonely woman. Just let me talk to her. I predict you'll be able to make your call to Childs telling him that we have her in thirty minutes."

He gave me a hug before relinquishing me to Landon so he could do the same.

"Don't underestimate her, Bay," Landon warned. "We've underestimated the enemy twice now. I don't want it to backfire on us a third time."

"It won't," I promised. "I've got this."

I kept my face impassive when I entered the interrogation room. I closed the door behind me and sat across from Natalie. She was cuffed, her shoulders sagging.

"Today wasn't your day, huh?" I asked as I shifted to get comfortable, resting my injured arm on the table.

"How did you find us?" she asked in a tiny voice.

I could've lied, but if she believed I was telling the truth she would be more likely to open up. "Your mother. We paid her a visit this morning."

"My mother didn't know where we were."

"She knew you'd been to Hollow Creek. She was with you, after all. You were giving yourselves power boosts with the fragments for some time."

Natalie worked her jaw. "I don't know what you mean."

"You're a terrible liar, but that doesn't matter. I don't expect you to ever talk about the fragments again. This will be the last conversation about them. If you do try to chat with others, they'll stick you in the sort of hospital you'll never get out of. This is a conversation for just us."

"Why is that?"

"My family is the reason those magical fragments were there for the taking."

Natalie sat straighter in her chair. "You did something to me today. You ... sent invisible people after me. I could feel their hands on my body, wrestling me to the ground. What was that?"

"Ghosts."

She snorted. "If you don't want to tell me, that's up to you."

"They really were ghosts," I assured her. "That's one of my abilities. Unfortunately, my best parlor trick did not work on Carl. Do you have any idea why that might be?"

Natalie looked taken aback. "I ... don't ... wait." Realization dawned on her face. "Did you talk to Carl?"

It was only then that I remembered she'd been passed out for the good stuff. I could use that to my advantage. "I did. He's an interesting guy. Smarter than I expected."

A rush of love washed over Natalie's face. "He's the smartest man I know."

"He also seems to be lacking a soul."

"No." Natalie vehemently shook her head. "Everybody has a soul. He hides his because he doesn't want anyone to see him as vulnerable. You can't be vulnerable in prison. The other inmates will cripple you, emotionally and physically."

"Is that a fact?"

"I've seen it numerous times."

I had to wonder if Carl was the first inmate she'd fallen in love with. "He left you without a thought."

"He had no choice. You were there. You were a threat to us. He had to run. I don't blame him."

"He could've easily crossed the creek and collected you. He had us in a very bad position. He could've killed us, saved you, and gotten away."

"He didn't want to kill innocent people. That's not who he is."

"He killed Ann," I countered. "I know you're aware of that because you were there. We saw the house."

Regret ignited in Natalie's eyes. "She lied to get him convicted. She was evil."

"No, she was a woman who made a choice," I countered. "She knew her husband killed the neighbor. I'm willing to guess she was suspicious about a few other murders. She did the right thing, and you helped Carl kill her."

"No." Natalie gripped her cuffed hands into fists. "I wasn't there, but she was an evil person, and she got what she deserved."

"And Carl? What does he deserve?"

"He's innocent. He deserves a life."

I kicked back in my chair, hoping I looked relaxed. Inside, I was coiled and ready for an explosion. "Well, if things turn out as he planned, he will get that life. He already has someone else lined up to meet with. Somebody in town."

Confusion knit Natalie's eyebrows. "You're making that up."

"He told us that he was going to break from you tonight. He always had another plan to fall back on. Us arriving when we did actually saved you because he was going to kill you."

"That's a lie." Natalie's voice shook like her hands. "You're just saying that to get me to turn on him."

Part of me really did feel sorry for her. She was broken, and there was no putting her back together again. She had a long, miserable stretch in front of her. Eventually, she would realize the truth of Carl Markham. She had nothing to offer us, though. Markham hadn't confided in her. He wouldn't have risked it.

"You lie," Natalie insisted. "Carl and I had a love story for the ages."

"Carl isn't capable of love. He said to tell you he was grateful for your assistance, that he couldn't have made his escape without you, but you're not to look for him. He'll kill you if he ever crosses paths with you again."

"But ... no." Natalie looked anguished. "We had a plan. We were going to build a life together. We were going to camp down by Hollow Creek because nobody would look for us there. I found a cave. It was going to suck, but in a few months, we would be able to leave without anybody looking for us and start a new life."

She really was pathetic. "He was going to kill you today, leave you down by the creek, and then take off with his true partner. Do you know who that is?"

"He loves me," Natalie insisted. "He's only ever loved me. I made him feel things he never felt before."

"You made him an offer he couldn't refuse," I corrected. "You actually came up with a plan to free him. You somehow managed to power magic he already had with the shards from Hollow Creek. I still don't know what he is—"

"He's a good man, with a good heart," she snapped. "He's been dealt a raw hand. He doesn't deserve any of this."

"I'm going to find out," I continued as I rose to my feet. "Someday you'll think back on all of this and hate yourself. I'm not saying anything that was done here is okay, but you should know that you never really had a shot.

"He read you the first time he met you," I offered. "He recognized that you needed love above all else. He was determined to make you think he could give you that love. He was always incapable of giving you everything he promised."

"No." Natalie closed her eyes, as if willing me to disappear. "He loved me. I know it. We're going to find a way to be together. One day, even if it's years from now, he'll break me out of prison, and we'll be together. Mark my words. It's going to happen."

Yup, she was definitely broken. "Have a good life, Natalie," I said as I headed for the door. "I really do hope you find some peace."

"You'll see," Natalie yelled at my back. "He'll find me. We're going to be happy forever."

# Twenty-Five

Landon and Chief Terry were responsible for taking Natalie to the prison to hand her over. Landon wanted to cover up my involvement in the takedown, but Chief Terry was adamant that couldn't happen.

"When she tells her attorney or the others interviewing her that Bay was there, what then?" Chief Terry demanded. "We'll look like we're hiding something."

"We *are* hiding something," Landon grumbled.

"There are medical records too," Chief Terry grumbled. "We have to be as honest as possible. You went to check Hollow Creek. You found them. Markham injured Bay."

Landon scowled. "I hate this!"

I reached over to touch his arm. "I'm sorry. I really am."

"Don't apologize." Landon pulled me in for a hug, careful not to jostle my injured arm. "I could've put my foot down when we got out there. I didn't. That's on me."

"We both have some blame on this one." I pulled back far enough to study his face. "We'll be okay. Even if Childs wants to make a stink about it, there's nothing he can prove. We're good."

Landon didn't look convinced, but he nodded. "What are you going to do?"

"I'm heading to The Overlook." I'd already made up my mind. "I have no idea what Carl Markham is. We can't fight him until we know, so I'm going to do some research."

He brushed my hair back from my face. "You're going to have a cup of tea and snuggle down under a blanket while doing your reading."

"Is that what you want to picture me doing?"

"Yes."

"Then that's what I'll do."

"Good." He gave me a kiss and then released me. "We'll be there in plenty of time for dinner."

**THE INN WAS QUIET. I FIGURED** my mother and aunts were tending to dinner. The Happy Holidays Players were nowhere in sight, but today was the dress rehearsal for the pageant. Tomorrow would be their big performance. I didn't expect to see them until shortly before dinner. That gave me plenty of time to read.

I was barely settled under a blanket, several aches and pains making themselves known, when Thistle and Clove joined me. "What's this?" I asked, as they each grabbed books.

"It's come to our attention that maybe you did what you did today because we haven't spent enough time with you," Clove volunteered, her eyes solemn.

"Yes, we're here to torture you with our presence," Thistle said on an impish grin.

I rolled my eyes. "Even if you guys had been there, I'm not sure it would've mattered. As for not spending as much time together, I guess that's true."

"Well, we're here to fix that," Thistle insisted. "What are we looking for?"

"I don't have a lot to go on. His eyes turned yellow. His hand turned into a claw. He seemed to be able to keep the ghosts at bay. I couldn't even order them to attack. They just floated there like idiots."

"Did he say anything?" Clove asked as she plopped down on the couch next to me.

"He said Natalie boosted her own powers thanks to shards from Hollow Creek. He also made it sound as if she somehow got those shards to him."

"We have a murderer who managed to get caught and needed a power boost," Clove mused. "If he had that much magic at his disposal, why didn't he use it to evade capture?"

"Or, once he was captured, why not use it to escape?" Thistle added. "Why did he need Natalie's help?"

I'd been rolling around possibilities on that front in my head for the better part of the afternoon. "I have no idea," I admitted. "None. I just don't know."

"You said earlier that he mentioned having someone else helping him," Thistle prodded. "Who do you think it could be? A parent?"

"Landon went through all the visitor log records for each escapee. Markham only had a handful of visitors during his time at Antrim Correctional. His lawyer visited twice. A reporter from down south tried to visit once because they were doing a profile on old murders, but Markham wouldn't see her. There was an aunt who visited twice, but her last visit was more than six months ago."

"So whoever it is, Markham has been able to keep in touch under the radar," Thistle deduced. "Is it possible Natalie got him phone privileges that weren't logged?"

"I'd say that's not only possible but probable," I replied. "Natalie is ... a broken woman. I felt sorry for her to an extent. I think she wanted love so desperately she was willing to believe all of Markham's lies. When I told her that he was done with her, she refused to believe it."

"Do you think she'll ever come to the realization that he was lying to her?" Clove asked. She was the romantic in the family.

I held out my hands. "I tried talking to her. She's not ready to believe anything I have to say. It's sad. She can't help us anyway. Whoever Markham is meeting, it's someone he never told Natalie about. That was by design."

"Okay." Thistle bobbed her head. "What are our choices? Could he be a demon?"

That was the notion I'd been cycling back to. "The yellow eyes seem consistent with that. It's the other stuff I can't wrap my head around."

"If he was a demon, why didn't he just break himself out of jail?" Thistle said.

I shrugged. "I don't get that part."

"What if someone bound his powers?" Clove asked. "Like ... what if the ex-wife was a witch and somehow stripped him of his powers, or dampened them, before she turned him in to the police. That might explain why he was so keen to track her down right away."

My initial reaction was to brush off the suggestion. Then I really thought about it. "Huh."

"It's interesting," Thistle agreed. "If the ex-wife knew what her husband was, maybe they hooked up over their shared magic, and then the wife grew tired of his demon ways and decided to screw him over."

"It would explain why he was so desperate to go after her right on the heels of his escape," I agreed. "That's a weak move in my book, but maybe he feared she would ultimately come after him and wanted to take her out before she could screw him over again."

"That would mean she knew what he was up to back then," Clove pointed out.

"I don't think you could marry that guy and not realize he's evil," I replied. "My guess is they were partners, and she turned on him because he got overzealous, or he somehow broke from the plan, and she figured she'd be better off without him. It would also explain why she declined police protection. She figured she could take care of herself better than they could protect her."

"That didn't work out very well," Thistle noted.

"But it does plug a few holes. Natalie didn't want to talk about Ann Markham's death. She kept saying that Ann had screwed Carl, and he'd been framed. She wouldn't look beyond that surface story."

"Probably because she couldn't," Clove offered. "If she admitted the man she'd fallen in love with was a monster, she would have to look inward to determine if she was a monster too."

"Where does that leave us?" I asked. "If we believe Ann somehow dampened Carl's magic, how did he manage to gain control of his powers again?"

"He could've managed it with Ann's death," Thistle suggested. "If she's the one who was behind binding him, maybe she needed to die to truly free him."

And there it was, the answer I was seeking. "Crap!" I pressed the heel of my hand to my forehead. "That's it. That's the answer to the riddle."

"What about the other escapees?" Clove asked. "They were magical. Wasn't Carl fueling them?"

"Only one of those prisoners was magical the first day," I replied. "I felt magic in Steve Mitchell's cell too, but two of the first three prisoners we took down were not magical. What if Natalie provided the magic at the start but didn't have enough to keep it going?"

"Why would that be?" Clove asked.

"Because as soon as Markham was free from the spell his ex-wife used on him, he absorbed all the power in his immediate area to fuel himself," Thistle surmised. "He took Natalie's powers."

"She didn't even try using magic on us at Hollow Creek," I said. "Carl didn't say when she provided him with the shards. She could've easily removed several from Hollow Creek and kept them to use as fuel for later.

"He would've lied as to why they were going to Ann's house, and Natalie has already proven she's willing to believe whatever nonsense he spouts," I continued. "They waited until the state police visited Ann, then they broke into her house. They killed her right away. She wasn't ready. She couldn't know that Markham had a vehicle waiting for him when he escaped, so she thought she had time."

"And as soon as Ann was dead, Carl started recharging," Thistle said. "It makes sense."

"What makes sense?" Landon asked as he entered the library. He didn't bother greeting my cousins, instead making his way directly to me and cupping my chin to look into my eyes. "How are you?"

"I'm fine," I assured him, wrapping my hands around his wrists. "Stop worrying about me."

"That's not an option now that we know this guy can beat us at will," Landon muttered. He pressed a kiss to my forehead and flopped onto the couch next to me.

"How did Childs take it?" I asked.

"He was understandably curious," Landon replied. "Representatives from the state correctional board were present, so he didn't have a lot of time for us. The other prisoners have been caught. All of them ... except one. They showed up in various downtowns—Bellaire, Shadow Hills, and Hawthorne Hollow—and turned themselves in."

"Well, that can't be a coincidence," I said.

Landon agreed. "Carl is relieving the pressure. He's the last inmate out there. The search will diminish now."

"We've figured out a few things too." I caught him up.

"All of that fits," he said. "Natalie was a pawn. Someone else is involved, and given who Carl is, I'm betting he covered his tracks. There won't be a mention in his records of this third party."

"He said that by the end of the day tomorrow, he'd be gone," I pointed out. "We have less than twenty-four hours to figure this out. If we don't, Carl will be long gone."

"Okay." Landon rolled his neck. "How do we kill a demon?"

"We have to bring in Aunt Tillie," I replied. "We need four of us to kill a demon." I glanced at Clove. "You don't have to if you don't want to. I can get my mom to help."

"No." Clove was adamant when she shook her head. "It's time I get back in the game. I appreciate that you guys gave me a break after Calvin, but the other day, something occurred to me.

"I'm his mother," she continued. "It's my job to keep him safe. I can't do that hiding who we are. Evil is going to come for us. It always does. It's time to be strong and start handling my fair share of the witchy duties around here. You've been doing the heavy lifting, Bay. We need to start shouldering our fair share of the burden."

"She's right," Thistle said when I flicked my eyes to her. "Your powers have been growing exponentially. That made it easy for us to sit back and allow you to do all the work. Scout and Stormy spending more time here made it easy for us to take a breath.

"I'm not saying we didn't need to take a breath, because we did, but Clove is right," she continued. "We all want to expand our families at some point. That means our magic must be shored up because the evil won't stop coming. Not ever."

"I don't want to force you guys into something you don't want to do," I hedged.

"You're not," Thistle insisted. "The truth is, it was easier to do this stuff when we were all living under the same roof. We've grown complacent because it's no longer easy."

Landon lifted his head. "If you think we're all moving in together like the freaking Brady Bunch, you're sadly mistaken."

Thistle chuckled. "Of course not. We all need our privacy. Bay was hurt twice this week because we've been keeping separate from one another."

"Part of that was Calvin," Clove interjected. "After he was born, I needed time to bond with him. And Thistle was just being Thistle. She's always been disagreeable. That's okay, but it's time we come back together."

"You guys couldn't have stopped what happened in the pot field," I argued. "We were just walking by. You wouldn't have been with us regardless."

"No, but we might have been at the inn if we stopped in for more meals," Thistle argued. "We've been slacking there too. We don't need to be here for every meal—I would kill someone if I was forced to do that—but it doesn't hurt to show up for a breakfast or dinner here or there. If we'd been at the inn, you could've called us for backup. Landon could've gotten us to the pot field in less than three minutes. He wouldn't have had to go through what he went through if help had been close."

"Hold up." Landon stirred. "Nothing would've stopped me from going into that field with Bay in danger. I knew what was going to happen. The pot field scenario was going to play out that way regardless."

"What about what happened at Hollow Creek today?" Thistle challenged.

"That's a different story." Landon slid his eyes to me. "I don't want to agree with your mother, Bay—especially on this—but she had a point earlier. Your ego is something to behold these days. I don't want you to be afraid, but a little common sense might go a long way."

I was sheepish. "I get it. Things have been going my way for a bit, and I let it puff me up. Markham beating us might've been a good thing. It brought me back down to earth. The problem is that even if you guys had been with us, we wouldn't have been ready for a demon. We need Aunt Tillie for that."

"Which means you have to make nice with her," Clove said. "My mother said you've been mean to her ever since Landon's little incident."

"Let's stop talking about my incident," Landon growled.

I ignored him. "I haven't been ignoring her. I just haven't wanted to see her."

"You don't have a choice," Thistle said. "We need her power."

"And she won't let you forget it," Clove said. "She's going to make you beg."

Now it was my turn to growl, which elicited a smirk from Landon.

"It's going to take all of us ... and maybe Stormy and Scout on top of that," Thistle said. "We're not used to facing demons. Something tells me Scout is."

"I think she's taken out her fair share," I admitted on a sigh. "We probably do have to tap her experience." I didn't like admitting it. Scout had her own problems to deal with. "Maybe we'll be strong enough to do it without her. I'll talk to Aunt Tillie. With Evan on our side to do the physical heavy lifting, our magic might be able to contain the demon."

"And then what?" Landon asked. "If you kill him, we have to hide the body. The public will assume he's always out there if we can't prove his death or capture."

"I don't see a way around that right now."

Landon didn't look happy, but he nodded. "We'll take it one step at a time."

"Yes, and Aunt Tillie is the first step." I wanted to find a hole and crawl into it.

"That's all you," Thistle offered. "I'm not even on her list right now."

"Me either," Clove said. Her smile was bright as she patted my shoulder. "Have fun."

# Twenty-Six

Aunt Tillie was in her easy chair in the kitchen. The fact that I would need to have this conversation with her in front of my mother and aunts was beyond disturbing. I steeled myself for her reaction and positioned myself in front of her.

"We think we have a demon," I announced.

Aunt Tillie narrowed one eye, screwing her face up into a weird wink, and sipped from the mug clutched in her hands. There was no way it was straight tea. "And this is my problem why?"

"Aunt Tillie." Mom's tone was low and full of warning. "We talked about this."

Aunt Tillie made a face. "And I told you this was my show. Stop being so bossy."

"You stop being such a pain," Mom shot back. "Bay has a right to be angry with you."

"Is this about that stupid ward again?" Aunt Tillie raised her nose in defiance. "He knew what would happen if he crossed those wards."

"He did it to save me," I pointed out. "I don't want to talk about those wards again." That was mostly true. She was never going to change, and I didn't expect her to. And, truth be told, part of me didn't want her to. We would need her stubborn ways to finish off the demon. "We need your help with the demon."

I caught them all up, stressing that the idea we were working with was just that. We didn't have proof. Aunt Tillie was already shaking her head.

"I don't see how he could be anything but a demon," she said. "It makes sense. All of it."

"We still don't know who the outsider helping him is," I pointed out. "It could be another demon. Either way, he has a plan to get out of here sometime tomorrow after dark."

"Then we'll have to stop him," Aunt Tillie replied easily. "If we're going to set a demon trap, we have to pick a spot away from people ... and we have to be smart about it."

I nodded stiffly. "Thank you." I turned to leave, but the sound of her clearing her throat stopped me.

"Maybe—I'm just talking *maybe* here—I should've considered your request when you made it all those months ago," she hedged.

Slowly, I turned back to face her. This felt like it was about to turn into an apology, something unheard of in this house. Because I didn't want to make the wrong assumption, I waited.

"I believe you have more to say," Mom told her pointedly.

The sigh that escaped Aunt Tillie was long and drawn out. "It never occurred to me that Landon would need to get into the field for any reason other than annoying me," she said.

"Is this you saying you're sorry?" I demanded. Per usual, my mouth got ahead of my brain.

"No!" Aunt Tillie looked scandalized. "I'm just saying that the problem has been handled."

I glanced at Mom.

"There are now exceptions for Landon and Terry in the field," Mom volunteered. "They can come and go as they please. So can we." Her smile was feral now. "Given the fact that Aunt Tillie has managed to create an area that will grow anything in the dead of winter—and forgot to tell us the good news because of her age—we're going to have some very good eats despite the snow this year."

I pressed my lips together to keep from laughing at Aunt Tillie's morose face.

"Of course, we'll have to cut back some of Aunt Tillie's plants to make room," Mom continued. "We'll have time when the Happy Holidays Players leave the day after tomorrow."

I worked my jaw as I turned back to Aunt Tillie. Obviously, this wasn't her day. "Thank you for making the exception for Landon and Chief Terry," I said. "I know that's not what you want, but it's not as if they're going to arrest you."

"I'm making exceptions for 'The Man,'" Aunt Tillie complained. "My entire life's mission is being flushed down the toilet."

"Well ... maybe you're starting on a new mission," I suggested.

"My old mission was fine."

"I still appreciate it." I leaned in and hugged her, earning a horrified glare. "You're a good aunt. You could do it professionally. As payback, I believe Thistle, Clove, and I are willing to help you with your yearly quest to ruin Mrs. Little's Christmas."

Aunt Tillie perked up marginally. "Now we're talking."

"We have to get rid of that demon first," I warned. "He's our priority. We don't have much time."

"I'll do some reading and thinking," Aunt Tillie promised. "If I get him, I win the competition."

I folded my arms across my chest. "How do you figure? I've caught way more than you."

"Yes, but he's the big dog. He counts as ten."

I thought about arguing, but there was no point. "Fine. If you help us take him down, you win."

Aunt Tillie's smile was wide enough to swallow the bottom half of her face. "Tomorrow is going to be a good day."

I hoped she was right.

I left them to their dinner preparations and headed into the dining room. Landon was in his usual spot, nursing a glass of wine. Clove and Thistle were at the table too, but the room was overrun with Happy Holidays Players.

"How were your rehearsals?" I asked.

"They went as well as can be expected," Mary replied. She had a huge glass of wine in front of her, telling me things might not have gone as well as she'd hoped. "The people in this town are ... interesting."

I smirked as I moved to the wine stand and poured myself a glass. "Running into trouble?"

"They're just ... very set in their ways. They have a vision of how they see things going, and if you disagree with that vision, they're unhappy about it."

"Well, I'm sure it will be a lovely pageant."

"I'm sure it will too." Her smile was tight. "Let's talk about something else. I heard they caught all the escaped prisoners. That must be a load off your mind."

My arm, which should've been numb thanks to Aunt Tillie's cream, twinged. "All but one. Carl Markham is still out there."

"I didn't realize there was still one on the loose. I was feeling relieved."

"I wouldn't worry much," Landon offered. "I very much doubt he'll interrupt your pageant."

"But one of them was caught here."

"The odds of another one showing up here are pretty slim."

"Still, it can happen." Her eyes were intense when they landed on me. "You've been involved in several of the captures. At least that's the gossip I heard."

"Really?" I worked overtime to keep my expression neutral. "Who has been spreading gossip about me? Other than my family."

"Margaret Little."

My stomach constricted. I could just imagine what sort of gossip Mrs. Little was spreading. "Well, you said it yourself, the people in this town are weird. I'd take what Mrs. Little says with a grain of salt."

"I take it with a stiff shot of tequila," Aunt Tillie volunteered as she swung through the door. Her chair, thankfully, was empty, and she groaned as she sat. "Did you tell him the good news?" she asked, inclining her head toward Landon.

He sat straighter. "What good news?"

"Aunt Tillie has decided to be gracious and open her new hydroponics station to you and Chief Terry." I was careful when replying.

"She's also opened it up to Mom and the aunts so they can utilize it all winter."

Aunt Tillie scowled. "Stop reminding me of that."

Landon smirked. "Well, that's very gracious of you."

"You have a hydroponics station here?" Lenny asked. "Can I see it?"

Aunt Tillie's expression was one for the record books. "No, and don't ask again unless you want me to turn your limp noodle into a stale hose."

I glanced at Mary, who looked more amused than anything else. "We're definitely eccentric in this town," I said. "I bet you're glad you came."

She shrugged. "Every town has a bit of eccentricity. You get used to it."

"Well, it will be over soon."

"Yes, and I can't wait."

**LANDON AND I WERE BOTH STUFFED** enough after dinner that we decided to walk back to the guesthouse. Landon risked getting close to the pot field to test if Aunt Tillie had really opened it up to him. He was wide-eyed and grinning when we moved past the wards together.

"You know, this field could be a godsend during winter," he noted.

"Do you want to spend all of January coming out here to get high? If so, I have to say I didn't see that coming."

He laughed as he slung his arm around my shoulders. "That's not what I had in mind, but we could bring a blanket out here. It's warm. We can see the sky. We could have winter picnics under the stars. Bring some wine. See where things go." His eyes twinkled.

"We could do that. I'll be curious how things go once Mom gets her hands on the space, but I can ask her to leave a spot open for us."

"It will be our own winter hideaway."

"I'd be up for that." I wrapped my arms around his waist and hugged. "Are you okay? After everything that happened today, it would be all right if you weren't."

"I'm good." He looked into my eyes, and a million emotions flashed in the space of an instant. "I was upset earlier—at myself more than you—but I get it now. We both have to get ourselves under control."

"We do. I have to stop thinking I'm untouchable. I *can* break."

"You can."

"And you have to stop believing that you're to blame whenever something goes wrong. We couldn't have known how that would play out today."

"I'm still frustrated. If I hadn't lost my gun..."

"If you hadn't lost your gun, we don't know that we would be standing here. The gun might not have done anything to him now that he's at full power."

"I just keep thinking that things might've ended differently. We might've been able to take both of them into custody."

"And then what?"

"It would be over."

"Carl Markham has a lot of powers to call upon. There's nothing to stop him from escaping again," I said. "Odds are we won't be taking him in."

He was quiet for a long time. Then he pressed a kiss to the top of my head. "Come on. Let's go home. I want to take a look at that arm, and I might want to dote on you a bit longer."

I laughed, as I was sure he'd intended. "I've had worse offers."

"And after that, I'm going to romance the crap out of you."

"Now we're talking."

**I SLEPT HARD THOUGH MY DREAMS** were jumbled. Carl Markham, in all his yellow-eyed glory, chased me through the trees near the bluff. I was breathless when I woke, and the first thing I saw was Landon's concerned gaze.

"Bad dream?" he asked as he stroked my hair.

"Pretty much what you'd expect," I replied. "Carl was chasing me."

"Were the others around?"

"No. Just me."

"That's how you know it was just a dream. This is a group effort going forward."

"Yeah." I managed a smile. "How did you sleep?"

"I slept hard. I had a bad dream too." He tugged me practically on top of him. "I couldn't find you in my dream. I lost you."

"It doesn't take a psychologist to figure out what your subconscious is trying to tell you." I ran my hand over his chest. "We'll make sure neither dream comes true."

"Any idea how we do that?"

"No, but I bet Aunt Tillie will have an idea. As for the where, we should try to draw him here. To the bluff."

"You already tried that."

"Yes, but at the time, I thought I was dealing with an enchantress. I had no idea I was dealing with a demon. Plus, we'll have help this time. When we set the trap, there will be four of us. Maybe we'll even tap Mom and the aunts for added help."

"You think that will be enough?"

"Don't you?"

"You could call in Scout." Landon looked hopeful. "She could probably kill this thing without breaking a sweat."

"She could, and I haven't ruled it out. But Scout has her hands full. Her parents are back. A member of her group turned out to be evil. Her emotions are running high. I don't want to bring her in unless I have no other choice."

Landon grumbled. "I just want to make sure that we've covered all our bases."

"Our big problem is this silent partner of his. It could be a magical being. It could be a human. We just don't know."

"If you draw in Markham, what happens to the partner?" Landon asked. "Can you set a trap that draws both?"

"Let's see what Aunt Tillie has come up with during breakfast and go from there. I think it's just family this morning, which is good. The Happy Holidays players are probably already downtown. It's a big day for them."

"I'm looking forward to them leaving," Landon admitted. "They bug me."

"You just don't like Ava."

"I swear she has eight hands."

I laughed. "It's not her fault that you're so hot she can't keep her hands off you." Something occurred to me. "Wait ... when did she touch you?"

"When didn't she? She keeps showing up when I'm at the wine bar or leaving the bathroom. She always wants to touch my arm or chest. It's like 'buy a clue, lady. I'm married.'"

"And to the best witch in the world."

"You've got that right." He rested his cheek against my forehead. "I want this finished today, Bay. I don't want it hanging over our heads any longer. I want it done."

"We'll finish it today," I promised. We had no choice really. "Markham plans to flee tonight. Before the sun sets, we need to figure out what his plan is and identify his partner. We have to talk to Aunt Tillie. She's better at this stuff than I am."

"Has she fought a demon before?"

"If you believe her, she has."

"Do you believe her?"

That was a question for the ages. Aunt Tillie liked to brag, and sometimes that bragging bordered on lying. Much like Twila and her assertion she'd been up for a role in *Titanic*, Aunt Tillie had been known to spin a yarn. "She wouldn't lie this time. She knows it's too important. She'll know what to do."

Landon wrapped me tightly in his arms and held so tight he almost constricted my breathing. "I want five more minutes of this, and then we'll hit the shower. We're both having big breakfasts for a big day."

"Sounds like a plan."

# Twenty-Seven

The walk to the inn was fun. Landon insisted on checking the wards at the pot field yet again. He was thrilled when he felt fine, even pulling me into a little dance. We were laughing when we let ourselves in through the family living quarters. Things were quiet in the living room.

Aunt Tillie wasn't on the couch watching the morning news. Peg wasn't running around demanding breakfast scraps.

It was quiet.

Things only got more confusing when we went into the kitchen. My mother and aunts, who were a fixture in the kitchen this time of day, weren't bustling behind the stove. Nothing was cooking. The familiar scents of home weren't present. The kitchen was simply devoid of life.

"No bacon?" Landon looked horrified.

I glanced around and then pushed through the swinging door that led to the dining room. The coffee carafe that was usually warming on the small table in the corner was empty. Nobody was at the table. The lights hadn't even been turned on. It was like waking up in a post-apocalyptic world.

"Bay, I don't like this," Landon complained from behind me.

When I glanced in his direction, I saw he'd drawn his gun. "What are you doing?" I hissed.

"Your mother and aunts are missing."

"We don't know that." Even as I said it, I wasn't certain. Where would they go? "Call Chief Terry."

"You call Chief Terry," he shot back. "I'm waiting for the monster to jump out of the corner."

I made a face but pulled out my phone. Chief Terry answered on the third ring "Where is Mom?" I demanded.

Chief Terry sounded harried. "What do you mean? It's eight o'clock. She cooks breakfast at eight o'clock."

"She isn't here. None of them are. Nothing is cooking. I think Landon might melt down over the lack of bacon."

"It's the end of the world," Landon intoned melodramatically.

"They were in the living room getting ready to make breakfast when I left," Chief Terry replied. "I had to come into town early. Margaret Little called to say that hoodlums were hanging out behind her store. I figured kids were screwing around back there—or Tillie—but nobody was there when I arrived."

I brushed past Landon, heading to the lobby. It was empty like the rest of the main floor. Nobody was in the living room or the bathrooms. I headed upstairs.

"This isn't right," I said to Chief Terry. "They're gone. We came in through the back door and they're just ... gone."

Chief Terry was all business when he responded. "What about the field? Maybe they couldn't wait the extra day to start planting."

"We stopped at the field on our way here," I argued. I poked my head into the first guest room. The door was open, the room empty. "Crap," I muttered.

"What?" Chief Terry demanded.

"I think the Happy Holidays Players are gone." I moved to the next room. It was cleaned out as well. "Their rooms are empty."

"I thought they were staying one more night."

"They were supposed to." I went from room to room. They were all empty. "The big pageant is today."

"It is." I heard Chief Terry scrambling. "Hold on."

I waited for almost two minutes, heading back downstairs to track down Landon. He was in the lobby, gazing out the window. When he looked at me, I saw the worry in his eyes.

"Your mother's Jeep is still in the lot. So are Marnie and Twila's vehicles. The Happy Holidays Players bus is gone, as are the two vehicles they were using."

A feeling of dread invaded my stomach. "What happened?"

Chief Terry was breathless when he spoke into the phone again. "Bay, all the people who got roles in the pageant are in the town square, but there are no Happy Holidays Players. They're not due for another hour, though, so nobody is panicking."

"I don't think they're showing up," I said. "I think ... I think..." What exactly did I think? I flicked my eyes to Landon, and something akin to panic licked my heart.

"It's okay," Landon assured me as he slid his left arm behind my back. "We'll find them."

I didn't think my mind was going to be able to formulate a plan, but then I snapped back to reality. "Chief Terry, I need you to check on Thistle," I said. "She's downtown. I'll call Clove and make sure she and the baby are safe."

"Okay." Chief Terry refused to let fear invade his voice. He was holding it together, and likely for my benefit. "Then what?"

"Then I'll call Evan. He can help us track them. If they were taken from here, we're probably going to need him and a good locator spell."

"Let's track down Clove and Thistle first," Chief Terry said. "I'll send Thistle to the inn. You get Clove out there."

"Okay. I..." I didn't know what to say. "You'll come too?"

"I'll be there with Thistle as soon as possible."

**CLOVE WAS CONFUSED WHEN I CALLED.** She couldn't wrap her head around what I was telling her, but she promised to be at the inn shortly. She opted to leave Calvin with her husband Sam, and I had to grin at the set of her shoulders and the obstinate tilt of her chin when she stormed through the door. "I guess you're ready and raring to go."

"I'm ready to find our family. I don't understand how this happened."

She wasn't the only one.

Chief Terry arrived with Thistle a few minutes later. Thistle looked furious. "Who the hell messes with our family?"

"It had to be the Happy Holidays Players," I replied. "It's the only thing that makes sense."

"Mary has been quite interested in the escapees," Landon noted. He was sitting at the dining room table, studying his phone. "I'm running her first. I'll have to run the others too. I have trouble believing Mary managed to kidnap everybody on her own. It had to be a group thing."

"I wonder why." Chief Terry stroked his chin and shook his head. "I left right around seven o'clock. I was going to come back for breakfast but got distracted replying to a few emails. They're replacing Childs today."

Part of me felt bad for the warden. The other part couldn't be fussed with caring. We all had problems. "Could they have known you would be out of the inn so early?"

"I don't think so." Chief Terry held out his hands. "I didn't exit through the inn. I didn't want to see anybody. I was tired and cranky about having to get up early because of Margaret."

"So you left through the back door," I said. "Where was everybody when you left?"

"Winnie, Marnie, and Twila were getting ready to head to the kitchen. I'm not sure where Tillie was."

I stilled. "She wasn't in the living room?"

Chief Terry shook his head. "No, and her bedroom door was open. I assumed she was out doing Tillie stuff."

I left them in the dining room and headed through the kitchen, not stopping until I was through the back door of the family living quarters and outside. Everybody followed.

"What are you doing?" Landon demanded as he struggled to keep up and type on his phone at the same time.

"Peg is gone," I reminded him.

"Yes, and she'd better be okay. If someone hurts that pig, I'm going to start shooting."

"Why would they take Peg?" I demanded as I stalked across the grounds to Aunt Tillie's greenhouse. "It's not as if she's an attack dog. She wasn't going to put up a fight to save Aunt Tillie. And how did they overpower Aunt Tillie?"

"She has a point," Chief Terry noted. He'd drawn his service weapon, which sent a chill through my body.

"They couldn't get the drop on everybody," I insisted. "There's no way Aunt Tillie would go down without a fight. Everything looks normal." I swung into the greenhouse and immediately made a face when a very obvious scent hit me like a slap across the face.

Aunt Tillie, dressed in fatigues and wearing her combat helmet, had her still churning. She stood at one of the workbenches, bottles spread in front of her, intent on her work. Peg ran between the workbench aisles making her Peg noises.

*Snort. Snort.*

"My girl!" Landon crooned when he saw her. He holstered his gun and dropped to his knees. "There's my beautiful girl."

Aunt Tillie had the gall to glare at me when she registered our presence. "This is a no tattletale zone," she snapped. "I see five tattletales, so you have to go."

Was she kidding me? "How long have you been out here?" I demanded.

"Why do you care." Aunt Tillie drew up her frame and squared her shoulders. "This is my greenhouse. I do what I want here."

"Nobody cares about the illegal hooch," Chief Terry barked. "At least, I don't care about it right now. Where are Marnie, Twila, and Winnie?"

For the first time I could remember, Aunt Tillie looked confused. "I don't understand the question," she said. "They're making breakfast. They said they would come out and get me when it was time to eat. Now that you mention it, it's been longer than it would normally be."

"That's because they're not there," Chief Terry fired back. "They're missing ... as are the Happy Holidays Players."

Aunt Tillie shook her head. "It's breakfast time. They're in the kitchen. They're always in the kitchen."

"Well, they're not." I was grim. Things were still bad, but nowhere near as bad as they could've been. "You had no idea the inn was empty, did you?"

"No." Aunt Tillie moved to the door to look up at the inn. "They're really gone?"

"Yes, and we thought you were too," I replied. "You're still here, which is good, but we have a problem."

"Obviously."

"I've sent out a be on the lookout," Chief Terry volunteered. "They're watching for the bus everywhere in the state."

"Would they really try to flee in that bus?" Thistle asked. "I mean ... that's not incognito."

She was right. "It's also not fast," I said. "That bus is huge."

"None of this makes sense," Chief Terry said. "The only good news is that they can't have gotten very far. At most, whatever happened at the inn went down an hour and a half ago."

"And I would've sensed if magic was involved," Aunt Tillie added. "Just because I'm focused on other stuff, that doesn't mean I wouldn't have sensed a magical assault on my own property."

"Then where are they?" I asked. "Where would they go?"

"I can't answer that," Landon responded. "What I can tell you is that had we run the Happy Holidays Players sooner we might've been able to get ahead of this." He was perplexed when he lowered his phone. "We have a problem."

"What was your first clue?" Thistle drawled. "The disappearance of our mothers wasn't enough to have you leaning that way?"

Landon shot her a quelling look. "Nobody needs your mouth, Thistle."

"I've been telling her that since she was born," Aunt Tillie said. "What did you find?" For a change, she wasn't looking rowdy or ready for a fight. Today she was put together and calm. I only felt all the more frightened because of it. Aunt Tillie wasn't a serious person. If she was serious now, we were about to embark on a righteous fight.

"Well, for starters, Mary Stratton is Carl Markham's high school girlfriend," Landon volunteered.

My mouth dropped open. "You have got to be kidding me."

"I wish I were." Landon pressed the heel of his hand to his forehead.

It was one of his go-to moves when he was feeling stressed. "She's mentioned in Markham's file. She visited him when he was first arrested down in Grand Rapids. That's where Markham and Ann lived before he was locked up."

Something occurred to me. "Did Ann move up here to get away from him?"

"There's nothing in the file that indicates that," Landon replied. "I checked when we learned she was dead. It's probable. I'm not sure how he ended up in Antrim given his violent record, but somehow, he was transferred up here despite all the safeguards that were supposed to be in place."

"Which was close to where Ann was living," I said. "I don't think it's a coincidence. Somehow, someone managed to pull some strings for him."

Landon went back to reading his phone. "Mary visited him often when he was incarcerated down south. She never visited here."

"That we know of," I countered. "Natalie could've doctored the visitation records."

"That's true." Landon's expression was flat. "I'm not sure how the rest of these Happy Holidays Players fit into the tale, but they have to be willing participants. There's no other explanation."

"Do we think Mary is a demon too?" Chief Terry asked. "Could that be the source of their bond?"

I didn't want to think about my mother and aunts being taken out by a demon, but I couldn't ignore the possibility. "I want to believe we would've sensed that," I said. "If we ate multiple meals with a demon, shouldn't we have known?"

"Not if she glamoured herself," Aunt Tillie replied. "She would've known what we were before coming here. I think the choice of lodging was purposeful. She wanted to keep an eye on us."

"Well, great. Do we assume we have two demons?"

"At least," Evan announced as he swept into the guesthouse. He looked a little windblown but otherwise unbothered.

"Thanks for returning my text," I said pointedly.

"I was on my way and turned my phone off so nobody would hear it." Evan, eternally calm, wasn't about to start panicking now. "I wanted to give the area a good sweep before catching up with you guys. It's a good thing I did. I know where your mothers are."

I practically threw myself at him. "Where?"

"They're on the bluff."

"The bluff?" That made no sense. "Why would...?" I trailed off and turned my gaze to Aunt Tillie.

"They're trying to tap into our magic," Aunt Tillie surmised. "They probably think your mothers can grant them access. They don't understand that your mothers don't have the power to do that."

"Who does?" Landon demanded.

"That would be me." Aunt Tillie sent him a smug smile. "This land is still mine. It reacts to me. It follows my orders. Winnie, Marnie, and Twila have always been dabblers. Even if the land was fully theirs, they wouldn't have the power to relinquish control to demons."

"Who has the power after you?" Chief Terry asked.

Her eyes moved to me. "There's going to be a specific power when I'm gone. You're not the boss yet, Bay. This is still my show."

"You said there's more than one demon," I prodded Evan. "How many?"

"I'd say all of them." Evan flashed a smile. "The good news is I think there are only two who are powerful."

"Mary and Carl," I said.

He nodded. "They're out there trying to force your mothers to tap into the power of the land. Your mothers are putting up a fight."

"What about the bus?" Landon asked. "Where is that?"

"That's on Perkins Drive. I saw it when I was coming in through the woods. That's why I entered where I did."

"So they only have about a five-minute run to get to safety if they decide to scatter," I said.

"Yes, but they're not going anywhere. I took care of that." Evan pulled a clump of cables from his pocket. "They're dead in the water. None of the three vehicles are going anywhere."

I smirked. "I still don't know how to beat a demon," I admitted. "What are we going to do? We can't wait for Scout to get here. We don't have time. They could hurt our mothers."

"They're not going to hurt your mothers." Evan was firm. "You don't need Scout either." Slowly, he tracked his gaze to Aunt Tillie. "It's time you break out that secret weapon."

I was about to ask the obvious question when realization struck me. "The grenade!"

Evan nodded. "You've been looking for a reason to use it, Tillie. I think we've found it."

"What does it do?" I asked Aunt Tillie, who was suddenly fidgeting like a cat with fleas.

"There's no choice," Evan said when Aunt Tillie didn't respond to my question. "We need a big dose of magic to incapacitate them."

"Will it work?" Landon asked Aunt Tillie.

"It will work," she said, "but I was hoping to use it on Margaret."

"This is more important," I pressed.

"Yes, well, your mother is going to owe me." She straightened. "I say we get my grenade and get it done. I can't remember the last time breakfast was this late."

I managed a smile, even though my insides were clenching. "Yes, let's get this done. Sooner is definitely better than later."

# Twenty-Eight

There was no playing it coy making our stand. We knew the land better than anyone. Evan was the only one who could camouflage his approach. He went to the trees, leaving the rest of us to march to the bluff in solidarity.

Mary had some of her followers watching for us, because they were alert and ready when we crested the top of the bluff.

The Happy Holidays players were spread out, Carl and Mary positioned together at the center of the group. My mother and aunts were on their knees in the middle of the circle. They looked unharmed—mostly—and there was a fierce determination to the set of Mom's jaw. She met my gaze as I closed the distance.

"Well, hello." Mary beamed at us as she wiggled her hips. "I was hoping you'd join us."

"You were not," I shot back. "That's the reason you attacked when you did. You figured taking my mother and aunts would be easiest. You planned to come here, tap the magical reserve to bolster yourselves, and get back out."

Mary's smile dimmed. "Yes, but once we realized that wasn't going to work, the plan changed. You fell right into our hands."

"I'm sure." I shook my head. "I don't know how you think this is going to go, but it's best you surrender now."

Carl laughed. "Is that how you see things going? The only reason you're alive is because I let you live. What makes you think this will go differently?"

"We didn't know what we were dealing with at Hollow Creek yesterday," I replied simply. "We were under the impression that Natalie was the power. We'd yet to put together that you were a demon. It never occurred to us that your powers had been clipped thanks to Ann. Things make more sense now."

Carl's eyes narrowed. "What is it that you think you know?"

I wanted to stretch things out to give Evan time to get in position. That meant conversing with a demon I was ready to smite. With that in mind, I flashed a patient smile and launched into it.

"Well, we've figured out that Ann was a witch, and you're a demon. You were likely killing all over Grand Rapids before you went after the neighbor. She was either exasperated by that time or plotting against you. She had the spell ready and bound your powers right after you did the deed. Then she turned you in."

Carl's scowl was pronounced. "She turned on me. I didn't see it coming. I thought she was weak. She proved me wrong."

"You showed her, though, didn't you?" I challenged, hating his smug smile. "You managed to wrangle a transfer up here once you found out where she was living. I bet you were behind that." I lobbed a dark glare in Mary's direction. "And then you started putting things together.

"It took me a while before all the pieces fit into place," I continued. "Natalie had magic. Not much, but enough for what you had planned. You convinced her that you were innocent, offered her the love she never got anywhere else, and then carefully laid out your plan.

"The magic at Hollow Creek helped quite a bit. It bolstered Natalie and allowed her to tuck some of the fragments away for when you were free. You needed to kill Ann for your plan to work, and I guess you spun a pretty story for Natalie about why you had to go to Ann's house before hunkering down in your hiding spot."

Carl's chuckle was bone chilling. "I guess you have figured out quite a bit of it. I didn't want to hide in a cave at all. That was Natalie's idea. She thought we could live on love the entire winter. What an idiot."

It took effort not to cringe on Natalie's behalf. I still felt sorry for her. "You didn't really care," I prodded. "You knew it would only be for a few nights. Your getaway driver was already in town. That was a stroke of genius. The acting troupe's arrival was scheduled six months ago. Why would they ever be suspects?"

"The plan was solid," Carl agreed. "That is until you decided to insert yourself into everything."

"We knew you would," Mary interjected. "It's not as if we didn't know your reputation. You've been involved in some pretty high-profile cases."

"That's why you made sure to put half your team at my mother's inn and the other half at my father's inn," I said. "You wanted to make sure you had us covered from every angle." I glanced around. There were no faces I didn't recognize. "Where are the other members of your team? The ones who were staying at the Dragonfly."

"They've left already," Mary replied. "We wanted to go in two groups. We knew there wouldn't really be a pageant. We're essentially retiring. It's been a nice run, but we have bigger and better things going for us now."

"Oh, yeah?" I didn't like her breezy tone. She'd been irritating me for days, but this was beyond that. "I'm guessing you created the troupe to serve as cover. Who is going to suspect a bunch of Christmas carolers as demons?"

She smirked. "It *was* pretty ingenious."

"It would've been smarter to actually finish the job here," I pointed out. "Now everybody is going to be looking for you."

"Who is everybody?" Carl challenged. "Your entire team is here."

"Not our entire team," I replied. "Before heading here, we sent word to Hawthorne Hollow. They know what's what over there. Some are even on their way here, even though this will be done before they arrive. The information has already been passed up the line."

"They know what you are," Thistle intoned darkly.

Carl made a "so what" hand gesture. "I'm not afraid of them. I'm back to full power."

"Yes, because of the fragments from Hollow Creek."

"Power is power."

Now it was my turn to smirk. "There's just one problem."

"What's that?"

"Those fragments came from us." I gestured to Aunt Tillie, Clove, Thistle, and myself in turn. "We created them. We also eradicated them."

Carl blinked several times, as if absorbing the information. He didn't immediately respond. Mary did, however, and it was obvious she didn't understand.

"What's done is done," she snapped. "It doesn't matter how he bolstered his powers, just that he did."

"If you say so." I knew Carl was figuring it out. "Just out of curiosity, does this all stem from a high school relationship? Were you really willing to give up everything because you loved him when you were seventeen? That seems a bit ... well, I think the word I'm looking for is pathetic."

Mary's rage flashed hot, and her eyes turned yellow in an instant. *Ah, there it is.* That was the demon she managed to dampen enough that we didn't pick up on what she was despite being in her presence for days.

"You don't even know what you're talking about," Mary fired back.

"Carl knows what I'm talking about," I countered on a smug smile.

"I have no idea what she's getting at, Mary," he growled. "Don't listen to her. You know you're my girl."

I choked on a laugh. "Oh, Mary, you're such a simpleton. He's going to do to you what he did to Natalie. He's going to absorb your powers before he goes. He understands that he's about to lose that power boost he was so happy with until I popped his little bubble, and you're too enticing of a target to ignore.

"You can't see it," I continued. "You're lost in his thrall. I don't know if that's part of the magic he possesses, but that's really none of my business."

"Yet you're still here," Carl growled. "Why?"

"You have my mother. Did you really think you could take members of our family and we'd do nothing?" I was incredulous. "All that research you conducted, did anything you uncovered lead you to believe we wouldn't come for them?"

Neither Mary nor Carl responded. The looks the former was shooting the latter were telling, however.

"What do you want to do, guys?" I demanded. Evan had to be in place by now. He was above us, ready to swoop down and free my mother and aunts.

"We want the power," Carl replied. "I feel it flowing beneath us. Your mothers were supposed to release the power to us. We were supposed to be gone before you knew they were missing."

"And were they supposed to be dead?" I demanded.

"Of course not," Mary said at the same time Carl uttered, "Does it matter now?"

Mary sent Carl a sharp look. "You said we were going to let them go as soon as we'd drained the property."

"And leave them to tell the cops?" Carl challenged.

Mary looked momentarily bewildered. "They already know it was us. They were always going to know. You said it didn't matter." The veil was finally being lifted from Mary's eyes, and it was a sight to behold.

"Have you figured it out yet, Mary?" I prodded. "Do you see it? He was going to leave you guys holding the bag when he made his escape. He never shared that loving feeling that you thought would last a lifetime. You were just a means to an end."

Mary took an extended step from Carl. She might've been a moron, but she was finally seeing the light.

"I'm going to give you a choice, Mary," I said in a low voice. "You can take the members of your troupe, go back downtown, and put on your pageant. You were involved in all of this, but I don't think you would've made some of the choices you have if you were seeing clearly."

"What's her other choice?" Carl sneered.

"We'll kill you all."

Mary's shoulders jerked. "How do you think you're going to manage that?" she asked in a soft voice. "We're more powerful than you."

"Are you?"

"You can't throw your ghosts at us, Bay," Carl snapped. "We've neutralized that threat."

"You shouldn't have let me know that before the final fight," I replied. "They're not even part of the plan."

"You don't have a plan," Carl shot back. "You didn't even know what enemy you were fighting until just now. You're blowing smoke at Mary, and she knows it." He turned to her. "You're the queen of my heart, Mary. Don't let her make you doubt me."

I recognized the moment we'd lost Mary to Carl. Much like Natalie, she couldn't force herself to see the truth. She needed to believe Carl loved her. If that illusion disappeared, she would have nothing left.

"You're going to regret this, Mary," I whispered.

Her gaze was steady when it locked with mine. "Some things are meant to be." She raised her hands, claws expanding.

Aunt Tillie tugged the pin from her grenade at the same moment the Happy Holidays Players shifted to pounce.

Carl's eyes went wide when he saw the weapon. Then he began to laugh. "Where did you get a grenade, old lady?"

Thistle, Clove, and I sucked in our breath at the same time.

"Did he just call me old?" Aunt Tillie demanded.

"I believe he did," Thistle replied evenly. "That puts him at the top of your list, right?"

"Not for long." Aunt Tillie reared back to throw the grenade.

"That won't work on me," Carl bellowed.

Aunt Tillie didn't hesitate. "Yes, it will."

The grenade landed like ... well, a grenade. The explosion was deafening, and the magical cloud that enveloped the demons made me rear back. Purple, pink, blue, green, yellow, orange, and red dust exploded outward, engulfing our enemies—and our mothers.

From up above, Evan dropped into the cloud. Exclamations of excitement reverberated from inside, but we couldn't see what was happening.

"What do we do?" Landon asked. He had his gun out, leveled at the dust cloud.

"I don't know." I took a step forward just as a figure came hurtling out of the dust. It was Carl, and he looked murderous.

I reacted without thinking and grabbed him by the throat. "*Glacio*," I intoned, pounding a mountain of magic into him.

He went rigid, his eyes going wide, and the magic of Hollow Creek started oozing out of him once my magic started interacting with his. I glanced at Aunt Tillie, uncertain.

"Why is that happening?" I asked.

She smirked. "Because I make one hell of a grenade." She raised her fist, let loose a whoop, and then plunged into the mist. Thistle and Clove matched her, raised fist for raised fist, and ran in after her.

I remained in my spot, open mouthed and gaping, and then put my full focus on Carl. "You should've killed me when you had the chance," I noted grimly. "I guess now it's my turn." Killing him when he was frozen was alien to me, but it had to be done. He couldn't be allowed to leave.

"No." Landon moved in front of me and shook his head. "This one's not on you." He raised his gun and pointed it at Carl. He looked horrified at what he was about to do.

Then Evan appeared. "It's not on you either," he said, nudging Landon's gun away. He had a cut on his face but otherwise seemed fine. "This one has to die. The others are down. Tillie says she can strip their magic, and she can do it before the day is out. I'm content letting her do that. Are you?"

I hesitated for a moment. "Yes." I didn't want to wipe out the entire acting troupe. Yes, they were all demons, but if Aunt Tillie could neuter them the way Carl had been neutered, I would be content with that. Carl, of course, was another story.

"Let me do this one." Evan shot Landon a smile and then slid his eyes to Carl. The demon seemed to understand what was coming. No matter how hard he fought against my magic, he couldn't free himself. "It's been nice knowing you, Carl."

Evan was calm as he moved behind the demon. Rather than snap his neck, he wrapped his hands around it and cut off Carl's oxygen. The demon's eyes bulged, forcing me to look away, but it was over much faster than I anticipated. When Carl dropped to the ground, there was no movement. He was dead weight, already gone from this world.

"You can say you found him this way," Evan said to Landon and

Chief Terry. "You can say whoever his third partner was did this to him. Or it can go down as a mystery. It's up to you."

Landon nodded stiffly. "I would've done it. I could've said he tried to flee, and I would've been justified."

"That doesn't mean you had to do it," Evan argued. "Landon, you're a good man. It goes against your nature to shoot someone who can't fight back. The problem is, if we'd let that guy fight back, he might've hurt someone we care about a great deal."

"He already hurt Bay," Landon pointed out. "I could've killed him just for that."

"But you don't have to." Evan smiled. "I've killed my fair share of people. Many of them didn't deserve it. I didn't have a soul then. I do now." He jerked his thumb toward Carl. "This one deserved it. You can't risk him getting loose again. He's already showed us what he will do.

"Those people in there, inside the dust, he would've killed them all to make his escape," he continued. "He was soulless. There was no bringing him back. I don't feel guilt for what I did."

"You shouldn't," Landon assured him as he holstered his service weapon.

The magical mist had begun to dissipate, and when I stepped into the melee, I was dumbfounded by what I found. All of the Happy Holidays Players, each and every single one, was on the ground, mindlessly staring at the sky.

"What did you do?" I asked Aunt Tillie. She was leaning over Mary, who was so still she looked dead.

"The grenade did most of it. I just froze them in place. We need to burn out their powers and modify their memories."

I was caught off guard. "How do we burn out their powers?"

"I believe we know a witch who just managed that feat with a bunch of witches less than two weeks ago."

*Stormy.* Of course. "I'm sure she'll come and help."

"We'll empty them out—in a way that means they'll never get their magic back—and then send them on their way," Aunt Tillie said. "It's the best outcome for all of us."

I agreed, even when my eyes landed on Mom, and I saw the bruise on her cheek. "Are you okay?"

"We're fine," Mom promised. She looked annoyed more than anything else. "They jumped us in the kitchen. We weren't expecting them. We won't ever let that happen again."

"That's good." I meant it. "Landon is upset he missed breakfast."

That elicited a smile from Mom. "Well, we can't have that. Maybe we'll have brunch today."

"Will there be bacon?" Landon asked.

Mom smiled. "What do you think?"

"I think you should get to cooking, and we'll finish cleaning up this mess."

Mom's smile didn't waver, even as Chief Terry pulled her in for a rather intimate hug.

# Twenty-Nine

Once the Happy Holidays Players had their memories wiped—a suggestion to do good deeds implanted just for the heck of it—and were on their way downtown thanks to Evan putting their vehicles back together, we headed inside. Chief Terry called for backup from the prison task force, and he and Landon waited for it to arrive.

Evan happily pitched in to help with breakfast preparations. He excitedly told Mom about how he used to cook for Scout because she was a menace in the kitchen. He seemed pretty happy, given the circumstances, and after a bit of thought over coffee, I realized it was because this death was delivered to protect people he cared about.

By the time Landon and Chief Terry came back inside, breakfast was ready, and everybody was more than happy to group around the table and stuff their faces. I was halfway through my eggs and hash browns when something occurred to me.

"The Happy Holidays Players packed up to leave but didn't pay you." I hadn't even thought about it before sending them on their way.

"We already charged their cards," Mom replied. "We got half at the beginning of the week, and I charged the other half when we returned to the inn today. Given the 'do good deeds' idea that was planted in their heads, I very much doubt they'll kick up a fuss over it. All the charges went through."

I nodded and let out a breath. The thought of my mother and aunts doing all that work and not getting paid would've made me irrationally angry. "Well, that's good at least."

"We should probably head downtown to watch the pageant later," Thistle suggested. "I don't particularly want to see them again, but it can't hurt to watch them from afar and make sure the spell is working."

I agreed. "We can do that."

"And take another trip to the kissing booth," Landon said as he handed me one of his slices of bacon. It caught me off guard. "Only three slices today," he explained to my unasked question. "The one thing that's become ridiculously clear this week is that I want a very long life with you."

The sentiment was sweet. "Yes, well, I don't think four slices of bacon will kill you on a day when we took out a bunch of demons."

He blinked twice and then immediately reached to the bacon platter for another slice. "You're the best wife ever," he announced around a mouthful of meaty goodness.

I smiled and shook my head. "The kissing booth sounds fun. Maybe, to give everyone a break, we can eat dinner downtown too."

"We're fine," Mom assured me. "We can put dinner together."

"I know, but it will be fun as a family." I meant it. "The big Christmas tree downtown will be lighted tonight. The carolers will be out singing. They're putting the giant mistletoe up."

"Now we're talking." Landon winked at me.

"We can do it as a family," I insisted. "This is the last festival until the big Christmas festival at the end of the month. Calvin can get bundled up and see the lights. This is something we can all enjoy."

"And it helps that we're putting up a united front for Margaret," Mom surmised. "I heard you and she went at each other a few days ago, Bay. You really shouldn't let her get to you."

"She's a hateful woman," I replied. "It took me a long time to see it. I believed that Aunt Tillie kept pushing her to do some of this stuff.

The truth is, she's just not good." I flicked my eyes to Aunt Tillie. "I'm all in for whatever you plan to do to her this holiday season."

"Me too." Thistle pumped her fist at the end of the table. "Let's take that craggy old witch down."

Aunt Tillie's smirk was a thing of beauty. "I have a few ideas. I need to shore them up."

"Something tells me Christmas is going to be something to behold," Evan said from his spot next to Twila. A month ago, it would've been weird to have him at the table without Scout. Now he was part of the family. "Scout said they're putting the Happy Holidays Players on the watch list. They shouldn't be a problem any longer. If something happens to change that, we'll know fairly quickly."

"They all seemed appropriately confused when we walked them to the bus," Clove said. "Mary almost seemed agitated, but it was as if she couldn't understand why she should be agitated."

"I think Mary had more powers than the others," I replied. "She probably figured out right away that her magic was gone. She couldn't very well announce that in front of us."

"I'm guessing the Happy Holidays Players are going to have a confusing two weeks," Mom agreed. "Once they hear about Carl Markham's death, things will only get worse."

"Yeah, what did they say about Markham?" I asked Chief Terry. "How much trouble are we in?"

"You're not in any trouble," Chief Terry promised. "If anybody asks, you were outside walking with Landon when you saw movement in the woods. You followed it and found Markham. He was dead on the ground. The movement was animals." There was a sternness to Chief Terry's steady stare.

"I've got it," I replied. "How about you?" I asked Landon. "Are you okay with this?"

"Yes." Landon answered without hesitation. "This is the way it has to be, so I don't want to hear any lip. I don't want any more attention on you."

"As it stands, Childs is probably the only one who will be suspicious," Chief Terry said. "He's out of his position—that's official now

—so it won't matter if he starts flapping his gums. He can cry to whomever he wants, but nobody will believe anything he says. He was fired in disgrace."

"Part of me feels sorry for him," I admitted. "He clearly didn't want this to happen."

"He didn't," Chief Terry agreed, "but he's responsible for the complacency that took over the prison. There will be some changes with the new guy coming in. They're also looking at all the prisoners again. I wouldn't be surprised if the violent ones are sent back south."

"What about the prisoners who were magically enticed to escape?" Thistle asked. "By the way ... who did that? I somehow missed the explanation for that."

"I think Natalie created the trigger without realizing what she was doing," I replied. "She thought the prisoners would serve as a few minutes of distraction so she and Carl could get away. She had no way of knowing about his other plans.

"As for who pulled the trigger, I think she did it with Barker," I continued. "The only reason he managed to exert any control over us is because he got his hands on me. Overall, the magic fueling him was weak. It grew stronger with each subsequent escapee they threw at us. That was Carl and Mary."

"Some of those prisoners didn't want to escape," Thistle pressed. "What's going to happen to them?"

"Unfortunately, there's not much we can do for them," Landon replied. "It's not as if we can explain that they were taken over by demons. It's sad, but it is what it is."

"I guess." Thistle looked troubled, but because Landon was right, she merely sighed. "What's next?"

I finished chewing what was in my mouth before responding. "What do you mean? Life is pretty much back to normal for us."

"No." Thistle was firm when she shook her head. "I meant what I said earlier. It was nice to have some downtime the last few months. Moving in with Marcus was a big deal, and I wanted to focus on him for a bit. But we need to get back to the witch stuff." She motioned between herself and Clove. "We've been slacking."

"We have," Clove agreed. "I needed the time away to get used to being a wife and mother, but it's time I started helping again ... and not just because I think I should be doing it. I want to do it. All of this shouldn't fall on your shoulders, Bay."

"You'll end up like Aunt Tillie if you keep at it the way you've been going," Thistle added. "Your head will be so big it's a wonder that your brain won't start rattling around."

Aunt Tillie's eyes narrowed.

"You'll start stalking Mrs. Little on your own and muttering to yourself," Clove said.

Aunt Tillie's eyes turned into glittery slits of hate.

"You'll start wearing a combat helmet and sharpening sticks to use on your enemies," Thistle said. "Everyone in town will start referring to you as Aunt Tillie Jr." She shuddered. "The freaking horror. You don't want that."

"You need us," Clove said. "And we need you. It's time we get back to what we're good at."

A smile rushed to my lips. "That sounds nice," I said. "Hopefully, we won't have to test our new bonds until after Christmas. I'd like a few weeks of quiet."

"I think we'd like that too." Landon slung his arm around my shoulders and slid his eyes to Aunt Tillie. "Right? We're going to have a quiet Christmas."

"You're all on my list for that one," Aunt Tillie replied. "Each and every one of you. If you want to survive, you'd better start running now."

Landon grinned. "And everything is back to normal."

"I'm going to make you all eat dirt sandwiches for Christmas dinner," Aunt Tillie continued. "You'll be weeping and cursing my name when I'm finished with you."

"That's the Christmas spirit," Landon enthused. His eyes shifted back to me. "Tell me about the huge mistletoe you mentioned earlier."

I wasn't surprised he hadn't forgotten that tidbit. "Maybe I should show you later. It might lose something in the telling."

"Now we're talking."

"You're all going to smell like fruitcake when I'm done," Aunt Tillie snapped. "Rotten, bad fruitcake. No more smell of bacon."

"Don't terrorize your family on what should be a good day," Landon shot back. "Christmas is the time for giving. Don't be a grinch."

"You're on my list too," Aunt Tillie fired back.

"Yup, things are definitely back to normal," Chief Terry sighed.

They were, and I couldn't have been more grateful for it.